BARBARA RADECKI

MESSENGER

The publisher gratefully acknowledges the support of the Canada Council for the Arts and the Ontario Arts Council for its publishing program. We acknowledge the financial support of the Government of Canada through the Canada Book Fund (cbf) for our publishing activities, and the Government of Ontario through Ontario Creates, an agency of the Ontario Ministry of Culture, and the Ontario Book Publishing Tax Credit Program.

LIBRARY AND ARCHIVES CANADA CATALOGUING IN PUBLICATION

Title: Messenger 93 / Barbara Radecki.
Other titles: Messenger ninety-three
Names: Radecki, Barbara, author.
Identifiers: Canadiana (print) 20190230746 | Canadiana (ebook) 20190230738 | ISBN 9781770865686 (softcover) | ISBN 9781770865693 (HTML)
Classification: LCC PS8635.A3365 M47 2020 | DDC jc813/.6—dc23

United States Library of Congress Control Number: 2019955759

Cover design: Angel Guerra
Interior text design: Tannice Goddard, tannicegdesigns.ca

Printed and bound in Canada.

Manufactured by Friesens in Altona, Manitoba, Canada in February 2020.

DCB
AN IMPRINT OF CORMORANT BOOKS INC.
260 SPADINA AVENUE, SUITE 502, TORONTO, ON, M5T 2E4
www.dcbyoungreaders.com
www.cormorantbooks.com

THURSDAY, APRIL 12

SEVEN DAYS UNTIL THE FALL

1

HOW DO I EXPLAIN how it started? Putting it into words is like looking at the sky and saying it's blue. *Blue* doesn't account for gradations of color, or shifts in weather, or my eye seeing differently than yours. *Blue* is basic. It doesn't reveal the truth.

On Wednesday, April 11, after another day of incognito drifting between classes and my locker — Nobody Here, Nothing To See — then playing the part at home of diligent student — an act as much for me as for my parents — I went to bed and fell asleep like I always do. Exhausted from the effort. Not daring to hope for a better day. Pen in hand, sketchbook perched on my stomach.

It was the middle of the night when I woke up and saw it. It was absolutely clear. Not a waking dream. Not a hazy sort of what-is-it. No. It was distinct and real. It was *there*. Materializing through the sooty skeins of darkness above my head.

A crow.

It was hovering over my bed, directly underneath my starburst-glass-and-bronze ceiling light. Its wings were spread, the feathers glossy black. Its eyes, black and red-rimmed, stared at me. I stared back, intensely aware of the physical world. How a million tiny goosebumps fanned over my skin. How my breath huffed out and in, rhythmic and locomotive. How the nighttime shadows erased everything in my room but the crow.

My body had turned into a block of ice. I could feel the weight of my sheet and blanket over me, the slight added pressure on my abdomen of the sketchbook.

The crow drifted closer, as smooth and stealthy as a military hovercraft. It was maybe three feet away now. Touching distance.

"You are Messenger 93." A voice in the dark.

My amazement reeled and multiplied. Goosebumps and breathlessness.

"You must find her."

Its pointed little beak didn't move, didn't snap open and shut or have superimposed lips like in those CG-phony movies. But I was certain it was the crow speaking.

"She will fall in seven days."

It didn't sound male. It didn't sound female.

"As she falls, so do we all."

My mind didn't search to understand. I didn't try to talk back.

"Only you can save her." The crow flapped its wings one time — I could feel a whoosh of warm air against my cheek. It said, "Save her, save us all." And then it folded itself inside its feathers and sank into the darkness like a corpse on water.

The paralysis ended instantly. I sat up and took stock: I was awake; there had been a crow in my room; it had spoken to me.

I flicked on my bedside lamp. Its light glowed orange over the walls and ceiling, into every charcoal corner, and I checked around for traces of the crow. It was just my usual room. Bed underneath me, desk on the opposite wall, above it my fake-painting of a highway disappearing into the distance. My window was closed and the three glass shelves that were slung across it were still intact. So were the ten air-plants lined up along the shelves in their little glass terrarium jars. Underneath, on the windowsill, my flock of waving cat figurines waved without movement.

Had I imagined the crow? Dreamed it?

It hadn't felt like a fantasy or a dream.

You are Messenger 93.

Why had the crow called me that? Why not my actual name? Which was as plain and simple as me. As thin and white and unremarkable. As hunched into itself as a question mark.

You must find her.

Find who?

She will fall in seven days.

Seven days? The exactness, the precision of the number, was like a sword in a rock.

As she falls, so do we all.

Fall rang in my ears like a bell. Its terrible meaning rippled through me.

Only you can save her. Save her, save us all.

That was hilarious. I was sixteen. What power did I have to save anyone?

Besides, there was no one I cared about enough to save. In fact, as a general rule, I hated all people. Except my family, I guess. And none of them needed my help.

A small metallic *tunnk* on the floor startled me, and I nearly whiplashed my head into the wall. I peered over the edge of my bed and saw it was just my pen, dropped out of my grip as it always did after I fell asleep, rolling lazily in a semi-circle. I cleared the ache from my throat and reached for it.

My sketchbook was still open and propped on the blanket over my lap. The storyboard for the imaginary series I was never going to film was still there. A scrawl of stick figures inside rows of panels across *heavyweight ultra-smooth superior-contrast* paper.

Unrecognized, unheralded superhero. *Infinity Girl.* A walking infinity mirror, Infinity Girl travels the world reflecting back to people what they want to see. But her power is that when the person is ready, the reflection morphs into who they really are.

Her target in that night's storyboard was a guy who sees himself as a brave warrior. But when he coaxes his best friend into a street fight with a rival gang and the friend dies, the warrior loses it. Infinity Girl finds him, and this time he recognizes himself as the tyrant he's always been.

No one ever sees Infinity Girl. All she has to do is stand there.

Pages and pages of scribbled panels — misguided losers, exotic locales, epic struggles. Infinity Girl's quest repeating over and over. And I still hadn't figured out how to make it cool enough to film. According to story rules, no one will care about a girl-hero if she isn't beautiful enough and if she refuses to fall in love. And there was no way I was falling into that trap.

You are Messenger 93.

Only you can save her.

I stabbed my pen into the page and sketched out a square for the next panel. I had to come up with a final act for the Tyrant's story. What would he do now that he knew the truth about himself?

She will fall in seven days.

I grabbed my headphones from the bedside table and clamped the padded ear cushions around my head. It was soft and comforting, like the best little-kid plush toy. I plugged into my phone and scrolled through my favorite artists — Tandem Acorns, Deleese Felicia, Last Sunny Day. I tapped into the Tandem Acorns playlist and chose their most intense song, dialed up the volume. *Boom, steady, boom. Boom, boom, steady, boom.*

But the memory of the crow's voice played over it like a counterbeat.

As she falls, so do we all.

You must find her. You must find her. You must find her.

2

I DON'T REMEMBER FALLING into sleep again, but I guess I did because my alarm startled me out of deep and blissful peace. I enjoyed maybe twenty seconds of sleepy calm, and then the crow incident inhabited my body. It was like how you'd imagine one of those spaceship transporters would feel if they were real: cells dematerializing, scrambling in limbo, then rematerializing you somewhere else. Because that's what had happened: I'd landed in a world where the crow had come, and I would never be the same.

But there was no way a crow had come, and obviously I was exactly the same.

Either way, I still had to go to school.

I got up and got dressed — my usual jeans and logo-less sweatshirt — and stuffed my eleven hundred schoolbooks and notepads into my backpack. Okay, not *eleven hundred* literally, but enough that my bag sagged under their weight and girth. Fanatical studying had become a means to an end. The only escape I'd come up with.

I heaved a backpack strap over one shoulder and headed to my bedroom door.

A small oblong shadow on the floor near the window caught my eye.

Before I knew what it was, that dark gash on the hardwood, my whole body tensed as if it were warning me.

Don't look at it, get out of there, run.

I looked anyway.

A black feather, as honed and sharp as the edge of the moon.

Somewhere in my chest, my heart seized.

I crept closer. Careful. As if the feather was about to burst from its spot and crush me. I plucked it up by its hard end and turned it over between my fingers. It was real. Super-light. Smooth and silky. The kind of gossamer thing you might make a wish on.

As she falls, so do we all, the crow's voice had whispered.

You must find her. Left-behind echoes caught in the bristles.

Seven days.

I made my way along the upstairs hall and listened to the usual banging and jingling coming from my parents' bedroom as they got ready for work. Drawers and zippers and jewelry. Water running in their bathroom.

Downstairs in the kitchen, my little brother Trevor was at the table, hunched over his new-edition manga, eating cereal. I poured myself a bowl and ate it standing at the counter.

"Hey, Trev?" My voice sounded normal. Easygoing. "Did you go into my room yesterday?"

"Gross," he said through a mouthful of cereal.

"It's okay. I just want to return this to its rightful owner." I dug into my back jeans' pocket and pulled out the feather. "Did you drop it in my room?"

Trevor side-eyed the feather for two seconds. His eyebrow lifted. "No." He went back to reading.

I flourished the feather. Just a little. To get his attention again. "But it's yours, right?"

Instead of answering, Trevor stuck an enormous spoonful of cereal into his mouth.

"Okay, cool." I slid the feather back into my pocket. "I guess the crow left it in my room for real then." Since Trevor wasn't listening anyway. "Yeah, because this crow came to me last night. It called me Messenger 93. It told me I have to find a girl. That I have seven days to save her.

"*Save her, save us all*, it said." I rinsed my bowl, stuck it in the dishwasher. "Hilarious, right?"

Trevor turned a page, eyes intent on the next chapter. The breath coming out of his nostrils rattled a bit. It made me strangely sad.

"Okay, well." I gave him a farewell wave, which he didn't see or acknowledge. "See ya."

In the front hall, I checked out the window. It was a questionable morning. Murky spring non-weather. I grabbed my raincoat, shoved my feet into my steel-toed boots.

I was in the middle of tying my boots when Trevor's voice, loud and monotone, intercepted me. "If the crow says you have to go, then you have to go."

I DON'T KNOW HOW long Trevor's pronouncement tasered me.

If the crow says you have to go, then you have to go. But I was still standing in the hall, statue-like, boots half-tied, when my mom ran down the stairs, clipping her earrings on, late for work again.

"Hey," she said, barely registering me. "I don't have time to drive you to school."

It was okay, she never did.

But it jolted me back to real time. I finished tying my boots, zipped up my coat, and opened the door. The outside air assaulted me, cold and wet.

I was standing on the front porch when my mom's voice called out. "Oh, hey, hey, before you go!" I stopped mid-door-close. Mom had stepped back into the hall. She was fumbling with a button on the cuff of her blouse. "Do you know a girl named Krista? From your school?"

There was a startling buzz in my head. Intense enough to block out reasonable thought.

"I got a call from Hattie's mom. No one's seen Krista or heard from her since lunchtime yesterday. They're reaching out to everyone, just in case." Mom made a sad face. "Looks like she might've run away. Do you know anything about it?"

I managed to shake my head.

"I didn't think so. That's what I told Hattie's mom." She tucked her blouse hem into her skirt and gave me a distracted smile. "So scary. But I'm sure she's fine. A little teenage rebellion." And she swished away, into the kitchen.

The front door closed between us, and it was a robotic moment later when I realized it was my own hand doing the closing, and then my feet moving me away from our house.

THE MORNING WAS WEIRDLY quiet. Like it had been stuffed with bubble wrap. There were no people walking dogs, no cars passing by or pulling out of driveways, no roar of city buses huffing down the main avenue a few blocks over. My footsteps tagging the pavement was the only sound I heard.

Do you know a girl named Krista?

I wandered by myself through sooty half-light, down the

home-lined streets of our neighborhood, past architectural trimmed hedges and budding garden plots and wrought-iron gates.

No one's seen Krista or heard from her since lunchtime yesterday.

I approached the school through the back way. Over the football field, along the track, past the old oak tree that presides over the backyard of the school. There was a crow in the branches. Small and black. Silent. It was staring out into the far distance. I kept a close eye on it as I got closer. But it ignored me, twitching its head to stare off in another far-off direction. So I kept going, keeping my breath in check. Telling myself it was a harmless coincidence.

It wasn't until I rounded the side of the school and hit the parking lot that the quiet stillness was ruined. The lot was teeming with cars, students hopping out, heading inside. There was a police cruiser pulled up on the curb by the doors, no officers sitting in the seats, no blazing lights.

Anusha, L.J., and Hattie were getting out of Hattie's mom's SUV that had been queued up among the other cars. I could tell, even from a distance, that the girls were messed up. They were agitated, ranting and gesticulating. But also tugging at each other's sleeves as they entered the school together. Small gestures of belonging. Of being in this as a team.

I got to the doors and pushed in alongside everyone else. I clasped my backpack stuffed with my eleven hundred books in front of me. You have to choose armor that isn't obvious, or it loses its power to protect you. I switched the din of chatter and shouts into white noise, as I always did. Better not to hear specific words. Better to disappear into the stream like just another one of its blind, submissive currents.

THE REFLECTION IN THE bathroom was not a mirror-image of a Girl Unhinged. I looked okay. A little tired maybe. My pupils weren't dilated or anything. My skin hadn't broken out in hives or rashes. I looked like a sane and ordinary person. Unremarkable. And why shouldn't I? There was no history of visions or voices, no misguided illusions of grandeur in my past. Okay, maybe for a couple of years when I was four/five, I was sure I was a fairy. But I didn't think that counted as evidence of mental instability.

Messenger 93. You must find her. Only you can save her.

If the crow says you have to go, then you have to go.

People believed in all kinds of things, didn't they? In gods and goddesses. In multi-verses. Telepathy. Laws. Astrology. Signs. Omens. Borders. Love. None of these things were certain. Immutable. And no one said *they* were crazy.

I washed my face, then filled my water bottle and drank a long swig. My stomach gurgled a bit. The morning's cereal wasn't sitting well.

I faced the bathroom exit and girded my shoulders and stepped out.

There was a droning excitement in the hallway that I tried to ignore. But it was hard. What I couldn't avoid seeing, even peripherally, was the disconcerting arrival of the principal and a police officer. They marched purposefully through the throngs of students and stopped side by side at a locker. A small woman, as slight and billowy as tissue, was waiting for them in front of it. I didn't need to get closer to know it was Krista's mom. I'd met her once, the year before.

My first class was on the other side of their huddle, and so I had no choice but to wander by. Me, another witness to the wreckage. Another eavesdropper. I took my time, bowing my head, threading between people. An invisible stitch.

The principal had a lock cutter in her hands. While the police officer looked on, his face set with passive interest, Ms. Drake angled and leveraged the cutter until she'd severed the bolt. She was talking to Krista's mom the whole time, who listened with tissue-like nods of her head. Ms. Drake pulled the metal door open and Krista's mom bent inside. She took her time touching, then gathering Krista's stuff.

There were a bunch of mood board images taped to the inside of Krista's locker door. My eyes honed in on one as I passed — a picture stuck to the upper left-hand corner that I'd never noticed before. It drew my attention like light to an event horizon.

A ripped scrap of paper with a silhouette of a black bird on it. The kind of simple drawing that looks like you've taken the letter M by its bottom feet and stretched it out.

So what made it stand out? All the other pictures were very *Krista*, for lack of a better word. Basic sunsets, basic inspirational quotes, basic instant photos of Krista and her friends making sexy, pouty faces. But what did the bird mean to her? A thick, black, single-lined wave of a bird. It was a totally different kind of keepsake. A paradox.

"Clio!" I recognized L.J.'s commanding voice. She and the other girls were swooping in on Krista's mom. "Are you okay, Clio?" That was Anusha. There was an edge there already. "Did you hear anything?" Hattie sounded breathless and shaky, on the verge of tears. "Did she call?"

"No, not yet." Clio had her arms full of Krista's stuff, but she reached out and stroked Hattie's arm. It was all so emotional and tender. "Just that one text."

"We asked around," Hattie said. "No one's seen her since yesterday morning."

"Lunchtime, actually," said Anusha, throwing it off like it was useless information. "In the park across the street."

"Sitting on that bench," said L.J. "No one thought anything of it. No one saw her leave."

"That's where they found her phone, right? In the trash?" Hattie was pale, her eyes circled as if she hadn't slept.

"Yes," Clio said, her hand still resting tenderly on Hattie's arm, tethering her. "Don't worry, we're going through everything now. We will find her. Everything will be okay."

Passing kids were staring wide-eyed at their little group. If it wasn't so awful, it could've passed for a stage production, or a reality show.

Clio stepped away from the lockers. She clutched Krista's stuff to her chest. "Thank you for everything, you guys." She turned and hurried away down the hall, the principal and police officer in step behind her.

"Can we do anything else to help?" Hattie fluttered after them.

Clio glanced over her shoulder. "Yes, girls — please go to your classes. I'll text you the minute I hear anything."

The girls hung back, dismissed, and Hattie pulled them into a worried clutch.

I hunched over, hoping to merge into the throng. Who knew what they would do or say if they saw me gawking?

3

ALL THROUGH HISTORY CLASS, I doodled wonky bird silhouettes and *Messenger 93* across loose-leaf sheets in my binder. Ms.
Stathakis's lesson on the destructive forces of colonialism played
a droning background soundtrack to the whirring monologue
inside my head.

Krista had run away.

She had run away.

She had *disappeared*.

I knew sort of how it would work. They'd be out there looking
for her. Tracking every digital lead. Posting gone-girl pleas on
social media. Scrutinizing her feeds and posts. Contacting anyone
she'd ever talked to.

But I couldn't make sense of *why* Krista would run. She had
everything anyone could ever want: Status and Love. She ruled
the school — or at least grade ten. She had Boy, and they were
inseparable. Dating for a whole year now. *True love*. She had a
million friends, or friends of friends who knew who she was and
thought she was cool. She had *my* friends.

Hattie, L.J., Anusha, and Boy. I'd gone to elementary and
middle schools with them. The five of us had been a solid unit.
Obviously there had been fights and drama and tears, but we
were loyal throughout. Unbreakable.

Krista showed up when we transferred over to T. Emmet High
School. As Niners, we were the bottom of the food chain. You
know that dynamic exactly, so I don't need to get super-explicit
about it. A curse is cast the moment you enter those hallways. You

begin your excruciating larval transformation. You pretend to be a well-adjusted human. Sometimes you turn out pretty good, sometimes you become a spirit crusher, and sometimes you disappear. One vital part of you erased at a time. Face. Voice. Heart. Soul.

Krista was the Spirit Crusher. I was the Erased One.

She'd zeroed in right away on our friend group. Probably because of Boy. At first she seemed fun. She had a wicked sense of humor. She could toss off a sharp zinger about almost anyone. She seemed to see through bullshit.

I liked her in those early days with a kind of shocked awe. Oh, people talk like that? They see that stuff? They don't pretend it doesn't exist? Your weaknesses, your yearnings, your secrets.

Pretty soon, when we were hanging out at our lockers in our tight new Group of Six, she started talking over me. And I let her. Then she started sidestepping in front of me as she performed her stories. I let her. She'd grab my phone and go into my socials and edit my feeds. She would never heart or comment on anything I posted. I let her do that too.

In the second month, whenever I spoke, she would zing me: *That's so pathetic/sad/catty/callous/gross/stupid/fake/mean/wrong.* At first, if someone called her on it, she'd say she was joking, *Get a sense of humor.* Then it became a funny bit she did. It didn't take long for me to stop chiming in.

She was super-nice to the rest of them. Hattie was a *goddess*, L.J. was a *genius*, Anusha was a *superstar*. She didn't tease Boy or label him — no, she was *deep* with him, *sensitive, honest, real.*

By month three, the other girls started turning on me. In person at first: *Why didn't you show up — you're the one who asked to meet? Why did you send that text to Tyron — you know I'm into him.* Then through private messages: *Thanks a lot for telling everyone my business. F U for calling me a bitch behind my back. Stop talking shit about me and other ppl you call "friends."*

I never knew what to say — because I couldn't explain it. I didn't set up those meets, or send any of those messages, or start any of those rumors. But it didn't matter that I denied it. They never believed me.

About five months into grade nine — not long after the holidays — I stopped existing for the girls in our group. Like Krista, they'd turn their backs on me when I approached. Step in front of me. Ignore me when I spoke.

I'd lurk their social streams. Scrutinize every photo of their *awesome, amazing hangs.* All the experiences I'd once taken for granted, now excluded from. Razor-cut out of their lives.

Then I stopped existing for everyone else.

I'd built up a small but respectable following on my platforms, especially on Ittch, but then the followers started dropping off. It didn't really hurt until Anusha left, and then L.J., and then Hattie. When my follower list was down to only Boy and a few other randos, I deleted all my accounts. If I didn't exist, then I wouldn't exist.

Krista and my old crew became one big happy family. Laughing, joking, fastening onto each other, whispering into each other's ears.

End of March, Krista and Boy were dating.

They couldn't keep their hands off each other, they were so in love. I didn't want to, but I snuck glances as they pushed against lockers or ducked into stairwells. Eyelashes curling closed like feathers, pink-cushioned communion of lips, glistening-darting tips of tongues.

Pretty soon I stopped existing for Boy too. Maybe not on

purpose, but by virtue of design. If he was with Krista, how could he see me?

You can't fight these things. You can only succumb.

I accepted my place. Became a Nobody.

For the rest of that year, then all through grade ten, I sat by myself, streamed music, pretended to scroll my phone, got deep into studying, scrawled stupidly ambitious storyboard panels.

By then Infinity Girl had found her nemesis. Double Kross arrived on the scene like hellfire and anthrax. She had demon powers. She could zero in on the invisible force-fields that connect you to every other living being and set them ablaze. Scorching the pulsing threads of humanity until all that is left is your charred and panting body, alive but alone inside a lifeless circle of eddying ash.

Double Kross had it in big-time for Infinity Girl. And Infinity Girl's only protection was the optical camouflage provided by her mirrors.

Krista had run away.

There was no question in my mind: Krista was *fine*. She was too smart and too mean to be at anyone's mercy. I could easily picture her hanging out in some den of empowered girls, laughing at us, formulating a plan to conquer the world.

I hated Krista. *Hated* her.

And maybe that was why the crow had come to me, and maybe that was why I had to be the one to find her. Which was just too unbelievable, too unbearable, to accept.

BETWEEN CLASSES, I CASUALLY searched the halls for Boy. No one had mentioned him being gone. Police and principals weren't breaking into *his* locker and going through *his* stuff. So he obviously hadn't run off with Krista. And if Boy was still around, Krista's mom would obviously have talked to him. If he knew anything about where Krista was, I assumed he would tell her. He was a good person.

I went to his locker and stood near it, hoping for some sign of him. Waiting for him like a lost girl on a city sidewalk with my hand out.

Kids streamed around me like I wasn't there.

Boy would never be okay with Krista taking off by herself. He would be devastated.

That's not how life was supposed to be for him.

Boy was *that* guy. The smiling, swaggering one. The one who acts like he's first across the finish line no matter how he places, who can't walk under a doorway without dunking on the top jamb, who can't pass up a chance to wrestle his buddies in the middle of the hall, holding and spinning and hurling them until they're basically doing one of those pairs figure skating routines.

I waited by his locker as the few minutes between classes ticked down.

But Boy didn't come. His friends — the other ones I might try to ask if I could channel the nerve — were nowhere around. It was just me, by myself, inside a useless, mindless stream of kids.

I pulled out my phone. Boy's number was still in there. I could call him. My thumb hovered over the prompt. But it felt twisted and mixed-up and wrong. What right did I have to bother him? Especially now.

A chill ran over my neck, like when you sense a presence. I looked up. There, at the other end of the hall, through the crowd, eyes trained hard, seeing me, was Remy.

Perfectly symmetrical features, brown-black skin, rows of gold-ringed braids lacing her shoulders. A vegan activist, Remy was probably the coolest person in our school. I couldn't remember the last time she'd spoken to or looked at me. We'd been friends in elementary school, but hadn't hung out in the same circle for ages.

We locked eyes as other people's bodies picketed the space between us.

I couldn't translate what she wanted to communicate with her intense and piercing stare. Or what she wanted to hide.

The bell screamed and I jumped and spun away.

IN MY NEXT CLASS, Anusha was sitting a few rows ahead of me. I watched her in half-profile. She had her phone out, silver acrylic nails scrolling through Ittch, tapping into profiles, onto photos, zooming in, zooming out, scrolling on.

I played with all the ways I could interrupt her. Question her.

Hey, Anusha, it's been ages. By the way, if you want, I know this imaginary crow and it might help us find Krista. Hey, Anusha, I love your outfit, it reminds me of Krista. Oh, which reminds me, maybe I can help you guys find her? Hey, Anusha, if a crow came to you and said you should find Krista but you secretly hated her, would you look for her anyway?

"Nice work." Mr. Roberts' voice startled me. My English essay with a red-penned A on it landed on the desk in front of me.

Anusha shot me a look at that exact instant. As if I'd spoken my thoughts out loud and she'd heard them. My face went hot. Almost burned my fingers when I hid it behind my hands.

"Do I have to say it again, people?" Mr. Roberts raised his voice to address the rest of the class. He dropped essays onto more desks. "Please pay attention to the *clear* and *simple* instructions I set out for you. *Before* you write."

Anusha turned away and stared purposefully at a point of air in front of her. She would never agree to talk to me.

"You were asked to explore the relationship between the writer's intent and the level of language used to convey that intent. If you're analyzing Tennyson's *The Eagle*, I'm not looking for how much you know about *eagles*."

Anusha hated me because she thought I'd badmouthed her behind her back.

"Let's examine the sensory appeal of the words Tennyson uses. The sound value. Literary devices like —" Mr. Roberts was at the blackboard now, writing across it with chalk. "Symbol. Connotation. Allusion."

I knew I should be taking notes. But when I pulled out my binder, I worked on practice notes to Anusha instead.

There's something you need to know.

There's something I need to tell you.

We have to talk. It's important.

Meet me at lunch break. Football field. Come alone.

If you care about Krista, find me. It's a matter of life and death.

It all sounded so hostile.

The bell rang. I started and checked the clock. I couldn't believe class was over already. Everyone burst out of their seats. Anusha stacked her books and balanced her phone on top. She started texting someone.

I opened my mouth to say her name. Nothing.

Swallowed and tried again. Nothing — I mean, *nothing* — came out.

"Remember," Mr. Roberts announced over the shuffling,

banging chairs, books, bodies. "Your Creative Writing assignments are due next week!"

Anusha, eyes trained on her screen, stepped into the exodus.
My window of opportunity was slamming shut. I fumbled with
the loose-leaf in my binder and ripped into one.

We have to talk. It's important.

It seemed the least ominous.

"Go ahead and write your poems in any style you choose!"
Mr. Roberts was shouting to be heard.

I scrambled to fold up the scrap of paper, and pushed into
line behind Anusha. Blood was whooshing in my ears like
floodwater.

"But marks will be based on your use of *language* and *symbols*!"

Just as I reached the note into the space between me and
Anusha, I realized I'd forgotten to sign it. I started to pull it back,
but someone knocked my arm and the note fell out of my grip. It
sailed over Anusha's right shoulder and down onto her stack of
books. As if the whole thing had been preordained.

"And please, people, let's explore outside the box! No more
snakes and ravens, okay?"

I gulped for sweet, nurturing air, and squeezed past the others
to get through the door. Krista's fate was in Anusha's hands now.
It was all on her.

AT LUNCH BREAK I pretended to work on a storyboard for
Infinity Girl while I waited for Anusha to arrive at the caf. We'd
known each other for so long, I told myself, she would recognize
my handwriting and realize the note was from me. I pictured
her reading it, then catching my eye across the room and doing
one of those subtle head-jerks to get me to follow her.

Instead I saw this: Anusha walked in without looking for me, got a spot at the table where she and her friends usually sat, pulled out an apple, took a bite, saw my folded note poised on her pile of books, plucked it up like it was a piece of public-bathroom toilet paper, didn't open it, didn't read it, threw it on the ground as if that's where it belonged, waved at L.J. and Hattie when they came into the caf together, then connected to the life-support that was their devastated-best-friend-huddle.

I didn't know what to do with my disappointment. Its claw plunged into my mouth and its long silver nail stretched down my throat towards the gag-trigger.

I took it out on Infinity Girl.

Establishing shot: school hallway. *Three girls enter frame.* Superstar, Goddess, Genius. *They walk the superhero slow-mo formation walk. Hair blows in improbable wind. Outfits show off their marketable bodies. Best friends, impervious to the usual threats of lust or jealousy or degradation. Their power is each other.*

Infinity Girl watches from the sidelines as they tell each other stories of lust and love. In the reflections off Infinity Girl's mirrors, the girls see only the indestructible power of their union.

Cut to: archetypal party. Smoking, drinking, grinding, puking. *Superstar, Goddess, and Genius arrive and rule. But Infinity Girl is there too. She intercepts. This time, the refracted lights off her mirror-plates work as lasers that divide the girls. They're thrown apart and stumble about in dark corners. They weaken with every passing second. No one sees them. No one helps them. They can't find each other.*

Genius understands it first, then Goddess, and then Superstar. They are alone, always have been, always will be. The indestructible union was an illusion.

Superstar clutches at the shadows and gasps for breath, close to her lonely death. Speech-bubble: *"Messenger 93!"* Second speech-bubble: *"Help me, Messenger 93!"*

No no no. I scratched out the bubbles. There was not, nor would there ever be, a crossover between Infinity Girl and Messenger 93. It was a super-error-brain-malfunction brought on by the trauma of the day.

I smoothed my hands over the storyboards. Poor fragile page. No match for the exasperated fury of my pen. The recklessly inked lines — squares of scenes, multitudes of stick-people — had turned the loose-leaf into shreds. I yanked it out of the binder and crumpled it into a ball.

A chill ran across the back of my neck and I looked up.

It was Remy again. This time, watching me from slightly behind the hard edge of the open cafeteria door. She couldn't hide a tremor that crossed her face from one side of her lips to the opposite eyebrow.

I stood up. Something about her expression made me want to demand an explanation. Instead, I grabbed my stuff and whirled in the opposite direction, leaving the caf through the side exit.

4

MESSENGER 93. MESSENGER 93.

The name kept pinballing inside my brain.

Why that name? What did it mean?

Maybe I'd seen it somewhere and it had entered my

subconscious. Maybe there was subliminal significance to it that could actually lead me to Krista.

But what was it?

By the time I got to Computer Science class, the noise in my head was so loud, I couldn't hear anything else. I waited until Mrs. Fariah went back to her own computer where she did whatever she did while we worked on our independent assignments. Our *masterpieces of grand design*, she called them. I was developing a music program: *Easy Soundtracks for Beginner Filmmakers*.

I clicked on the file, but then opened the browser over top. The empty search field gaped at me. I hesitated, then typed in: *Messenger 93*.

Nothing interesting came up right away. A radio station, a year in the last century, an airplane crash. But digging deeper, I found hit after hit of weird and interesting stuff.

Like, did you know there are *93 million miles* between Earth and the sun?

That the diameter of the universe is *93 billion light years across*?

In DNA there are molecules that carry genetic information. One of them — *miRNA-93* — is a micro-molecule *messenger* that scientists believe can stop the growth of cancer cells in the human body. So you could actually say there's a Messenger 93 *that has the power to stop cancer.*

There was once this old religious philosophy that calculated the numeric value of words. Apparently the number-values for "will" and "love" add up to 93, so 93 became that religion's power number. It became their *message of love*.

Love. That manipulative, coercive word.

Messenger brought up a billion hits.

Get this — *messenger* also means *prophet*.

"In religion, a prophet is an individual who claims to have been contacted by the supernatural or angelic. The prophet then serves as an intermediary, delivering a divine message to humanity."

Contacted by angels? Divine message to humanity?

Messenger 93. Only you can save her. Save her, save us all.

There were too many prophets to search every one, so I looked up the most famous. Jesus, Buddha, Muhammad, Moses, Joan of Arc.

All of them died horrible deaths. Jesus: staked to a cross; Buddha: violently ill, possibly poisoned; Muhammad: violently ill, possibly poisoned; Moses: wandered the desert for forty years, died just short of the Promised Land; Joan of Arc: burned alive at the stake. She was nineteen. *Nineteen.*

There was a tap on my shoulder and I practically punched the computer screen. Mrs. Fariah was beside me, giving me one of those scrunched-mouth-disappointed-head-tilts. She pointed pointedly at my screen and I fumbled to quit out of the search. She waited while I pretended to get back to work on my music program, and then she moved on down the aisle.

But terrible words had been planted inside me. Galactic questions.

AFTER MY LAST CLASS, I rounded through the side doors and out towards the track, and came up against the circle-wall of L.J., Hattie, and Anusha. All four of us stalled to instant and stiff attention. Them staring at me, me taking them in, the football field behind them stretching away like some empty airstrip at the edge of the apocalypse.

It was ominously quiet. No teachers. No students running by. No breeze buffeting over the short-mown grass. No birds, no crows in the giant oak.

"I'm looking for Krista." It was a blurt. Not the words I'd wanted to speak if I saw them. Definitely not the words I meant. Because I was *not* looking for Krista. But now it was out and I couldn't take it back.

Hattie stepped towards me. "Why?"

"I don't know." There was a slight breathlessness to my voice, which I worked to fix. "Because I have to?" Except I didn't, did I? I still had a choice.

"You *have to*?" Anusha stepped in beside Hattie and stared me down. "Is this another one of your backstabbing moves?"

"No   " Tears twitched at the rims of my eyes. "No — I wouldn't —" But that was all I could get out. I hunched my shoulders and pushed to move past them.

L.J. stepped in front of me. She said, hard, certain, "Krista doesn't want to be found."

Hattie smacked L.J.'s arm. "Stop saying that."

"Why should I when it's true? Krista *chose* this. Why am I the only one who respects that?"

"Because it's *dangerous*."

"Yeah, and she's doing it anyway. She's doing what she needs to do, and she doesn't care about anything else." L.J. flicked her hand at Hattie and then at me. "Leave her alone. Let her work it out."

"But we don't know *for sure* that she chose this." It looked like Hattie was going to cry. "Someone could've taken her."

"C'mon. It's Krista we're talking about. She texted her mom before she ditched her phone. She literally said she was okay."

"But what if she's running away from something bad and she can't talk about it? Like, some sort of abusive situation?"

This time L.J. smacked Hattie. "Clio is not a fucking *abuser*. Clio is an angel."

"Right, right." Hattie was full-on pacing now. "And her dad's dead. So it can't be that."

"What I don't get," Anusha emphasized each word, "is how you guys don't see this whole thing as a huge betrayal."

Hattie stopped and looked at Anusha like she had become the sun. "Betrayal?"

"She never said anything to us." Anusha was seething. It shocked me. Locked me to my spot. "What does that say about our friendship? That she doesn't trust us. She's leaving us hanging like everyone else. And Boyd? You ever think about him? What kind of person does that? Leave their boyfriend like that?"

"It's okay, Anusha." Tears were streaming down Hattie's face. "You just feel guilty because you can't help her."

Anusha reeled on her. "I don't feel *guilty*! This is not my fault. I'm saying — she betrayed us, and she betrayed him, and I hope she's having fun on her *sparkly adventure*, but she's dead to me."

Hattie gasped. She splayed her hands in front of her mouth like she'd caught the sound.

Anusha spun around to face me. "And what are *you* doing here? We didn't invite you to our wake. Or are you loving this? Karma for some traumatic shit you think Krista did to you."

The other two girls turned to stare at me too. Riveted, waiting.

"I didn't —" I shook my head. The inside of my mouth was sand. "I'm not —"

"How are you better than her, huh?" Anusha leaned at me. "You are two sides of the same coin."

She stared at me for a really long time.

I mean like when one second extends into eons and eras.

What was I doing? Why was I here?

I forced myself upright, forced myself to look at each of them. I said, veering from word to word to get them all out, "I know you guys think I started those rumors, that I set you up, or back-stabbed you or whatever, but I swear — I didn't do any of it. You were my best friends. I would never break that."

Anusha's face distorted — sarcastic pity. "Well, too bad for you." She spoke through gritted teeth. "Because everything breaks, doesn't it?"

That razed me. A hand at my throat.

Somehow I managed to turn and hobble away. I pictured them watching me, rolling their eyes, condemning my uselessness. My legs were gelatin. I was drenched in a feverish sweat.

Joan of Arc, nineteen, nobody special before turning self-proclaimed prophet. Burned at the stake.

My rubbery legs somehow got me to the track, then across it, then over the football field and down the path to the residential street that backed onto the school. It wasn't until I was out of eyeshot that a semblance of composure returned to my limbs.

I made it to the bus stop, got onto the next bus, and pushed down the aisle to a seat at the back. I just needed to get to my headphones-on-music-cranked-sketchpad-armored normal life.

And maybe I would've made it too, maybe it would've all ended there — except I had to be looking out the window, didn't I? Had to be replaying the epically weird day against the backdrop of the unraveling world. Because that's how I saw Remy sitting on the sidewalk, cross-legged, leaning against a mailbox, scrolling her phone.

I was out of my seat before I could even think about what I

was doing. I rang the bell to get the driver to drop me at the next stop, and before I knew it, I was standing on the sidewalk not far from Remy, staring at her like a stalker. She didn't notice me — she was too busy checking her screen. And that's when I noticed where I'd landed: at the intersection to the street where Krista lived.

I'd been to Krista's house once, back when I was still a part of their friend group. She'd invited us over because her mom needed her to babysit her baby brother and Krista didn't want to be alone. Her mom — *Clio* — had been nice. She'd paid attention when we were introduced. She noticed little things like Hattie's exquisite handwriting, Anusha's necklace from her grandmother, L.J.'s thrift shop menswear jacket, the fact that my eyes are very subtly two different colors, Boy's firm handshake.

She left us to look after the baby, who was maybe a year old, chubby and cute and constantly getting into stuff. Krista rolled her eyes after her mom was gone and huffed about how much she hated her. We all laughed and pretended it was another one of her witty jokes. Because everyone was shiny-in-love with Clio. She'd been kind to us. *An angel.* More exotically, she was a *widow.* A woman alone in the world by circumstances outside her control.

I took another look at Remy, sitting on the sidewalk, curled over her phone, unexpectedly small. I could ask her why she'd stared at me at school, what she wanted. I looked again down the street towards Krista's house. There was a police cruiser parked in front by the curb.

The neighborhood was way nicer than ours. Bigger yards, grander homes, sportier cars in fancier driveways. A police car was like a bruise. It didn't belong. It spoke of injuries that weren't supposed to happen in places like this.

Instead of confronting Remy, I was drawn down the block. I guess I had to see it for myself.

Krista's house was a princess castle of French doors and dormers and topiaries. The front door was open, so I crossed to the other side of the street and wandered a little farther on so I could get my bearings without being seen. I certainly didn't want to talk to or be questioned by the police.

In an effort to look/feel inconspicuous, I pulled out my pen and a scrap of paper from my pocket — a receipt from True Blue-locity for Tandem Acorns's latest 12-inch.

Establishing shot: *Infinity Girl stands in front of a decrepit mansion. She's found Double Kross's secret lair. Except it's not within her power to destroy a person, even for the betterment of the world. She must find another way to stop Double Kross before Double Kross finds her and takes her down.*

A crow flies in. It lands on Infinity Girl's shoulder. She is taken aback but doesn't shoo the bird away. Speech-bubble: *"Messenger 93, face what most frightens you."*

No no no. But before I could scratch it out, there was some movement across the street in the front hall of Krista's house. Shadows and striking bursts of light. And then there were people coming out. I crumpled the receipt and shoved it into my pocket.

It was the same uniformed police officer as that morning in school, and another man — grizzled, white, bald and mustached, wearing a wrinkled brown suit. They were talking to someone inside the house — I assumed it was Clio. They made grim, respectful gestures of goodbye and headed to the cruiser.

Clio stood in the doorway and watched the car drive off. Her face seemed to dissolve in the late afternoon light, paling into frail distress like a tissue in a puddle. She looked so alone. Abandoned. My heart ached for her. *This was Krista's fault.*

But there was another person in the house. And he came out then too.

Boy stepped onto the front stoop beside Clio. He didn't see me. Or anyway, he was looking down the street in the other direction. His face was ashen, eyebrows winched up in sorrowful misery, hair tousled in a way that showed he hadn't thought to brush it.

His sadness cut me. *That was Krista's fault too.*

He waved at Clio in the same grim, serious way that the cops had, and Clio gave him a weak smile. Hands in his pockets, he trudged down the stairs, down the front walkway, down the sidewalk. As if the crushing weight of every lost girl everywhere had landed on him.

I crossed the street and followed him, hypnotized by his scrunched back. I was about to call out when he pulled his phone from his pocket, punched in a number, and put it to his ear. I worked to break free of my rattling nerves, willed myself to go after him, when someone suddenly touched my arm in the softest, gentlest way.

Clio. She was looking up at me with an exhausted expression. She laid the tips of her fingers against my cheek. "Thank you so much for coming. It means the world."

"Oh, hi!" It was all I could say. The possibility that Clio remembered me was mindboggling.

She took my hand. I glanced back at Boy. He was walking faster now, still talking on his phone, too far away to notice me.

Clio led me up the walk and then up the stairs to her house.

Her hand was dry — sharp edges from pulled hangnails scratched at my fingers — and there was something childish about the way she gently tugged at me to come inside. Like we were going to see something marvelous together.

"They've been here for hours," she said as she led me down the grand entrance hall. "We've been going through all her things." She sighed as she spoke, tiny puffs of miserable air. "Her phone, her room, her computer, her locker. They took her hard drive. Do you know what that's like for a mom who promised to respect her child's privacy? It's — It's — I can't —" She shook her head and escorted me down another hall.

"I'm so sorry," I said. Useless. Somehow responsible.

It was sumptuous but gloomy inside the house. No sunlight streaming in through windows. No artificial light radiating from chandeliers. We arrived at a family room, and it was gigantic — expensive furniture, toys strewn everywhere. Blocks, trucks, picture books, stuffed animals, a rocking horse. There was a plate of cookies on the coffee table, crumbs from some having been eaten, four mugs of coffee in various states of emptiness/fullness.

Clio pushed aside some tiny car models on the couch, and they clattered noisily to the hardwood floor. "Please sit," she said, flopping into the luxurious cushions. "Forgive the mess."

I sat down beside her, sinking deep. It was warm and I unzipped my coat.

"Krista didn't take anything with her. She needs her medication —" Clio lifted a knuckle to her lips. It was terrible watching her try to erase her emotions. "She just left us."

She will fall. Seven days.

"I'm so sorry," I said.

She reached over and took my hand. Her hand started squeezing,

probably unconsciously because she squeezed too tight and it hurt.
"I drove the streets all night looking for her. Like you do for a lost
dog. Isn't that —" She let out a gaspy, half-hysterical laugh.

"You must be so tired," I said. This was outside my realm.

"I am," she said, sinking into herself, half-laughing again.
"I am very tired." She ran her fingers lightly over her cheeks.
I noticed for the first time that she had a light spray of freckles
across them, like aerosol-paint spatter. "I don't know why she
left." She slumped. "No one knows why she left." She seemed to
surprise herself with a thought, then turned to me. "Do you know
why?"

"I —" There had to be a reason. A good one. But I couldn't
think of any. Krista had everything. Including this — a loving,
worried, searching mother. "I'm sorry," I said. "I have no idea."

"She gets so —" She clawed at the air. "*Angry*. For no reason.
Ever since her dad —" She stopped. Her fingers wilted. She
gathered her hands in her lap and lingered on them.

"Yeah ..." I said, drawing it out to fill the silence.

"Did you know they took her toothbrush in for DNA evidence?
I mean — no expense spared. And I am so, so grateful. But —"
She looked up at me. Looked through me, really, to some infinite
place beyond my eyes. "If they find her, if she doesn't want me
to know where she is, then they are legally bound *not* to tell me
her whereabouts. *Me* — her own mother. Isn't that the most —?"
Her focus came back to this reality, and she grabbed my hand for
the third time. "Do you know where she is?"

"No, I'm sorry," I said. "I *wish* I knew where she was." I was
weirdly scared now.

She will fall in seven days.

"Aw, sweetie," she said. "I know how hard this is on you kids."

She let go of my hand. I was embarrassed at the hugeness of my relief. She bent over and gathered up a handful of little-kid puzzle pieces that were skittering under her foot. "Krista always loved puzzles," she said as she very carefully stacked the pieces one on top of the other. "Riddles. That kind of thing. I think that's why she sent that strange message. I think it's her way of processing since her dad died."

Everything inside me vibrated. "She sent a strange message?"

"Oh, maybe you'll understand it!" She jumped up. "They found her phone in that garbage can at school—" She disappeared around the corner, into the hall that led towards the back of the house.

She will fall. She will fall.

Clio came back a few seconds later holding Krista's phone. It was the same model as mine, protected inside a glitzy black-and-gold cover.

She plopped onto the couch beside me and said breathlessly, "Oh, I hope you can figure it out." She powered on the phone. The unlock screen came up. She glanced at me guiltily. "They hacked her passcodes. Don't judge me — we have no choice." Her fingers were trembling. She keyed in Krista's code. *9393.* "I wonder if you have any idea   " The screen unlocked — "what this means?" She tapped into the messages, then into a text, which she presented to me.

But I couldn't register the text or her question. My entire brain was occupied by a flashing set of numbers.

9393.

Was that really Krista's password?

Of course I couldn't ask Clio why Krista would've chosen that, or what it meant.

Messenger 93. You must find her.

But Clio was staring at me so directly it felt like a drill to my head. She was waiting for me to understand. "I'm sorry, what is it?" I said. My voice echoed. Someone else speaking.

You must find her. Only you can save her.

But I didn't want to save her. I couldn't.

Clio pointed at the phone. "These are the last two texts she sent before she left." She clicked out of the first text and into another one. "This is the one she sent to me."

I leaned in and begged every one of my brain cells to co-operate. To pay attention.

Don't worry, Mom, Krista's text read. *I'm okay. Not coming home til I work it out.*

"See," Clio said, pointing to the time-stamp. "She sent this at 12:45 p.m. yesterday. And then there's this one." She clicked back to the other text. "This is the message she sent Boyd right after, at 12:46 p.m."

I looked closely. The text to Boy was made up of the words *Only you*, followed by four emojis: the single eye, the finger-pointing-up, the scissors, and the tiny paired stars.

Clio hysteria-laughed again. "You see? Riddles! She wants him to find her, doesn't she? Aren't these little pictograms meant to show where she is? Aren't they clues?"

"Mm-hm, mm-hm," I could hear myself saying as she spoke. My head was nodding.

"He came over today — he's in such a state, oh my goodness, I feel so badly for him. He doesn't understand the clues! He doesn't know where she is, or why she's doing this."

"Boy, you mean? He doesn't understand her message?"

"No! None of us understands it!" Clio turned slightly away. Her mouth twitched. She didn't cry, but her eyelids puffed out

as if they'd instantly filled with tears.

"I'm so sorry." I looked into my lap — I couldn't face her fragile expression anymore. I had to get out of there.

Clio's eyes flicked to look behind me and her whole face softened. "Hey, buddy," she said. "Did we wake you?"

I turned around. Her kid was standing at the entrance to the family room. He wasn't a baby anymore — weird that I'd expected one, hadn't factored in the past year and a half. He had the soft jowly cheeks and pudgy fingers of your basic-model toddler, and pale skin with a paint-spatter of freckles, like his mom's but lighter. Freckles-in-training.

"Mommy?" he said, looking at me, tears pooling on his lower lids. "I don't feel good."

"It's because you need to go back to bed," Clio said.

"Thwoat hewt." He had that funny accent so many little kids have, where they can't pronounce their Rs. "I'm *sick*."

"It's okay, Eddie," Clio said. "You're not sick. You're just tired. It's been a long —"

And then he puked. It squooshed out of his mouth and dribbled down his chin and onto the front of his pajamas.

"Oh gosh." Clio was up.

The kid began to cry. Clio picked up a random cloth and used it to wipe his face and chest. She murmured at him, "It's okay, sweetie, it's okay." But he bawled like a baby while she threw the cloth to the floor and pulled off his pukey pajamas. "Sh-sh. You're just surprised." She threw the pajamas down too and picked him up. "It's okay. Everything is fine." The kid was naked except for a diaper, and she wrapped her arms around his diapered butt and walked him over to me. "Please, do you mind?" She released him onto my lap. He was incredibly heavy. "He just needs a little

comfort while I —" Clio went back for the pajamas and cloth. "I'll just be a minute." She bundled them together and retreated down the hall towards the back of the house.

Eddie stopped crying and stared at me with weepy eyes, tears and snot rolling down his pudgy, almost-freckled face. He hiccupped and took in a tragic gulp of breath. There was a thunking sound from down the hall of a washing machine being opened.

He said, "De bewd wants you to go."

I didn't want to scare him. I said, "What?"

"De black bewd said it." His eyes were tiny little swimming pools.

Then I remembered — the baby couldn't pronounce his Rs. "The *bird* said I have to go?

"Yes."

Everything liquid inside me crystalized.

"What bird, Eddie?"

"It said de boy will help you."

I stood up. The kid rocked happily in my arms.

I didn't know what to do. What I wanted to do was bolt.

There was a sudden loud rush of running water as Clio started a load of laundry.

I noticed Krista's phone in its black-and-gold case. Clio had left it on the couch.

Krista's life would be in her phone. Information. Important places. Significant people. Her phone could potentially point to where she was. The cops, Krista's mother, they already had all the data. But what if they didn't understand the clues? And what if I could? Eventually, with time and quiet focus.

Honestly, I don't know what got into me, but I was suddenly bending over, heaving the kid with one arm, and reaching around

his padded butt to rifle in my backpack for my own phone. I angled my back to the hallway because I didn't know how much longer Clio would be gone. I thought I heard a door open and close somewhere.

I pulled my SIM card out of my phone. I popped Krista's phone out of her glittery case and rammed mine inside it. But my phone didn't snap into her case right away, and I grunted and pushed at the corners. The kid started to giggle. He thought we were playing a game.

"Eddie! I guess you're feeling better." Clio's voice behind me.

I dropped my phone, now in Krista's case. It landed softly on the sumptuous couch. I bolted upright, tugging the kid close to me. "I'm sorry," I said, fighting tears. "I don't know what I'm doing."

"Aw, you're doing great." Clio had her eyes on Eddie. She looked like she'd been crying. "Thank you so much."

I grasped Krista's stolen phone against my palm.

Clio took the kid from me and tugged a onesie over his bare parts.

"I'm sorry," I said, cringing away from them, fumbling with my coat pocket, dropping Krista's phone and my SIM card into it. "I have to go." I grabbed my backpack and headed to the front door.

"Wait, wait." Clio called out. I squirmed and looked back. She was lifting the plate of cookies off the coffee table. There was a small pile of business cards underneath it. She brought me one. Actually tucked it into my same hand that had, a second before, been hiding her missing daughter's phone.

Detective Stanzi, the card read, then his precinct, address, and phone numbers.

"We're handing those out to everyone. Please, if you think of anything ..."

If you think of anything. Just like a real-life murder mystery.

I really, really had to get out of there.

"Bye, Eddie." I waved clumsily and half-stumbled down the hall and through the grand entrance towards the front door. I can't say for sure if Clio was watching me the whole time, but it was a super-long hallway.

I BASICALLY RACED MY beating heart down the street. *What was I doing? What was I thinking?* I'd just stolen a phone that was a mother's connection to her runaway daughter. Was I *supposed* to take it? Was that it? It was a dire situation, and I'd been asked, or commanded, or ordained, to help. *The bird wants you to go.* The *black bewd*, he'd called it. *It said you have to go.*

But, no. Just no. I couldn't help them. Because I didn't know what I was doing.

Daylight had changed again. Somewhere behind the matte of clouds, the sun was dipping into early evening. I ran all the way to the bus stop. I hailed the next bus without checking the route. There were people on board — there must've been — but I was so inside my own mess, I didn't register anything except the few inches in front of my face. The bus doors levering open to usher me in, the fluorescent lights tinting the air blue, the smeared floor of the aisle as I walked down it, the free seat against the window.

I reached into my coat pocket. Krista's phone, my SIM card, and Detective Stanzi's business card came out clinging to each other. I tossed my SIM. Punishment for my stupid recklessness. Detective Stanzi went back into my pocket. *If you think of anything.* And now there was only Krista's phone in my hand.

9393.

The screen came to life.

I clicked into her texts first. The one to her mom: *Don't worry, Mom. I'm okay. Not coming home til I work it out.* And the one to Boy: *Only you.* Single eye emoji, pointing-up-finger, scissors, two tiny stars.

It looked like Clio was right: that Krista was playing some kind of warped hide-and-seek with Boy. Of course she'd leave clues. Like a serial killer hiding in her secret lair who wants to be found. Or admired. Or both.

Still, I played with interpretations.

Eye emoji: Definitely, *Look for me.* Up-finger: Probably, *I'm over here.* But where? A high-up place? North of the city? Scissors: Maybe, *We'll cut ourselves off from the world.* Either that or, *I'm hiding at a crafts store.* Stars: There were no observatories or planetariums that I knew of, so it couldn't be, *Let's look at the stars together.* So probably she meant, *Follow all these clues and I will blow your mind.* Obviously, it was supposed to be romantic.

I clicked into her social media. Her Ittch grid was full of selfies of Krista-in-all-her-glory, or snuggling with Boy, or her and her friends performing seductions for the lens. Parties, hangouts, shopping, coffee, new outfits, new makeup, new hairstyles. She was beautiful. I had to accept it. Or at least, pretty. Or maybe it didn't even matter how she *looked* — she had something that I didn't. Sparkle. Lustre. Fierce determination to be better than everyone else.

I spent an embarrassing amount of time staring at the pictures of her and Boy.

I don't even want to talk about it.

By the time I looked up again, it was dark out, and I was somewhere in the city that I didn't recognize. Artificial lights had powered on inside buildings and glowed from streetlamps and passing cars.

I flew off the seat and rang the bell. Jumped off the bus in a whirring panic. *Where was I?* Probably just a few steps from the scene of my death.

I'd definitely ended up all the way on the other side of the city. It was the kind of street lined with grungy Mom-and-Pop stores and unappetizing restaurants. Where the streetlights don't make much of a dent to the nighttime dark. Sketchy old people wandered around or leaned against buildings.

I pulled my coat hood over my head and dipped into a beat-up diner. It was bustling inside and I pushed up against the front plate-glass window and pulled out Krista's phone. I would call my dad to pick me up on his way home from work. He always worked late. Nine/ten usually. He'd be pissed, and probably confused, but so be it.

The smell of fried food — chicken, fries, eggs — filled my nose and reminded me that I hadn't eaten since the bowl of cereal that morning. Thirteen hours ago. My stomach rumbled. Loudly. My mouth watered. I was sure I was lightheaded, or low-blood-sugared. Maybe Dad and I could stop for fast food on the way home.

My fingers hovered over Krista's keypad ... But I couldn't remember Dad's phone number. I started and stopped dialing a dozen times. I'd never had to phone him without using one-touch. Same with my mother. Same with our home line. If I'd known their numbers at some earlier point in my life, maybe forced to memorize them for circumstances exactly like this, they were gone from my brain now. Replaced by a million more urgent, necessary, life-saving details.

"Table for one, sweetheart?" It was a tiny older woman with a super-cool bobbed haircut.

I was voraciously hungry.

"Yes, please."

I followed her to the next empty booth. She handed me a laminated menu, and I was so hungry, I didn't even let her leave. "Veggie burger and fries, please. An apple juice. And a coffee." I wasn't much of a coffee drinker, but I needed the caffeine hit.

She smiled at me in a knowing way — like she knew I was an imposter in her land, but she'd be hospitable as long as I didn't cause any trouble.

I contemplated Krista's phone again. I could dial Information, or 911, or message my parents through their socials and hope they checked. There were options for help.

But I didn't do any of that. I lurked Krista's private life some more. Ate my wondrous meal in glorious solitude. Pondered all the strange developments of that strange day.

It said de boy will help you.

What had Eddie meant by that? Was it truly another message from the crow?

The boy.

Was I supposed to contact *Boy*?

And really, that would make sense. If anyone knew Krista's secret thoughts, it would be Boy. Although I assumed that was the reason he'd been with Clio all day. Telling her and the cops everything he knew.

Krista's phone didn't offer anything useful either. Nothing in her search history, or feeds, or texts with her friends. It was all so ... *boring*.

"Ooh, that's cute."

It was the waitress picking up my empty plate, dropping the bill on the table. I followed her pointing finger. Krista's Ittch feed was on the screen again, but this time it was showing one of the profiles she'd "liked" the most. Some random girl who lived on the west coast, who mostly posted photos of herself in tiny bikinis.

The waitress's finger landed on the screen. She was pointing at a photo of the the girl's perfect bare legs. "Adding that one to the mood board," the waitress said, her finger outlining a tattoo on the girl's ankle, just above the bone. It was a simple silhouette of a black bird. Kind of like the drawing on the torn scrap of paper inside Krista's locker.

The paradox.

Clio hadn't taken any of those pictures off the locker door that morning. No one had investigated them. What if there was something there that everyone had missed?

I grabbed my wallet. I didn't have any cash, so I pulled out the family emergency credit card. The server brought me the machine and I made sure to key in a nice tip.

If I could just get a look inside that locker, at that picture of the bird, maybe all questions would be answered, and this weird quest would come to its final and fated end.

Only you can find her.

AN HOUR AND TWO bus transfers later, I walked into Emmet Park — the largest park in our neighborhood. Haphazard pools of light illuminated a patch of playground sand here, or a curve of sidewalk there. I avoided the light and ran through the dewy grass. I remembered how our dog Pepper, before he got hit by the car, used to suck on the longer blades whenever I took him for a walk.

I went all the way to the far end of the park. Across the street, my school rose up like a prison. I slumped onto a bench and caught my breath. I was getting tired now. It was late — 11:00. Then I realized I was sitting on the exact bench where Krista had sat on her last day, in her last recorded moments, and I launched up so fast, it was like escaping a monster. Or the ridiculous but so-possible possibility that the bench had sucked Krista into another dimension.

I ran to the main doors of the school and wrenched at the handles. They were locked. I ran to the side doors, and they were locked too. I walked around to the side of the school that faced the football field. Without the light of day, the field was almost totally black.

I peered through the dark and saw a yellow rectangle gleaming on the grass between me and the school's back wall. *A portal to an enchanted underworld. Its gate had swung open and it was luring me over. Oh hello, Crow. I'm coming to get you.*

When I was only a house-length away, a small red ember arced through the air and landed on the portal's gleaming force-field. The ember hissed and expired, and the illusion broke. Just a cigarette stub on a reflection of light. I looked over and noticed there was a recess in the school's back wall. Inside the recess — now it all made sense — someone was ending their smoke break at an open door. Shadows moved across the reflection on the grass — whoever it was had turned and was stepping back inside.

The rectangle of light began to slowly narrow. The door was closing, pulled by one of those pneumatic arms. I ran towards it, sprinting over the last few feet, and dove into the alcove just in time to squeeze my toe under the door before it locked into place. Gulping air as quietly as I could, I hoped that Cigarette Smoker wouldn't notice the door hadn't fully closed. I waited a few minutes before daring to move, then contorted my body to replace my toehold with a fingerhold, and then my finger with my hand.

I inched the door open and peered inside. At the far end of the hall, there was a pail on wheels with a mop stabbed into it and, beside it, a trolley of cleaning products. The janitor was nowhere to be seen, although I could hear echoed shuffling in the distance. I'd never met the nighttime custodian and had no idea if he could be trusted not to kill me.

Still, I edged myself inside and squinted against the staggeringly bright fluorescents. Shielding my eyes so I could see where I was going, I ducked down the hall that led away from the mop and bucket, and into the hall with Krista's locker. Just a quick peek inside and I'd be gone.

Except they'd put a new lock on the door.

Respecting her privacy, or something.

The outside of her locker had been plastered with messages and plastic flowers and taped-on stuffed animals. *Krista, come home! Krista, we love you!* Homages to everyone's most cherished friend.

I pulled out her phone and launched the browser and searched how to break a combination lock. It looked surprisingly easy. Apply pressure to the shackle, spin the dial, note the numbers where it catches. Rotate both ways until you find the single points of resistance, then try combinations of combinations until you get the right order. *Five minutes*, they promised, *It can be done in under five minutes*.

I found a pen in my bag and began the process — rotating the lock clockwise then counterclockwise, feeling for each slight notch where the dial caught — a single point of resistance — then writing each possible number on my hand. I tried a combination and tugged on the lock, but the shackle clunked in the case. Listening for the janitor, I tried another set of numbers. I spun the dial and tugged on the lock. Again the shackle clunked and stuck. Another combination. Clunk, stuck. Then another. Clunk, stuck. Different arrangements of numbers. Dialing left past zero, then right again. Clunk stuck. Right, left, right. Clunk stuck. Right, left, right. Clunk stuck clunk stuck clunk stuck.

More than five minutes.

More minutes.

Even more minutes.

Too many minutes.

I had to give up. I couldn't do it. Why had I ever thought I could do it?

The lock clicked and slipped open.

I almost whooped, but I didn't. I pulled the locker door as quietly as I could. The clang and grate of metal on metal echoed and I cringed and looked both ways down the hall. All coasts were clear.

Inside was a neat stack of Krista's binders and textbooks. I remembered Clio going through everything that morning, then returning the pile to its place and tweaking and adjusting until it was all perfect for Krista's return.

The ripped scrap of paper with the bird silhouette was still there, still taped to the upper left-hand corner on the inside of the door. I worked gently at the tape so I wouldn't tear the paper. It was just a regular drawing, something like the one on the girl's ankle in the Ittch photo. I turned it over. The back was blank. *Nothing. A dead end.*

I was about to close the locker when I noticed one of those eight-by-ten plastic envelopes on top of Krista's neatly investigated pile of stuff. The envelope was clear and logoed — *Go-go Go-go Go-go* stamped in rows across the front and back. Through the clear part, I could see it held a collection of instant photos. Ever since I'd known her, Krista had had one of those cameras.

I couldn't resist: I had to open the envelope and check inside. Just in case.

But it was only a bunch of dramatic modeling shoots in theatrical locations featuring Krista and her friends.

A rumble echoed through the hallway — the janitor was just around the nearest corner. The shock made me bumble the envelope. A bunch of photos skidded out and along the floor. I froze. It was deathly quiet in the halls — the janitor maybe frozen and listening too.

I scrambled to gather up the mess, shoving the photos back into the envelope, trying not to make a sound, or lose my balance, or whack my head against the open locker door.

Go-go Go-go Go-go written across the plastic envelope. *Go. Go. Go. Go. Go. Go.*

It was still absolutely quiet, the janitor maybe still listening, maybe sneaking up on me now.

The last photo was in my hand. I was almost free.

Before I could throw it inside the envelope, I was startled to see that it was one with Krista and me together. She was grabbing my face, which was squished and cringing, my eyes squeezed closed, my mouth stretched into a wincing smile. Krista was in profile, her lips were pressed against my cheek.

I couldn't remember the photo being taken, or who had taken it. Had it been Anusha? Hattie? Boy? I couldn't confirm the location, or even the timing — except that it would've been sometime after we'd started school together and before the moment Krista had decided to erase me.

. Krista and me. Her kissing me. My own beaming surprise caught on bleached-out laminated film stock.

I stood up and my shoulder banged against the metal door. The sound echoed down the hall. "Hey!" His voice echoed back at me from around the corner. Now I heard the beat of his footsteps advancing. But something else too. A rhythmic *whack* like he was using a long-barrel rifle to propel himself towards me.

Go. Go. Go! Go!

I threw the envelope back inside Krista's locker and closed the door. Fumbled to get the lock back into the holster.

"Hey! Hey!" He was thunking faster now, getting closer.

It was too far to the exit at the end of the hall. I tested the doorknob of the nearest classroom. Open. I cranked the door as quietly as I could and ducked inside.

It wasn't a classroom I'd been in before, and it was like every classroom I'd ever been in. I crept to the back and camouflaged myself in a huddle on the ground, amid the skeletal legs of desks and chairs.

The photo of Krista kissing me was still in my hand. I stuck it into my coat pocket along with her drawing of the bird silhouette. I held my breath, filling with doubt that I would make it out of there alive.

FRIDAY, APRIL 13

SIX DAYS UNTIL THE FALL

1

I DIDN'T LET MYSELF fall asleep. Actually, I tried everything in my power to *not* fall asleep. But, I fell deep. When my eyes fluttered open, it was dark in the classroom, and still dark outside through the windows. My body had twisted fetal underneath a desk. I began to shiver, chilled from so many hours curled on a hard tile floor.

"Messenger 93." There it was. The female/male voice. Its reasonable and patient tone. "She will fall in six days."

I bolted upright and looked around.

But I couldn't see the crow.

The shadows in the room were epic. Like the set of a horror movie.

I fought my body's urge to blindly run.

"Hello?" I whispered. "Are you there?" I unfolded my limbs slowly. "What do you want me to do?" Slowly pulled myself up into the terrifying darkness.

Shoot the messenger. Wasn't that an actual expression?

"What am I supposed to do?" I whispered, louder this time.

But the crow was gone. Or it wasn't speaking to me anymore.

Maybe I'd achieved a whole new level of invisible. Erased by my own haunting voice.

She will fall in six days reverberated through my mind — a menacing countdown — as I stealth-crept out of the room.

The janitor was clearly gone — all the lights in the school had been turned off — so I ran full-tilt. Nothing but echoes to chase me down the hall and out the side doors.

I RAN THROUGH THE night. There were no buses running at that time. Whatever time it was.

Before I knew it, I was standing in front of Boy's house.

The bird wants you to go. The black bird. It said the boy will help you.

I stared at his house, remembering the old days — how we'd started off as kids in sandboxes, then graduated to school-yards, and eventually to long bouts on his couch playing video games. By the time Krista showed up, his house had become our group's central hangout because his parents were almost never home — his dad was setting up some huge office in Singapore, and his mom would go visit for long stretches. Just the nanny to watch us, who was too sweet and too busy to challenge any of our exploits.

Except for some security lights, all the windows in the house were dark.

Boy's room was on the second floor, one window facing the street and one facing the side garden — a narrow strip of land occupied by a single, sturdy maple. It was the middle of the night, so I couldn't just knock on the door and request his company. And I wasn't going to ping stones at the window until he opened it and let me in.

I contemplated the maple, its branches arcing upwards like a fluted ladder. For a few years when we were young — eight, nine, ten — the maple had been our favorite point of entry into Boy's house. We felt like we were accessing a secret club or fort. One at a time, we'd wriggle up the trunk and across the strongest branch. The first one up — usually Boy — would jam a binder edge into the bottom lip of the window and lever it up. Then, one by one, we'd each spill into his room.

The sound of our laughter — cascading, ecstatic, pure — came back to me.

If the crow wanted me to talk to Boy, if *Boy was going to help me*, then it must've meant he and I were supposed to find Krista *together*.

A startling possibility.

Except — what if I told him about the crow and he made fun of me like he used to?

Maybe that would be okay too. Boy's teasing would help me shake the crow off. I could get on with my life.

Or what if talking about Krista devastated him? What if he didn't want to be reminded that she was gone? He might be triggered to guilt and shame — he hadn't been able to stop her from leaving.

But then there was the possibility that Boy would be able to figure out the crow's messages. He knew Krista better than anyone. There was a genuine chance — if I asked the right question in the right way — that he would understand everything.

That would be a good thing, wouldn't it?

The boy will help you.

I headed towards the maple as if I'd been training for that moment my whole life. In the opalescent midnight dark, the tree looked like a multi-limbed deity. My feet scrabbled against its trunk and I grabbed at the lowest branch. But with zero upper body strength — wearing a thousand-pound backpack and dedicating yourself to homework and streamed music will do that — I lost my grip and fell.

I unstrapped my backpack and tried again. Then I tried again. And a few more times after that. Until I finally managed to lift myself high enough to hook my arm around the lowest branch and winch myself up. I caught my breath and began to climb higher, crouching up and hoisting myself onto the next branch. And then the next higher branch. That was the one I needed. The one that curved towards Boy's house, brushing against the brickwork near his window. I wrapped my legs around it and scooted along until the window was within touching distance. His curtains were closed, and behind the curtains it was dark. Asleep, or not at home.

A wave of willful belief surged through me. Boy would be there and he would talk to me and he would get it. He'd grasp a key piece of information that would help all of us see what needed to be seen.

I'd forgotten to bring along a binder to pry the window open, so I fished in my coat pocket for my bus pass. I stretched off the branch as far as I could. The tip bowed and rocked. I was a lot heavier than I'd been at ten. If I was going to survive the jump into his window, I'd have to use quick and accurate movements.

I slipped the bus pass under the bottom edge of the window-pane and jerked around until the pane lifted ever so slightly. Then I braced my fingers under the sash and pressed up. The window slid open as easily as if I were inside on a summer day and just wanted a cool breeze.

Before I could second-guess my decision, before Boy could wake up and maybe defend himself in some violent way, I launched myself off the branch and into his room.

There was a commotion. Grunting, a stifled scream, thumping, stumbling, a bang, and a soft thud. But I hardly made a sound — I landed clean on the broadloom, like a cat. The air was humid; it smelled stale and salty.

A reading light clicked on and Boy was staring at me from his bed. My heart tilted in its familiar, sickening way.

He blinked a few times, like he couldn't make sense of what he was seeing — not "who is that?" but "*what* is that?" His thick, loopy hair was rumpled, sticking up. The sheet was pulled tight against his waist. He wasn't wearing pajamas, or at least his chest was bare, and there was a blotch of bright red on his white, hard-muscled skin. He didn't look like he'd just been woken from a deep sleep. Actually, he looked pretty alert.

"It's okay, Boy. It's just me. It's me."

Being with him in his room brought me straight back to the old days when we used to hang out, flopped on his bed, laughing until I thought I'd burst. A feeling of pure joy came over me.

"What is — What the —" He rattled his head.

"I know, Boy. I'm sorry. I had to come —"

"You can't just break into my room —"

"I know, I get it. But wait till I tell you "

"It's like the middle of the —"

"Just hear me out for a minute —"

"Middle of the — It's fucking —" He fumbled with his phone. Checked the screen.

"Please, Boy — I just need to talk to you about this one thing —"

"Are you high?"

"No!"

He leaned on his arm to look behind me, as if the shadows in his room were explaining why I was there. "Aw shit." He slumped and ran a hand through his rumpled hair. "If I hear you out, will you leave?"

"Trust me. If you hear this, you will get it."

He sighed. "Okay, whatever, go on."

But I couldn't have stopped it from coming out if I'd tried. My heart was pounding so fast, it was a volcanic eruption.

"I had this dream yesterday night, Boy. Not a regular dream. But a mind-blowing one. I dreamt that this giant crow came out of the sky and it had this really important message it had to give me. In my dream, I watched it fly closer and closer, and it was creepy and weird, but also really magical and cool. And then the whole thing started to feel really real." Chills and goosebumps threaded over my skin and up over my head. I couldn't believe it was finally okay to tell someone. "But then I could feel myself wake up, and when I opened my eyes, the crow was right there. Like, it was actually hovering over my bed. And it spoke to me. I could see it and hear it *in my room*. It called me Messenger 93. It told me that I had to find Krista. That if I don't find her in seven days —" I took a breath. "Then she's going to *fall*, Boy. It told me I had to *save* her. That saving her would save us all. That's exactly what the crow said, I swear. *As she falls, so do we all*." The edges of reality softened and smudged, like a vintage film shot. "And then today, Boy? Clio's kid — the baby? — he said that a *crow told him* that you're going to help me." I pointed out the open window at the maple tree. "That's why I had to come here, Boy. It's like a sign or something. We can't ignore it. We're supposed to do this together."

Boy had such a look of amazement on his face. It was disorienting and thrilling to have him see me again. No excuses, no Krista pulling him away.

"We have to find her, Boy. We still have six days. We can save her."

A smile suffused my whole being. I felt beauteous. Krista wasn't even a person anymore. She was a *mission*.

"C'mon, Boy, say something." I smiled at him. Let his incredulous gaze penetrate me. "What do you think?"

"For fuck's sake." The hardness of his voice startled me. Those were the last words I expected to hear in that sacred, awe-filled moment. "My name is Boy*ddddd*. *Boyd*. With a 'd' at the end." My body went cold as his words serrated the stale and salty air.

Boy. It was my nickname for him.

"A *crow*? *Messenger 93*? You know that's crazy, right?"

The story of the crow recoiled back inside me like a pulled cord. I could feel it winding tightly inwards, into my deepest emptiness, away and out of his sight.

But I nodded and managed a smile. "You're right, Boyd. I'm so sorry." I was very small. A cricket. "I haven't had much sleep." I was hyper-conscious of my blinking eyes. How Boyd disappeared and reappeared, disappeared and reappeared. "Okay, I'll get out of your hair now."

"Good." He flopped his head back, cringed like he was in pain.

"Okay, well —" A cool breeze swirled in through the open window. "Before I go —" I readjusted my clothes like they were somehow stopping me from leaving right away. "It's just that — Can I ask you one more thing?"

"Seriously?"

"Can you think of anything about Krista that you haven't told anyone else? Something that might help find her? Even if it seems random or insignificant?"

"You don't think her mom and the cops and everyone asked me that already? You don't think I told them? They downloaded all our data. They have *everything* we ever did or said. They *searched my house*. Homicide and Missing Persons. That's what the department is called. Like I hid her body in the walls or something."

"Wow," I said. "That is — That's terrible."

He scrunched the hem of the sheet against his bare chest. His expression lost its edge. "I swear, I have no idea where she is." His voice lost its edge too. He sounded more like the Boy — Boy*d* — I remembered. "Other than the text," he said, "I haven't heard from her at all since she left."

"And what about the text?"

"What about the text?"

"*Only you*? The emojis? The eye, finger, scissors, stars?" Yes, I'd unintentionally memorized it. "What do you think it means?"

"I don't know," he said, exasperated. Traumatized maybe. "That she was pissed I broke up with her?"

The flow of blood to my head stopped. I reached for the windowsill. "You broke up?"

Boyd collapsed into a deep, despairing slump. He said, so low it was almost a whisper, "It happened right before she left. The night before." He groaned and rubbed at his face, his eyes. "Aw shit! I shouldn't have said anything." He threw his head back, scrunched at the sheet along his chest. "This is my fault."

"No, Boyd, it's not. It's not your —"

"Please don't tell anyone, okay?" He looked at me and there were actual tears brimming along his bottom lids. "Her mom doesn't even know yet. I was going to tell her yesterday — But there was too much — She was crying — Expecting me to — Please don't tell anyone! I'll do it. I swear. I'll tell her today."

"Sure, of course. I would never tell." I fumbled with my coat. It was impossible to process.

"I'm not smart like you guys." He stuck his thumbs into his tears and jerked them away. "I'm not a *detective*. I don't know what any of your messages mean."

I tried to clear my head. "I thought there were no other messages."

"*Your* message. I don't know what it means either."

I racked my brain — somehow I'd lost track of what we were talking about. "You mean the stuff about the crow and saving Krista?"

He threw up his hands in frustration. "Krista hates you. Why do you even care what happens to her?"

It was too much. I didn't know *what* I wanted right now, what I was supposed to do, what any of this meant. I looked out the window and measured the distance to the maple's reaching arm. If I missed, it was a long way down. Falling might actually be less painful than this.

I tried a low-key impression of my brother Trevor: "If the crow says you have to go, then you have to go." And before I could speak another tragically miscalculated word, I launched myself out of Boyd's window and into the night.

2

THAT WAS IT — I had cracked. It had been one too many things and I had cracked and I would be forever broken. And my brokenness would be glaring to everyone and it would be the only thing anyone would ever see and I would be accused of being nothing but eggshell for the rest of my life.

I hooked my backpack over my shoulders and ran blindly down the street. Boyd's words kept repeating in my head.

I have no idea where she is. She was pissed I broke up with her. I hid her body in the walls. Krista hates you. Why do you even care what happens to her? Fucking crazy.

I collapsed on someone's driveway behind their giant burgundy SUV. Didn't people self-harm when it got to be too much? It suddenly seemed like a solid approach. If you hurt yourself, all other hurts would pale.

I slapped the pavement. There was a radiation of heat. Tiny pebbles imbedded my palms. I slapped the pavement again, harder. The ache was metallic. Electric. I slapped again and again. There was something to it. Boyd — his scorn, his despair, his distractingly bare chest — receded with each fresh blow.

"Hey, hey, stop."

I turned around to find a woman standing over me. She was backlit and mostly a silhouette, but I could see she was fussing with her jacket, zipping it up. As my vision adjusted to the dark, she began to rack into focus. Not a woman — a girl. Rows of smooth gold-ringed braids framing her face. "Remy?"

"Hey. Hi." Everything about her was tense. On high alert. "I just came from Boyd's."

The stifled scream when I jumped in — it had sounded high for Boyd.

"You were there?"

"It freaked me out when you came in through the window." She was pulling out her phone, tapping into the screen. "I kind of ended up on the other side of the room."

Mortification filled me. It set me on fire. "You heard all that?"

I remembered Boyd eyeing that one dark corner behind me.

"He needs my help right now, okay? This has been really hard on him." Bitterness seemed to ignite off her, drifting through the air and landing like tiny alien beings on my skin. She stuck her illuminated phone in my face. "Why did you send this to him?"

I stood up. It was a screencap of a message in Boyd's inbox. An owl emoji, *Fri at 2* beside it.

The message was from my Ittch account. The Ittch account I had deleted a year ago. Sent the morning before. Around the time I was loitering in front of Boyd's locker. "I didn't send that."

"At first I thought it was because you had something to do with Krista being gone."

"*Me?*"

"Because you hate her so much."

"I don't *hate* — I don't —" But I did. More than anything.

"I was going to tell the cops about you, but Boyd wouldn't let me. He couldn't figure out what you wanted, but he didn't think you, like, *kidnapped* her or something."

I remembered how Remy had lurked me at school all day. Like she was at war with me.

I could hardly speak. "Well ... Good. Because I didn't."

"Yeah, I know that now. After what just happened."

All the things I'd said about the crow.

"Are you trying to get with him?" She looked so serious, I almost laughed.

"No," I said, just as seriously. "That is so —" I couldn't think of the right word — "gross."

She took a breath. Seemed to relax.

I examined my palm. The pavement had left a mosaic of tiny indentations. "So you and Boyd are together?"

"I — I think so."

Remy sitting on the sidewalk down the street from Krista's house. Waiting for Boyd to finish with the cops and Clio. There to help him through his trauma.

"Does Krista know about you?"

"God, no!"

All the new pieces of information were still floating in. Landing one by one.

Boyd had broken up with Krista.

Boyd   had broken up   *with Krista.*

Boyd   *had broken up with*   Krista.

It didn't seem like a possibility. And I don't mean a *possibility* in this story of Krista, I mean a *possibility* in all the manifestations of the space-time continuum.

They were the perfect couple. Soul mates. Destined to be together always.

But they had ended. And now he was with Remy.

"He's such a mess," Remy said plaintively, as if she'd heard my thoughts. "I don't know what's going to happen."

I ran my fingers over the indentations on my palm. "It's not Boyd's fault that Krista ran away," I said. "He's allowed to break up with her. He's allowed to be with you."

"That's what I keep saying!"

And he was. Remy was a thousand-million times better than Krista. Anyway, it would never be me.

Remy seemed to consider something. Her expression changed — she was older than me suddenly. *The mature one.* "You said you wanted to know everything about Krista?" she said. "Even if it seemed random and insignificant."

"Yeah?"

"I don't know what this is." She huddled her chin into her jacket collar. "Or if someone told the cops or Krista's mom about it already."

"What?"

"The day she ran off, I saw her at the park with that dell girl." She raised her eyebrows, waiting for me to react.

"From the deli? On Twentieth?"

"No. *Dell*. You know, *Dell*."

My brain scanned over all the school-famous names and faces I was supposed to know. There was no Dell in any memory track. "From Careers and Civics?"

"No. *Dell*. *Dell*. You don't know *Dell*? She's that social media star. The one on Ittch with all the followers."

Except I wasn't on Ittch. Despite owl messages sent from my account the day before.

Remy said, "She goes to Fairdale Collegiate?"

I still had no idea who we were talking about.

"I couldn't believe it was her," Remy was saying. "I'd never seen her in real life before. And there she was with Krista."

If Remy knew who Dell was, Krista must've known too. It should've impressed her. Meant something to her. "What time?"

"Like, 12:30. Lunch break."

Everyone already knew that Krista's last confirmed sighting was lunchtime in the park in front of our school. But I hadn't heard anyone talk about seeing a famous girl named Dell.

"You talked to them?"

"No. God, no."

"You saw them talking to each other?"

"She was posing."

"Krista posed for her?"

"No, Dell was posing. Krista took a picture of her, then she gave Dell her phone back and then she left with her friends."

"Krista left?"

"No, *Dell* left ... Here, wait." She tapped into her phone again, clicked into her Ittch account, and angled the screen towards me.

Dell was gut-wrenchingly pretty. Her style was late-last-century: tousled white-blond hair; calligraphic eye liner; tight top, loose pants or tight pants, loose top; various vintage leather boots; strategic skin. She had more followers than kids who went to all the high schools in the city combined.

Remy clicked on the latest post. Sultry cool-weather look. Pale pink full-length cashmere coat fluttering open to reveal a tight, black, belted one-piece. It was one of the few long shots on her feed. Framed, I guess, to show her arm sticking out and her thumb pointing down. Behind her was a short stretch of park grass, then the street, then our school. Underneath the photo, there were thousands of likes, hundreds of comments.

"She does this thing," Remy said, pulling her phone back to look at the photo herself, "where she picks a school and challenges the girls to beat her like-count. Then she gets shots of herself in front of the losing school." She waggled her phone at me. "Like this. Always taken by someone who goes there. But this post? The one Krista took? It went viral. Like, it sent Dell to a whole new level. *Everyone* knows her now. They just announced her as the host of that huge Influencers party next week."

I waited for some epic meaning to fall into place. A clue that would reveal Krista's true whereabouts. But nothing. There hadn't been a big fight between Krista and Dell. Krista hadn't run after them. Dell hadn't forced her into a van or anything.

Remy looked at me expectantly. "I mean ... Maybe *Dell* knows something. And — I don't know — maybe if it's a young person asking her questions, instead of, like, a cop or whatever, she might tell you something."

"You think *Dell* might tell me something?"

"Yeah, I don't know. Maybe? If she knows something."

"Hmm." I pretended to consider it.

Dell was clearly older than us. Not exactly the kind of person I could walk up to and investigate — if that's what I was going to do.

"Okay, well ... That's all I got." Remy slipped her phone back inside her jacket pocket and zipped it shut. "I should go."

"Yeah, me too." Although I didn't know where.

She eyed me. "I think it's pretty cool what you're doing."

That was mind-blowing.

She smiled, then took off, running away into the dark before I could smile back.

I PULLED OUT KRISTA'S phone and clicked into Ittch. My profile still existed. As if I'd never deleted it. But my grid was gone, and my follower count was 1. When I clicked to see who the follower was, it was me. I logged in with my old information — and it worked. I checked the inbox, and there it was — the owl emoji and the *Fri at 2* message, sent to Boyd.

It was so confusing, I almost wondered for a second if I *had* done it. Reactivated my account to send Boyd a luring message.

An owl. A day and a time. But they were meaningless to me.

Clio's voice floated in, her saying, *Krista always loved puzzles. Riddles.*

Krista. Of course it was Krista.

She knew my logins. The so-many times she'd grabbed my phone when we were still friends. Her going into my feeds, posting stuff for me in the name of fun and games. My friends turning on me for things they were certain I'd done or said behind their backs.

Krista had orchestrated it all. Sent messages from my accounts to make a point, then deleted them so I wouldn't find out.

I wanted to sink into despair. It was too unfair. Her taking everything away from me — using ploys and tricks — for some mystical reason I could never figure out. *Why? What had I ever done to her?*

But I didn't have time for despair. It was the middle of the night, and I was *so close* to finding the key. To getting out of this torturous nightmare.

At least now I understood why Krista had run away. She was a) heartbroken; b) humiliated; c) plotting her revenge; d) all of the above.

But why would she pose as me to talk to Boyd?

Because she wanted to see him. Because no one would think the message had come from her and use it to track her. Because I was never going to check my Ittch, and no one was ever going to question me about anything. She must've thought — for a reason I couldn't understand — that there was a real chance Boyd would meet me somewhere on Friday at two. *Today* at two. And instead she would be there in my place. And she would — *What*? What would she do? Woo him back?

Her text to Boyd took on a whole new meaning. Single eye:

Watch out. Finger: *I'm your one and only*. Scissors: *Find me or I will slice you*. Stars: *And this is where you'll end up*.

Krista was trying to correct the tragic course of her life.

But where was she? And what was she planning?

Eye. Finger. Scissors. Stars.

I'd always thought I was pretty smart. I did well in school. Could string lucid ideas together. Could write a mean essay. Had legit taste in music. Didn't get carried away by absurd romantic notions. Knew who had my back (nobody). Had reasonable expectations of life (none). It was kind of depressing that *Krista* had designed a clue I *couldn't figure out*.

She will fall in six days.

The girl-who-has-everything-but-runs-away wants to be somewhere completely different than the girl-who's-heartbroken-and-waiting-to-be-rescued. Everything Girl is going to chase some idea or dream. She could be anywhere. Hollywood. Yoga retreat. Fight club. But Expectations Girl designs a trap for her prey.

As she falls, so do we all.

I wasn't sure anymore if I was supposed to save Krista from some terrible fall, or Boyd from her heartbreak, or myself from her wrath.

But Joan of Arc went to war, didn't she? She probably didn't like it. Or think it was easy. There was every chance she was going to die. She went because she had to. Because the voices told her to. Because she was going to know what to do when it mattered most. At least that's what Google had said.

You must find her. Only you can save her.

I reset my backpack over my shoulders. It was heavy. Why did I always have to carry so many books? I headed the opposite direction from Remy — it would be too weird to run into her again. It was still dark out, but the sun was definitely pulling up to the curb of the world.

I walked the long way around to our neighborhood shopping strip. Morning commuters were already on the road. The whoosh of tires driving by was oddly soothing. Like memories of being little and getting driven somewhere, the bliss of not having to make any decisions, of not having to think, of barely being alive.

By the time I got to the shopping strip, the sun was rising. I'd never watched the sun rise before. It was pretty. Blush-line horizon, buildings and trees silhouetted against it, a dimmed-screen dome of sky containing us all.

According to the crow, I had *six days* left. But it hadn't told me what I would be doing with those days. I felt scuzzy, my mouth was slick with sleep. If I wanted to freshen up, I had two options: go home, or stay on the road and pick up some supplies.

Going home felt like failure. A destination for losers. Or targets. For worms waiting to get plucked up and eaten by crows. My bedroom was where this whole thing had started. For the first time not a refuge but a dungeon. A trap.

I went into the all-night pharmacy and found the clothing aisle with its slim assortment of the basics. I picked up two plain sweatshirts, two pairs of warm socks, and six pairs of underwear. At the cash, I added toothpaste and a toothbrush. I used the family emergency credit card to pay, and clocked that it should be the last time to use it.

By the time I was out on the street again, the morning light was brighter. As pale pink as Dell's Ittch-famous coat. I found an instant teller and slipped in my card. There was only $213.43

in my account. All that remained of my allowances and money-gifts after spending the rest on music and audio-gear and nonde-script clothing. I withdrew the two hundred dollars available through even twenties and stuck it in my wallet.

I walked a few more blocks and hit the Jo's Joe. A couple of kids in hairnets were working the counter. Customers were already lined up at the counter or hunched over coffees at tables. No one noticed when I walked in.

I ducked into the bathroom and avoided looking at myself in the mirror. I washed my face, brushed my teeth, combed my hair. There were smeared black marks on my left palm — numbers I'd written to break into Krista's locker. I washed those off too, then filled my water bottle. After ripping price tags off my purchases, I changed into a fresh pair of underwear and socks, and swapped yesterday's sweatshirt with a new one.

I tried to push the other new clothes into my backpack, but there were too many binders and books in the way. I didn't know where I was going next, but it seemed unlikely that my immi-nent future was going to include studying for school. Besides, the books were too heavy.

I pulled everything out of my backpack. There were only toilets and trashcans in the Jo's Joe bathroom. Nowhere to stash my stuff for safekeeping. I took a breath, and stacked my schoolwork, book by book, behind the garbage can. Maybe it would still be there when I came back.

Messenger 93.

I went to the counter and ordered a breakfast sandwich and a cup of hot chocolate. I paid in cash and slumped at the only free table. There was a socket in the wall and I rummaged for my charger and Krista's phone and plugged them together. The charge-icon flashed on, and then her screen switched over to the keypad. *9393* to get in. The strangest thing.

A tinny, barely audible voice spoke above me. "... human remains found in a shallow grave near highway 6." Not a crow's voice this time, but one coming from a TV suspended on the wall. The screen was tuned to one of those 24-hour news channels, and the shot was panning over an empty field near some woods. "... excavated during routine maintenance work." Cut to an announcer, dead expression, mic at her chest. "Police seek assistance in identifying the female body."

My mouth went dry. Of course there would be a serial killer on the loose.

"More information," the announcer said, "will be made available following a postmortem examination. Signing off from Betthurry."

I keyed into Krista's phone and searched *Betthurry*. It was a small place in the middle of nowhere, north of the city. Barely even a town. The only thing that came up about it was the news story about the dead body.

She will fall.

The crow had said there were six days left, hadn't it? *Six days*.

I glanced around, half-expecting to see it perched on a nearby table, ready to coach me. But it was only the usual coffee shop hubbub and digitally-absorbed customers.

So what was I supposed to do?

Remy's voice saying, *Maybe Dell knows something. She might tell you something*.

Remy hadn't told anyone else about Dell. Which meant I was the only one who would attempt to talk to her.

3

IT TOOK THREE BUSES to get to Fairdale Collegiate. By the time I was on the last stretch, I was sardined in with a hundred other kids commuting to school. When they all started jumping off the bus, I got off too. It was 8:45 a.m.

Out on the sidewalk, I pulled up my raincoat hood and hid inside it. I searched the student-packs for Dell, but there was no sign of her. A bunch of kids were hanging out on the steps and stone fixtures in the yard. Tight-knit groups were already heading into class.

I wondered what Infinity Girl would do with this crowd. Would she show them their slumped unhappiness? Their yearning eyes as they stared at themselves in bathroom mirrors, searching for a better face? *I know it's not enough*, she might reveal. *It's never going to be enough*.

I looked around for some easy targets. Two tiny girls were walking shoulder-to-shoulder towards me. They tried to walk in formation around me. I stood straighter. For once I would be the intimidating one. "Excuse me," I said. The girls stopped in unison and looked up at me. Their mouths had frozen into defensive pouts. "Do you guys know Dell?"

The girls looked at each other — their heads snapping at exactly the same time. I could read the subtext: *this is a trick question*.

"You know — *Dell*?" I said, adopting Remy's tone. "*Dell*?"

"Yeah?" said the girl on the right.

"Everyone knows Dell," said the girl on the left.

They started to walk on, as if they'd answered the troll's riddle at the bridge and were clear to leave.

"I need to find her," I said, stepping in front of them again. "It's super-important."

If anything, their frozen pouts embedded deeper. "We don't know where she is," right-girl said.

"We don't *know*-know her," said left-girl.

"That's okay," I said. I had to walk backwards now because they were trying to get around me. "I just need to know where she mostly hangs out. Like, a general vicinity. Caf? Library? Specific hallway?"

"Yeah," said right-girl. She was pulling discreetly at her friend's sleeve.

"Any of those," said her friend. And then they scuttled away.

I turned and faced the school. I'd have to go in there, unarmed, a one-person search party.

Weirdly, it wasn't that hard to insinuate myself among the students and pretend like I belonged. It was a trick I knew well, having done it every day in my own school. You didn't need friends or a gang if you didn't care about having them.

I knew the bell could ring any minute, so I trooped down hall after hall, scanning faces as quickly as I could. To be honest, I expected there to be a glowing aura around Dell, a choir singing, something consecrated that would open a path and lead me directly to her. But it was all so ordinary, so familiar. Just another school, just another hallway, just another swarm of weary faces.

I found the caf and the library, and she wasn't in either place. Kids were already collecting in classrooms, and I knew I couldn't check each one. I half-considered asking the school secretary to tell me which class Dell was in, but didn't want to risk getting kicked out.

The bell rang suddenly and, just as suddenly, classroom doors slammed shut and the halls were empty. Soon there would be a hall monitor, and no good explanation to give them for why I wasn't in class. I rushed towards the nearest exit and pushed through the door. It led me into an unremarkable courtyard. I stopped and let the door close behind me.

Dell was wearing her pink coat. It was buttoned up this time, with a heather-gray cashmere scarf triple-wound around her neck. Her skin was artificially luminous and light. Her hair was white, fanning upwards in breathless layers, sort of like the feather from my bedroom. Her eyes were closed.

I turned away and tucked into a corner and settled, pretend-casually, on a concrete ledge, pulling off my hood and shaking out my hair so I wouldn't look so intensely sketchy. Then I took out Krista's phone and pretended to engage. I didn't want to confront Dell right away — it had to be a nonchalant approach.

When I looked up next, I noticed for the first time that she wasn't alone. There were three other kids with her, all just as white and synthetic-looking. Two girls were splayed along the edge of a planter, totally absorbed watching Dell with a guy, who had his back to me.

I shifted on my perch so I could see what they were doing. Dell's hands were wrapped around the boy's forearms and his were wrapped around hers. Even though I couldn't see his face, I imagined his eyes were closed too. There was something formal about their pose — their backs straight and unmoving — that made it look like they were locked in prayer.

If I was going to ask Dell about Krista, I'd have to go up to them.

Interrupt them. Do the detective thing and show them Krista's picture: *Do you know this girl?*

I launched Krista's Ittch, and clicked into Dell's profile. The last photo she'd posted was the one Remy had shown me: Dell in front of our school two days before, posing with her thumb down. I enlarged it and inspected every corner. I don't know what I hoped to see. A scrap of paper lying on the grass with an exact address? A significantly shady person watching from the perimeter? But there was only Dell, a patch of grass, a short strip of road, and the front entrance of our school with its raised metal letters spelling out the name: *T. Emmet High School*.

I checked with Dell-in-real-life again. Just in time to see her serene, plastic expression break. Her lips twitched into a smile that revealed very white teeth. Then she started to full-on laugh, her voice high and wheeling. She opened her eyes and looked at the boy whose arms she was clasping. "So, do you love me?" She had one of those nasal-baby voices.

The guy started laughing too and broke away from her. "No."

Dell slapped him. "Get out!"

"Ow!" He laughed and held his cheek where Dell had slapped him, and then she slapped him on the other cheek. "Ow!" He reeled away, but he was buckling with laughter. "I'm sorry!" he said, cowering away from Dell. I could see his face now. He looked as pristine as a boy Barbie. "I kept thinking about other stuff," he said, and the two other girls started laughing.

"No!" Dell screeched. "It's supposed to work! You were supposed to be, like, connecting with me on a vibrational level."

"It did work! I was vibrationally connected to the samosas Lida packed me for lunch. I'm *obsessed*."

Dell smacked him again. "Well, I didn't fall in love with you

either. I was dreaming of that beaded halter at Celestial Inspo.
I *have* to have it."

I checked Krista's phone and clicked into her profile and
picked one of her close-up shots. I imagined the walk across the
courtyard, towards Dell and her friends, them looking up at me,
my hand shaking as I extended the phone and showed them
Krista's picture: *Do you know this girl?*

"Gawd," Dell said, running her fingers through her hair, flip-
ping the part one way then the other. "I totally have to make my
Ittch rounds again. Ugh. I *hate* it."

"Your terrible life," said one of her friends. She was the only
one with dark eyes.

"I have too many fans now," Dell said with a theatrical sigh.
"It's so stressful."

The dark-eyed girl stretched up off the ground. "I have to go
to class."

"Me too," said the other girl.

If I didn't ask them now, I'd be trapped there, forever clinging
to the bland brick courtyard wall. I stood up and Dell's eyes
flicked to me. "Ugh, I'm so bored," she groaned to herself. But
we were staring at each other. It stopped me in my path and I
couldn't move.

"Hello?" she said and the others spun to face me.

I was staked to the spot.

"I don't do guest shots." Dell pitched her voice higher and more
baby for me. Her *celebrity* voice.

"Or autographs," said Barbie-Boy.

"Def not." Dell was sugar-sweet about it. "But I'm doing a
giveaway next week. You should enter." She brightened, but it
wasn't a smile. She bared her teeth.

Shoot the messenger.

My hand with Krista's phone flew up, positioned so she could see it. "You know this girl," I said by accident not as a question.

"What girl?" Dell said. She didn't move towards me, didn't glance at my phone. None of them did.

"You met her outside T. Emmet," I said. "Two days ago." I checked the screen. A photo of Krista was up, one with no shadows on her face, only Plasticine contours. My feet finally unglued and I shuffled towards them. "Do you remember her?" I got close enough that Dell had no choice but to look at the photo. By some miracle, my hand wasn't shaking.

Her eyes shifted languidly from Krista back to me. "No, I'm sorry," she said.

I didn't lose it. Instead I went into the menu and scrolled over to Dell's profile, and tapped into the picture of her in front of our school. "She took this shot," I said, showing Dell her own pink-coated self.

"Oh right." A smile crept over her face. It was strangely sly. Either she knew something, or she liked pretending she knew something. "The response to that post was *lit*. I owe that girl big-time."

"What happened after the girl took it?"

Dell's smile turned sensuous. "Like, did we kiss?" Her friends laughed — although it wasn't equally funny to all of them.

"No." I tried to keep the edge out of my voice. "Did you guys talk to each other?"

She stood up and all her friends shifted and seemed to tense. "No, we didn't *talk*."

I took imaginary stock of where the exit was, how fast I'd need to run, how loudly I might need to scream. "Did she leave with you?"

"What? No." Her sly cool didn't break, but I could tell she was calculating something.

"Did you see her leave the park after?"

"No."

I looked at the other kids. "Were you there that day? Did you see where the girl went?"

They all exchanged glances and then settled back to look at me. My skin tingled. Something was brewing.

"No," Dell said. "I don't remember her. None of us do." The other kids put sorry expressions on their faces and shook their heads.

I dropped my phone-holding hand and looked at my feet. What could I do? I wasn't equipped with the Persuasion Superpower. I couldn't force them to tell me what I needed to hear. And maybe they didn't know anything at all. And maybe I should've been grateful they were talking to me at all.

"I'm so sorry," Dell said in her craftiest baby voice. She'd come close enough to touch my elbow. "Breakups suck. But your girlfriend is hot — you *should* try to get her back." She turned to her friends. "She should come to the party next week, huh?" Her friends shrugged and murmured half-words. Dell rummaged in her purse and pulled out a pen. She lifted my left hand and clicked the pen to write. Krista's phone was in my hand, so she wrote on the inside of my wrist. A date, time, address. The faint pressure tickled. "Password is *sweet-sweet*. You have to come. It'll be off the hook."

I remembered Remy telling me how they'd *just announced Dell as the host of that huge Influencers party next week*. No one ever invited me to parties.

"Who knows —" Dell clicked the pen and put it away. "Maybe

your girlfriend will even show. You guys can kiss and make up."
She studied my face. "You should check out Radiant Beam. It'll
make your skin super-soft and bright. You can find it on my feed."

"Okay." I wasn't thinking straight. "Thanks."

"Here, we'll do a before-and-after." With one slick move, she
pulled her phone from her pocket, unlocked it, and snapped a
photo of my face. "Order it through my link today, and we'll comp
you an 'after' at the party."

Barbie-Boy leaned in. "Yeah, and don't forget to like and leave
a comment."

"Hey," Dell said to me with a dazzling smile. "We can make
you famous!" And then she stepped back among her friends and
they became an artfully packaged pack as they walked towards
the door.

I don't know why I had to blurt it out. I guess the crow and its
over-the-top messages had screwed with my synapses. "You're
supposed to leave your eyes open."

Dell turned back first, and then the others followed — a fan of
fake-curious expressions. "Hmm?"

"The thing to make you fall in love. You're supposed to stare
at each other."

"For real?" Dell said. I nodded and she gave Barbie-Boy a smack
on his arm. "I told you we were doing it wrong!" Then she let out
a baby-laugh and spun towards the door. The other kids laughed
too and lined up behind her and, one by one, they disappeared
from the courtyard.

"IF YOU THINK OF anything …"

Clio had said it to me, and I had said it to Boyd, and Remy
had brought me to Dell. As I headed down the street away from

her school, I rummaged through my coat pocket for the card Clio had given me.

Joseph B. Stanzi. Detective.

Detectives have resources and power that I would never have. I could tell Joseph B. about Dell. Get him to look into her whereabouts at the time of Krista's disappearance. If I dropped Dell in his lap, he'd have to talk to her, right? He'd put the pressure on. And when he found Krista — and it would probably take less than six days — then I would deal with the *fall*, whatever it was going to be.

The thought of watching Krista go down took on epic, thrilling scope.

I rode the two transfers to Joseph B. Stanzi's precinct, got off the bus, and found my bearings. The road was really wide, with three lanes traveling in each direction. Gas stations, fast food joints, coffee shops, auto repair garages, big-box hardware stores. That kind of neighborhood. The police station was on the other side of the road, a brick and glass rectangle with sliding glass doors as a front entrance.

I crossed the busy street and walked inside. The lobby was state-of-the-art — leather and chrome benches, steel security doors, glass rooms-inside-rooms where, on the other side, female and male officers stared at multiple computer screens.

It wasn't clear right away how I should conduct myself. There were a few people waiting on the leather benches, and I decided to camouflage myself among them until I learned how the regulars handled the whole confessing business. Not that I was *confessing* to anything, but it would be helpful to see how it was done.

I slumped into one of the benches against the back wall and

hugged my bag to my stomach. It felt good to sit. I was tired in a way I'd never been tired before.

THE NEXT THING I knew, I was flying out of deep smothering black and into an alien world that was tipped on its side. Spaceship steel and glass. Blue robots patrolling high-tech consoles. Outcasts from dying planets huddled in corners.

There was a sharp jab in my ribs and I jolted up and rubbed my eyes. The police station came into focus and I had a strong and sudden urge to burst into tears.

"You can't sleep here." It was a gravelly voice near my left ear and I turned towards it. An old man and woman were hunched on the bench beside me, staring at me through squinted, crinkled eyes. They both wore oversized woolen scarves and sweaters that had been thrown on in musty layers. The man was closest to me and he had his elbow up and aimed for my ribs, as if he was going to jab me with it again. The woman leaned over him and said, "They don't like it if you sleep here. Word to the wise."

I tried to swallow, but my mouth was too dry.

"If you're here for the community meeting," the woman said, "the coffee's crap. I suggest you run quick and get a take-out." She lifted her hand to show me the paper cup she was clutching. "Right at the corner," she said.

I couldn't help eyeing my backpack. Was my wallet, my two hundred dollars, still in it?

"They's starting in a few," said the man. His eyebrow hairs were out of control, curling over his forehead and onto his eyelids. "Best hurry."

"I'm not here for the meeting." My voice was raspy with sleep-phlegm.

"No? Then why're you here?" The woman sounded astounded. Like there was no other reason to be sitting in the lobby of a police station.

"Gonna kick you out if you got no reason to be here," said the man.

I tried to pretend that my hand wasn't searching for my wallet among the new sweatshirts and underwear in my backpack. "I'm here about a girl."

"And who is this girl to you?"

The question, the whiff of suspicion, triggered some kind of brain malfunction. A sickening urge to justify myself. I blurted, "My sister."

"Your *sister*?!" the woman said like it was incredible a person could have one.

"She ran away," I said, cringing so deeply inside that my teeth could've chewed my toes. "I'm looking for her."

"You got a picture?" said the man. "Maybe I seen her. I get around."

There was nothing to lose at this point. I took out Krista's phone and tapped into her photo. The picture I'd shown Dell. The perfect one.

The old people huddled over me, their crinkled eyes maniacally close to the screen. The man tapped Krista's filtered cheek. "That there's a mask. No way she looks like that."

The woman reached over him and tugged my coat. "Oh hey! Kreeboy's also tryna catch a girl. Been here all day tryna get 'em to help. They keep kicking him out, he keeps coming back. You should talk to him."

"Who's Kreeboy?" I said.

"Got the raven on his back."

"No, it's a crow," said the man.

My skin prickled.

"Dropped a feather on his neck," said the woman.

A crow. A feather.

I tried to hide the slight tremor in my voice. "Is there a *crow* in here?"

The man leaned back so he could eye me. "I guess you gotta go to the march."

The woman leaned over his lap, towards me. "It's for missing girls."

"The boy's people are organizing it. He was just here tryna get us all to go." He looked around at the collection of huddled outcasts. "No one seemed too interested."

"Yeah," the woman said, lifting her coffee for a sip. "Felt kinda sorry for him."

"It's a sorry thing, that's for sure."

"He said they were meeting at the owl."

"Owl?" So much adrenaline surged on my tongue, it was as if I was being force-fed mercury.

"The bird of the city," the woman said.

I shook my head.

"You *know*," the man said. "The *important* one."

"With the wings." The woman lifted her arms to show me. Coffee sloshed out of the sippy part of her cup and landed on her sweater. I watched the stain sink into the faded, patterned wool. Then I knew what they meant. "Oh," I said, "you mean City Hall. The Celebrate Your Fears statue."

Even as I said it, my ears began to burn. Back in fourth grade when Remy and I were still friends, our class had toured City Hall. We were all too hyper to pay attention to the lectures about

local politics and who did which job for what reason. I was
following Remy around, giggling at everything she giggled at —
the stinky carpets, the guide's faint lisp, each other, ourselves. And
then the large bronze owl in the plaza with its stoic face and open
wings. It's no wonder I'd misheard the guide. *Celebrate Your Fears*,
I was sure he'd said. He paused at the statue so we'd take a moment
to contemplate its brilliance. And I did stop giggling for a second.
I did marvel. I had a lot of fears to celebrate. The unexpected twist
had been a revelation.

"Celebrate Your *Fellows*," I said to the old people, my whole
face burning. My revelations were always imploding. "That's what
I meant."

"Now you got it," said the man.

"When is the march?" I said.

"Today at two."

Owl emoji, Fri at 2.

Once, all of us had hung out together at City Hall plaza — me,
Krista, Boyd, L.J., Anusha, Hattie. There'd been some kind of
music festival going on — no performers I liked — and we'd traveled down by bus when we were supposed to be studying at
Boyd's. It had started out fun. Boyd and I running around the
square, playing tag while the others watched, him catching me,
me letting him. Krista coming up to us, vigilante-style, and pulling
out a water bottle she'd brought from home, filled with orange
juice and mostly vodka. I couldn't say no. Not there, like that, with
everyone watching. We took turns drinking. I was the first one
out. Sick and puking behind the pedestal of the owl statue. I
couldn't look at any of them afterwards as we rode the bus home.
Krista kept poking the back of my neck.

I checked her phone. Ten a.m.

"There he is," said the woman. She pointed her sweater-covered hand down the main hall.

A young guy, maybe a couple of years older than me, was walking towards the lobby, wielding a rectangle of poster board above his head. He was tall and lanky and wore a black zippered hoodie. Faded black jeans clung to his hips and a tweed newsboy cap was pulled over his short-cropped dark brown hair. His eyes were intent, focused. Not someone named Kreeboy, I realized. A boy who is Cree.

An enlarged printed photo was glued to the poster board in his hands. It was a picture of a girl with long, dark hair. Scrawled in blue marker above her: *Have you seen Jocelyn? Missing for 27 days.*

He arrived in the lobby and turned to face the pass-through door that secured the police station from the lobby. He angled his body in a way that allowed me to see the back of his hoodie. Fluorescent yellow eyes stared at me, fluorescent feathered eyebrows slanted sharply over them, a black beak was outlined below. *The crow.*

Even though no one paid attention to him, he stood his ground, aiming his poster one way then the other. He glanced back over his shoulder and for that one heartbeat our eyes met.

An electrical charge went through me.

It was the crow, I told myself. It was both of us looking for a girl on the same day in the same place. The chance of it. The wonder. Nothing more than that.

The front doors flew open and a force blew in. He was imposing enough that everyone looked over, watched as he headed to the security door by the front desk. The boy stepped in front of him. "Detective Stanzi—"

Detective Joseph B. Stanzi. The grizzled man, wearing the same wrinkled brown suit, that I'd seen coming out of Clio's house the day before.

Stanzi put up his hand to stop the boy. "We're working on it."

"Are you working on it though?" The boy took another step to block Stanzi's way in. "Because none of your guys are up there looking for her." His voice was deep and sure.

Stanzi tried to get around him. "And I keep telling you. That's a different jurisdiction. They have a team in Deerhead assigned to that case."

The boy took another step to block him. "There's no *team* in Deerhead looking for her. They haven't even put a trace on her phone! What if she's in the city? She could've come down here. She comes down here sometimes."

Stanzi took a step again and so did the boy. "If there's any evidence she came down, we'll hear about it and we will look into it."

"And I'm telling you, not one single authority is looking for her."

"Listen, kid, I don't have time for your politics."

"*Politics*? This is a missing girl!"

"Hey, hey!" Stanzi held up both hands like he was stopping himself from manhandling the kid. "Settle down or we're gonna have a real problem here."

The boy foisted his poster at Stanzi. "But you won't look for her! You never look for any of them!"

"Okay, I've had enough of this BS." Stanzi looked through the glass at the welcome desk. "Someone get this kid out of here." The officers behind the glass looked up, each for a half-second, then they went back to deciphering whatever was on their screens. Stanzi waved his hand like he was fed up with everyone. He pushed past the boy, opened the secured door, and went through it, stranding the boy in the lobby.

The boy glanced down at the poster board in his hands. He stared hard at the photo on it. An imaginary film of his missing girl — *Jocelyn* — played in my mind. Their idyllic but tragic-fated love. He is so into her, she is so into him. Him holding her, laughing with her, kissing her. Then she's gone, and he is devastated.

I felt a sharp jab in my side, and I started and looked over at the old people. "Now you gotta go for it," the man said, his elbow angled to jab me again.

I couldn't speak, couldn't decide what to do. I'd come here for Detective Stanzi. I was supposed to tell him about Dell. He'd walked by me only a few moments before. All I had to do was go up to the front desk and ask to speak to him.

But Stanzi was different than I'd imagined. Clio was *so, so grateful* to him. I thought he'd be reassuring. Concerned, determined. Not someone who challenged claims and said there was nothing he could do.

"Go talk to him," the old woman said.

I didn't know who they wanted me to talk to. The kid? Detective Stanzi?

The boy was hunched over now, spinning the Jocelyn poster into a roll against his knees. I could see the tension in his shoulders, the way his fingers flexed around the board. His anger.

He pulled out a backpack that had been shoved under one of the benches, slipped the rolled poster under the top flap. Then he strapped the backpack over his shoulders and stood tall.

I waited for him to look my way again. If he looked at me, it would be a sign. A *direction*.

But he didn't look at me. He shook his head with disdain and zipped his hoodie and set his expression. Then he walked to the main entrance and pushed his way outside. The glass double doors slid closed behind him.

"Is that you?" the old man jabbed me in the ribs again. I followed his pointing finger. Behind the police window, one of the officers had flipped her computer screen our way so she could get at something behind it.

My face was on her computer. A terrible photo.

It was really a picture that Mom had taken of Trevor at Christmas the year before. The shot had been framed to cut him out, but you could still see his hands cradling an unwrapped collection of manga. I was in the background, waiting for my turn. My face was too white — Mom had forgotten to turn the flash off — and my pupils were red spots. It surprised me that no one had bothered to fix that. My usual long hair framed my face, but bangs cut across my forehead. The bangs had been a desperate attempt to salvage my grade nine reputation. But they looked awkward, had made me feel awkward, and I'd grown them out.

There was a statement below my photo on the police screen, but it was too far off and I couldn't read the words. The headline above it was clear though, stamped out in bold black font: *Missing Teen*.

It had never occurred to me that I would be *missing* too.

The old man pointed his gnarled finger from the screen to my face. "Sure looks like you."

"No, no," I said, pulling my hood over my head. "That's my sister. The one I'm looking for." I hopped off the bench and hunched my way out of there before he or anyone could say another word.

THE BOY WAS RUNNING to catch the bus. He was fluid, athletic. Striding down the sidewalk, then leaping from the curb onto the inner step. My arrival was clumsy and stupid — missing the bar on the door and rearing in head-first, plunking down too hard on the step, breath grunting out. But he never turned, didn't see me.

I adjusted my hood over my head, hiding my face with my hand when I passed him. I went to the last bench and pretended to look out the window. He stuck earbuds in his ears. The metronome rock of his head in time to some song was mesmerizing. I wondered what the song was. If it was calming him down or ramping him up or making him feel better. If it reminded him of some blissful moment with Jocelyn.

It was a message, right?

Reassuring me that I was supposed to be there, behind him, on that bus.

We'd been cruising for about ten minutes when the boy got up and stood at the exit doors. I jumped up and hung back behind some other passengers. When the doors opened, I stepped out after him.

We were in a neighborhood famous for its thrift shops. I was tempted to check out the shop windows. Before that day, in another reality, I might've been content browsing indie vinyl and waving-cat figurines.

As he navigated the sidewalk, he kept up a strong, long-legged stride. His overstuffed backpack never slowed him down. The rolled ends of the poster stuck out of the top flap and I remembered Jocelyn's graceful smiling face. I couldn't see it because the backpack was strapped over it, but I thought about the fluorescent crow on the back of his hoodie, and how crows were everywhere, leading me.

He turned a corner and then another and we ended up in a back alley. It was secluded and quiet, and I reared back so he wouldn't see me, peered around the corner to watch him from the main street. He went halfway down the block, then stopped and looked in through an open back door. After a few seconds' hesitation — *was he nervous?* — he ducked in through the door and disappeared from my view.

I took a deep breath and went after him. There was no sign above the door, which was propped open with a large recycling bin. Behind it, barely lit with one Edison bulb, was a narrow corridor. Its walls were glazed coagulated-blood red.

I took a tentative step into the gloom. I could hear someone talking, the pulsated echo of words coming at me, garbled and bass, from the far end. Every step I took towards the voice felt like I was getting sucked into a slippery vacuum.

The hall ended at a soft wall of black velvet curtains. Through the split in the curtains, in the space beyond, small fairy-lights winked from the walls and ceiling.

The voice was clearer now. A deep voice talking in rhyme. *The boy*.

Except he wasn't talking. And the beat was good. Chills pricked over me. Like someone was hovering fingers over my shoulders and neck.

I fumbled in the dark for the crooked seam of light and peered through it. There was a small music hall on the other side. The seats in the audience were empty, so it wasn't a performance, but the boy was performing on a makeshift stage. His tweed cap was balanced on his backpack, which was on the floor beside him. His back was to me, and now I could see his fluorescent crow again. It was staring at me with its ferocious eyes.

I scanned the shadows and found another person — a man,

red bandanna tied around his forehead, long single braid down his back. He was leaning against a wall, listening, his eyes closed, nodding in time to the beat.

The words to the boy's song became clear to me.

You rip me from my home, write words that make it law.

Call your act a gift. "Don't ask for more, boy, it's impossible."

I didn't only hear lyrics. The words appeared, bright and sparking, in front of me.

I wanna fight you, but you don't pretend to give a shit.

Don't bother to loose your tie. Don't bother to raise your fists.

You got other things to do, man, somewhere else to be.

Why bother working it, it's liberating to be free.

I forgot myself. His music, his voice — smooth and sure — slid into my body.

Still run the race you want.

Bills only taste you got.

Cut your nose 'spite your face.

Spills your red blood too.

The ferocious crow on his back challenged me.

But it's okay. Yeah, it's okay.

You're not my nation, not my tribe.

I'm okay, yeah. On my way, yeah.

Creator never take a bribe.

The boy stopped and swung his hand as if to say that's all he had. I wanted to clap and cheer, but I caught myself.

The man stepped onto the stage. "Pretty good, bro," he said. "Try shifting the bars, mess up the rhyme. Play around with it. But, hey, it's a solid start."

The boy slumped. "Do you want it though?" He reached into the back pocket of his jeans, pulled out a folded piece of paper, and tried to hand it to the man. "I can let it go for sixty."

But the man didn't take the paper. "I thought you were looking to perform."

"No. Selling it."

The man softened. "I'm going to say something, and I don't want you to take this as a sign you should stop doing what you're doing — But our audience — They aren't going to listen to your words if you don't understand them."

The boy hung his head. "Yeah, I get it." His voice was less strong, less certain, now.

"It's a journey," the man said. "Keep talking to people. Keep your ears open. Listening is good. And you can always come back. Door's always open."

The boy scuffled sideways along the stage. He was taking it in, thinking. He looked back at the man. "I can let it go for forty?"

"Not buying songs, my brother. Not enough money in the game as it is."

The boy scuffled the other way. "It's just — I need to get up to Deerhead … There's a search going on. For a missing girl …" His voice trailed off. But then he tried again. "I can let it go for twenty?"

The man nodded sympathetically and stuck his hand in his jeans' pocket and pulled out a thin clip of bills. He counted off a twenty and handed it to the kid. A sorry expression shaded his face. "That's all I can do."

The boy hung his head and took the bill. Then he offered the folded paper one more time. "I'm done with the song," he said, his voice gruff with disappointment. "Give it to someone who needs a place to start." He hunched into himself as if he thought the man would reject his music again, but the man took the paper and tucked it into his shirt pocket, then laid a fatherly hand on the kid's shoulder. Without exchanging another word, they grasped hands and shook.

The boy leaned over to grab his backpack. He adjusted his cap to his head and heaved his bag over his shoulders, then turned to face the back of the room. To face me.

I launched away from my hiding spot behind the curtains, and flew down the red plastered corridor and out into the bright glare of the deserted alley. I scooted around the corner, and ran all the way to the main intersection.

Had the boy seen me? Would he consider me a threat?

There was a small patio outside one of the main street restaurants. I slid into one of their picnic tables and buried my head in my hands and pretended to be waiting for a meal.

A minute later, a blur caught my eye. I snuck a look. Someone passing by with a black hood pulled over his head like me. Both of us hiding inside our clothing-armor.

I didn't need to see the backpack with the Jocelyn poster rolled under the flap or the tweed cap on his head to know it was him. Everything about him was already familiar.

He didn't go far, just a few blocks, when he stopped in front of a storefront. He hesitated for a few seconds, so I also hesitated, kneeling down and pretending to tie my bootlace. When he decided to go into the store, I ran to catch up. I could hear the old-style wood and glass door clang to a close.

I tried to sneak a look inside, but there was so much stuff packed against the window — camo wear, portable chairs, propane cooktops and lanterns — that I couldn't see a thing. *It's just a store*, I told myself, *a public space where anyone can go*. I took a chance and slipped inside, making sure the chimes on the door didn't announce me. Dust and mothball fumes filled my nostrils.

It was an army surplus shop, rows of open metal shelves piled with new and used gear. The boy pulled off his hood, revealing his cap again and the slender stem of his neck. He chose an aisle and headed down it and I faked a casual amble down a parallel aisle, sneaking glances through the open shelving, idly running my hands over tied rolls of sleeping bags and foam mats.

He was searching for something specific and, soon enough, he stopped at a banged-up cardboard box and rummaged around inside it. At first I couldn't see what it was, so I eased aside some sleeping bags for a better view.

Tumbling around in his searching hands was an assortment of loose hunting knives. Straight blades, curved blades, folding blades, holstered blades.

He picked up a long knife in a battered leather sheath and pulled it out. It was menacingly curved and pointed at the end. He turned it over in his hands, weighed the leather-bound grip, ran a thumb lightly along the edge of the blade. He tried a quick jab, the steel refined enough to glance a pinprick of dull light.

I recoiled and pulled sleeping bags in front of me and dumped my head into one of the dusty rolls. A fierce dread ignited inside me.

The boy took the knife to the cash and pulled out the musician's twenty dollars to pay for it. *I need to get up to Deerhead*, he'd said to the musician. *For a missing girl*. He needed the money to save Jocelyn. Not so he could *buy a knife*.

The clerk took the bill and counted out change, while the boy turned the blade left then right. He seemed satisfied and pulled up his sleeve and strapped the holster to his left forearm and slid the knife into the holster. He fixed the sleeve of his shirt and then his hoodie over the holster to hide it.

He was about to leave when he stopped to grab something off a hook above the cash. I squirmed to get a look through the shelving. It was a cheap Halloween mask. It twirled on the end of his finger from its elastic strap, and I could see that it was one of those blank masks, the kind where the face is so *nothing* it's aggressively creepy.

The boy showed the cashier the mask and threw down another dollar to pay for it. Then he thanked the guy and left the store.

With a knife and a mask.

Was *this* the reason the crow had come to me? Was Krista just a ploy to bring me to this person? Was I supposed to stop something bigger, more terrible, from happening?

Save her, save us all.

Joan of Arc must've turned over in her sacrificial grave. Because I knew then that I couldn't step in front of a knife. Couldn't bleed for a greater good. The crow had picked the wrong Messenger.

"Can I help you?" said a voice behind me. I jumped and righted myself, but refused to look at the salesclerk. "Can I help you find something?" he said more loudly, stepping closer.

I shook my head and jerked away. I pulled myself along the shelves all the way to the front door where I yanked the knob and escaped into the cool outside air. The door clanged to a close behind me, its chime singing.

I took off down the sidewalk. I didn't want to see the boy, but I searched for him anyway.

He had crossed the street and was heading down the block towards a side alley. The brickwork on the alley's corner building had been totally painted over with graffiti-style art. Half of it was a giant color mural of cartoon characters — huge-eared mice with silver fangs, sword-wielding cockroaches, bright green tree-men. The other half was a black-and-white clock that was so big, it circled from roof to street-level. Numbers from 100 to 1 counted down beside the clock. Real-life birds — swallows, maybe, swifts, sparrows — flocked in circles in front of the mural. Looped up to the roof of the building and swooped down again.

I crossed the street, dodging cars in both directions, and gave chase. My brain was running too: *I couldn't let him disappear. I had to have proof he existed.* I pulled out the phone, clicked into the camera, and took photo-bursts of him as he walked away.

He slowed down. Behind him, the flock of birds flew in unison in low figure-eights through the alley. Against the bright mural backdrop, they looked like a spray of emoticons celebrating his arrival. I slowed down too and took another photo-burst.

I tried to act innocent — casually aiming my camera in subtly different directions. I was just some student snapping alleyway art for a school project.

It wasn't until I heard the hydraulic squeal of a bus settling at a stop that I noticed he wasn't heading down the alley with the mural, but aiming to get on the eastbound.

The bus's doors closed, the engine throttled down. I pocketed the phone and ran. But the bus was already pulling away from the curb. I stared hard through the side windows. Bodyless heads in profile. None of them his. The bus passed and gained speed. I fixed on the rear window as it drove away. Only backs of heads. None of them his. He was gone, swallowed by a void.

I ducked into the alley to catch my breath.

I couldn't do this. I couldn't do it.

I was leaning against the brickwork, against the mural, the part of it with the wall-sized black-and-white clock. *The World Clock*, it said. The numbers counting down, *100, 99, 98, 97, 96, 95*, lined up above my head, *30, 29, 28, 27*, going along my body, *12, 11, 10, 9*, and down to the curb by my toes, *4, 3, 2, 1*. The colorful side with the mice and cockroaches and tree-men was no friendlier. *This is our mess*, their bubbles read. *We will not renew unless we reject anger and follow the immaculate light. THE TRUTH IS HIDDEN INSIDE THE FALLACY. THE TRUTH IS THE WAY.*

The birds were suddenly gone and it was eerily quiet and still.

The boy took hostage of my mind. His intensely focused eyes, his wired body.

I tapped into Krista's phone, into the camera-stream. *Had I captured him?*

But he was mostly a blur — my hand had been shaking too much. Quarter-profile, half-profile, three-quarter profile, him against the mural, shifting edge-to-edge in the frame, almost a silhouette. The mural was really the star of each shot. The wall-sized black-and-white World Clock counting down from 100. The maniacal cartoon mice and cockroaches and trees. So many bossy orders on how to be a human.

This is our Mess	*95*
We will not Renew unless	*94*
We Reject Anger and	*93*
Follow the Immaculate Light	*92*
	91
THE TRUTH IS HIDDEN INSIDE THE FALLACY	*90*
THE TRUTH IS THE WAY	*89*

The flocks of tiny birds — the swallows or sparrows or whatever they were — were blurred in flight in front of the mural. Their wings erased some letters and numbers in the photos, and framed others. It made the images look surreal.

Or *planned*.

I stared hard at a couple of them. Painted letters, words, a number, stood out between parenthetical smudges of movement. Suddenly I could see actual sentences amid the blurs.

Mess

en

ger   *93*

Follow h Im

HE   IS   THE FALL
        HE   IS THE WAY

I almost threw the phone across the street.

What was happening? Why? Why me?

My thumb tapped into the browser, then typed in a search command. *Me*. Because, really, *why* me? And there I was — an instant result. At the top of the Missing Persons list. That horrible photo.

Police seek 16-year-old girl. Not seen at home since morning April 12. Last seen April 13, early morning, west-end neighborhood. Jeans, black hooded raincoat, black work boots.

Either Remy had offered up that "last seen" information, and/or that morning's emergency credit card purchase at the pharmacy had been traced.

At the bottom of the alert, there was a link to my mom's profile — a post she'd made public. I clicked on it. The same information, the same photo. But also this: *She's looking for a friend from school!* And then a link to Krista's profile. *If anyone has seen either girl, please contact us immediately!*

But here was the unbelievable part: even though they'd only put it up a few hours before, the number of shares on the repost-button was in the hundreds. My parents' friends, Clio's friends, Krista's friends, their friends, friends of friends, strangers, all sharing my story. Even Hattie was in on it.

The messages underneath were unexpected: I was on a *beautiful mission* to find my *missing friend*. I was a *hero*. I was *just a kid*. I was a *shining star*. I *needed help*. Their *hearts* were with me. Their *thoughts*. Their *prayers*. Their *light*. This was *love*.

I read and re-read and re-re-read every single comment, every post, every share. It was staggering.

Wait — *had I really become Messenger 93?*

Could it be possible? *Could I actually help people?*

What if it *was* true?

I had never done one good thing in my life. What was I doing every day beyond sleeping and getting up, going to school, eating, hydrating, hiding in my room, listening to music, lamenting my fate, and sketching stick figures into storyboard panels about impossibly luminous worlds?

What would happen if I found Krista?

The possibility of bringing her back — clutching her hand, everyone cheering, celebrating — played like a triumphant, tear-jerking movie.

You must find her. Only you can save her.

Maybe I was *powerful*.

Maybe I could do *anything*.

I could be *homeless, faceless, genderless*.

Save her, save us all.

The boy popped into my mind again. Hiding his blank mask and an army surplus knife. Heading somewhere fast.

The old people at the police station had told me where to find him: *Today at two. The march for missing girls.*

Krista's message had told Boyd where to meet her: Owl, *Fri at 2.*

The City Hall statue. *Celebrate Your Fears.* My stupid name for it.

The old man saying, *I guess you gotta go.*

The next eastbound bus rolled up. Adrenalin pumped through me so hard, I half-expected to lift off the ground and gain flight. The door squealed open and I stepped up.

Messenger 93. Follow him. HE IS THE FALL. HE IS THE WAY.

4

I ENTERED THE WIDE plaza in front of City Hall and looked around for the statue. A giant screen blinked at me from the far side. Its digital display of announcements and ads flashed obnoxiously — new cars, stale TV shows, supposedly exciting upcoming events. But the blinking lights also illuminated the owl, its bronze shape, its flared wings. *Celebrate Your Fellows.*

I bought a grilled cheese and a bag of chips from one of the food trucks and ate on a bench behind a row of potted cedars so I could hide and watch the owl at the same time. It was noon — still a while before the march was supposed to start. I hoped the boy would arrive early so that I could —

I had no idea what I was going to do with him.

I was going to *wait and see.* Literally.

It was a warm day and the plaza was full of people coming and going. Tourists, shoppers, suited business types. They crossed the square, or sat around eating takeout, or skateboarded over concrete slabs, or threw coins into the long reflecting pool.

Time disintegrated as I watched them. A force inside me radiated. Everything was brighter. Colors popped. Edges sharpened. I could imagine their lives, their secrets. I could see them being sent on their own missions by their own crows.

I had no memory of ever feeling that way before. No name for it — whatever it was.

It felt almost as if — as if I loved everyone. Like the possibility of saving one of them, any of them, all of them, made each person suddenly and intensely real.

And then it was two o'clock. Time was back, and now it was ticking down with cold determination.

I noticed that people had begun to gather for the march. Like the boy, they were holding signs and placards scrawled with messages over photos of women's faces: *Where Are Our Women? Too many missing girls!* A lot of posters were only names — long lists of names. *Tara. Polly. Catherine. Regina. Rita. Leanne. Francis. Glenda.* Too many names.

The dizziness inside me fell away and was gone. I braced myself and focused hard on finding the boy. *Something was going to happen. I had to be ready for it.*

More and more people arrived and crowded together. Some of them started to call out, "Save our lives!" "Find our sisters!" They brought out instruments and played music — drumming, jingling, singing, chanting. It was sad, but also powerfully beautiful.

There were suddenly hundreds of people in the square —

almost like a gate had been opened — all of them rallying together, crying out, chanting. A bunch of people linked arms and started to dance around the reflecting pool. Everyone wanted to join the loop, so hands unlatched and re-latched and soon they were circling the whole center of the square.

Police officers arrived and gathered in small groups off to the sides. I pulled up my hood and tucked close to a group of tourists so I could keep an eye on the area around the owl. When there were too many people for clear sightlines, I struggled through the crowd to get closer. Placards stabbed the spaces around me. Calls and chants echoed in my ears. Tourists and suits blocked my way as they stopped to watch.

Then I saw him. Standing apart from the crowd. In front of a potted cedar, outside the circle of dancers. Tweed cap, black hoodie, over-stuffed backpack strapped to his back. A knife holstered underneath his sleeve.

He took his backpack off and slid the rolled poster out so he could root inside. When he stood up again, the mask he'd bought at the surplus store was dangling from his finger. He adjusted the mask under his cap, over his face.

A white faceless mask hiding his identity.

He unfurled the poster board and raised it high over his head, directing it at the crowd like he'd done at the police station. Showing his girl to everyone: *Have you seen Jocelyn? Missing for 27 days.*

He turned to face my way. I don't know if it was my imagination but the mask's eyes seemed to find me through the crowd. Seemed to stare directly at me. Danger rose like a demon and howled at me. I couldn't move, couldn't breathe.

Something terrible was going to happen.

There were so many people in the square. Old people, young people, some in wheelchairs, some hobbling on canes. Little kids holding their parents' hands, babies being pushed in strollers. A lot of them had joined the large ring flowing in one direction around the pool. Drummers and singers underscored the shuffled steps. All of them too small, too defenseless. *They had to be saved.*

I girded myself and went after the boy, drawn to him like a zombie to brains.

The ring of dancers blocked my way, streaming past me, an elastic wall that I couldn't join. I skirted them, pushed past the owl, past the giant screen, through crowds of advocates and onlookers, moving as fast as I could.

On the opposite side of the square, the boy moved away from the potted cedar and trailed behind the circle dancers. He was jabbing the Jocelyn sign over his head in time to the drumbeat. No one seemed to notice him. Even though he looked packaged, packed with aggression. A guy in a mask, carrying an overstuffed backpack.

Someone had to stop him from doing what he came here to do.

It swarmed me in a cathartic rush: *HE IS THE FALL. I was Joan of Arc. Driven by purpose. Protected by armor. Marching into battle. I was doing what I was called to do.*

The force of knowing drove me forward. I wound around bystanders, focused only on him. But the boy was moving farther and farther away from me, sidestepping behind the circle dancers. Soon the crowd was just a blur and he was a flashing signal light.

I charged forwards, gaining on him. And then I was behind him, and his backpack was the only thing between us.

My hand was twitching to reach out, to yank him away from the others. *To make itself known to him.*

I couldn't take my eyes off the back of his head. The way the tweed cap fit around it. The short, ordered hairs outlining his skull. The sharp rim of the plastic mask against his cheek. The curve of his ear, the ear I could see as I walked on his right side.

I jerked forward to catch his arm. Jerked back to stop myself.

Below his ear, there was a tattoo: a hyper-delicate feather inked onto his neck. Each teeny barb along the vane had its own style — stiff or soft or spent. *A crow*, the old people had said at the station. *Dropped a feather on his neck*. I had a feather too, found in my room and secured inside the back pocket of my jeans.

The longer I stared at it — the fineness, the sweetness, of that tattoo — the more everything changed. It was as if the feather was threading inside my mouth to latch onto something beating and vital. I didn't understand what it meant. But I spoke. "Don't do it."

His head twitched in my direction and away again, as if he'd heard then dismissed me.

I moved in closer as we stepped in time behind the circle dancers. I put my mouth as close to his ear as I could without making contact. My heart was beating incredibly fast, my breath tight and shallow enough to almost strangle me. "Don't do it," I said as firmly as I could.

This time he pulled away from the circle and rounded towards me. The hardness of the mask's plastic features and empty expression was terrifying. I lurched back.

"Who're you talking to?" His voice was muffled by the mask.

I didn't want to cause panic in the crowd — unreasonably polite while defending humanity.

"I'm talking to you," I said. "Please don't do it."

He stepped towards me and I stepped back.

"Don't do what?" He took another step towards me and I stepped back again.

Joan of Arc disappeared. I was myself again — pitiful and pathetic. A target.

He took another step and another, and so did I. We kept taking more and more steps away from the crowd, somehow avoiding demonstrators, somehow moving farther and farther into obscurity. I tried to steel myself as we moved, tried to measure where the closest cops were, tested my resolve about getting — or not getting — their attention.

"I saw you buy the knife." I made my voice husky with defiance. "It's strapped to your arm."

In an instant, his forearm was pressed against my chest and he was pushing me backwards. I didn't cry out. Didn't scream or fight him. I'd always imagined I'd be a model victim — I'd yell and flail loudly enough to get people's attention. Or the adrenalin rush would fill me with super-human strength. Or exactly the right words would come so I could change my attacker's mind: *There are cameras everywhere.* *I'm sorry the world has hurt you.* *My ghost will haunt you till your dying day.* But nothing. I was a bug under his heel and all I could do was watch my own death in horrified silence.

"You're following me?" He was still pushing me and I was throttling backwards, all the way to City Hall. My back came up hard against the concrete wall. I gasped for breath. "Why are you following me?" His voice was muffled but audible. "Who are you?"

An answer came out of my mouth before I could stop it. "I'm Messenger 93, and I have to stop you from bringing harm to these people." Even as I said it, I cringed. Had I stepped out of my brother's manga?

"*Messenger 93*?" he repeated.

I didn't know where to look — the mask was too creepy and lifeless.

He dropped his arm from my chest. "What harm am I bringing to these people?"

"The knife. The backpack. I have to stop you. That's all I know."

"My *backpack*?"

I felt suddenly sick. I tried to look into the holes that hid his eyes, but I couldn't see through them. *What had I done?*

He laid the poster on the ground and pulled off his backpack. Jocelyn stared up at me, her features distilled in black and white on printer paper. Wide eyes, sweet smile, a dimple in one cheek. A better person.

"I seriously gotta do this for you?" He unzipped the backpack and tugged the sides open, jerking the nylon flaps a couple of times for effect.

I could've run then. There was nothing stopping me. But I looked inside the unzipped parts. Compact bagged tent and sleeping bag, rolled clothes, packs of freeze-dried food. For the first time I noticed water canteens in both side pockets. Camping equipment.

"But the knife." At the store, in his hands, it had looked like a weapon.

He was zipping the bag closed again, quietly grunting because too much was in it and the teeth would barely join. A tiny droplet of sweat trickled from under his cap and trailed the edge of the mask. "The knife is for the woods," he said. "For food."

Of course you'd need a knife for camping, for food.

Shame burned me up. He was just a kid, worried and searching for someone who meant something to him.

What had I done? What had I done?

And how did I look coming at him? Wound up, aggressive, hiding inside my hood?

I bent to pick up his Jocelyn poster — it seemed rude to leave her lying on the dirty pavement. I brushed my hand across her face.

"Can I go now?" He didn't wait for an answer, but heaved the backpack over his shoulders, grabbed the Jocelyn poster from me, and trudged away.

I could've left then, forgotten all about him. But I ran after him. "I'm sorry!" He kept striding away. "You have to believe me!" *He didn't have to believe me. Of course, he didn't have to believe me.*

He was heading back towards the circle dancers and the crowds around them, waving the Jocelyn poster in the air. Calling out from behind his mask. "Has anyone seen this girl? Help us find Jocelyn!" But we were in a pretty empty part of the square, not close to the advocates, and it made him stand out. People started sizing him up — the backpack, the mask. A few of them exchanged whispered comments. A woman clutched a small child to her legs.

"Have you seen this girl?" His voice shouted louder. "Has anyone seen her?"

Suddenly a dark blur scooted past me and landed on him. It was a short bleached-blond woman wearing a dark, too-tight suit with a security badge stitched to one sleeve. She yanked the boy by the arm. "What the hell are you doing?" she yelled at him.

He didn't resist her like he had me. He stood obediently in the spot she'd chosen and tilted his head down to see her through the mask.

She jabbed her finger at him. "Take that thing off right now."

He did as she asked. The mask dangled by its elastic from his neck. Even from where I stood, I could see sweat droplets on his cheeks and across the bridge of his nose.

"You trying to get yourself shot?!"

"No, ma'am." He was composed. Careful.

"So why the hell you wearing that?"

"For the invisible girls who disappear off our streets every day. If they're nobody, I'm nobody."

Oh, I thought, sinking deeper into myself. *Right*.

"Sweet Jesus," the security guard said. She switched back to attack-mode. "Get out of here."

The boy didn't get agitated like he had with Detective Stanzi. He stood tall. "But I'm taking part in the march. It's my right."

"So get rid of that mask and stop showboating."

"I have a right to look for this girl."

"You have no right to harass people."

"I'm not harassing anyone." He showed her his sign. "I'm looking for her." Photocopied Jocelyn stared angelically from the poster board. "Have you ever seen her down here?"

"You back-talk me one more time and I'm calling the cops."

"I'm not back-talking you. I'm asking if you've ever seen this girl." He aimed the sign at her.

The woman swatted the sign away. "We're not *babysitters*."

"A *missing* girl, ma'am. She needs our help."

"That's it." The woman wheeled around and pulled out her cellphone. She shoved it in his face and held it there. She wasn't calling anyone — she was diminishing him.

"Okay, okay." He stuck the Jocelyn poster under his arm and held up his hands. Their standoff lasted long enough for me to wonder if I should do something. Run over and tackle the woman. Order her to properly look at Jocelyn's face. I wanted to scream at her to pay attention to Jocelyn.

The boy eyed the guard for another moment, then turned and walked away. She marched off too, probably looking for someone else to harass. But the boy was heading straight towards me. At first it was obviously an accidental direction choice — until his eyes met mine through the crowd. Then he narrowed in.

I didn't run away. I *wanted* to talk to him. Wanted to have his attention, even if it was full of rightful loathing. I pulled off my hood, loosened my hair, smoothed it over my shoulders.

"Is it you who called the dogs on me?" he shouted.

"No, no, I swear!" I waved my hands in surrender as he charged up to me. "I'm sorry. It was a mistake what I said to you."

He stopped. He was only a few feet away. His skin was in touching distance, warm and pulsing. His intent, shining eyes looked at me. Interstellar planets.

"Are you undercover or something?"

A burst of laughter escaped me. "No." And it was gone. "It's because — It's because I'm looking for a missing girl too."

He used his sleeve to wipe the crystalline beads of sweat from his hairline. "Who is she to you, the girl you're looking for?"

It was too complicated. Too weird.

Also, I was *missing*. So I couldn't be *me*.

I blurted the same lie I'd told the old people at the precinct. "She's my sister."

"Your sister." His body, the muscles of his face, shifted the slightest bit. "She's been gone how long?"

"Two days. Since Wednesday."

"And you're following me because you think I had something

to do with it?"

"No!" I almost put my hand on his arm.

"You're following me because you think you're this Messenger 93 and you had a vision that I was going to blow up the crowd?" His eyes were penetrating. "With my camping gear?"

I looked down at Jocelyn's black-and-white face. She was still smiling.

"Or what? That I was going to pull out this shitty knife and stab everyone?" He lifted his sleeve and flashed the holster at me. "And you're part of some magical plan where you're supposed to save everyone from me? That by stopping me, you win your sister back?"

"No!" I couldn't look at him. "No I —"

A crow on his back. A feather on his neck. The birds in the alley. Eddie's little R-less voice, *The bird wants you to go, the black bird said the boy will help you. HE IS THE WAY.*

I tried again. "I came after you because you're looking for Jocelyn and — And there might be a connection."

His eyes widened. "A connection? Between Jocelyn and your sister?" He looked at me as if he wasn't sure he'd heard right. "You know Jocelyn?"

"No," I said, confused. I'd forgotten how I'd gotten us to this point. Him, the crowds, messages on murals, they were messing with my head. "But there might be a connection — There *might* be."

"Really?" Hopeful expectation opened his expression. "What is it?" He looked so young at that moment. Like I could see him as a little boy. I could see us playing in a park, on a seesaw, swinging our legs, laughing at each other, not a care in the world.

But I had to give him an answer. *What connection?* A good answer. A rational one.

For some reason, the word Deerhead rung in my head like a bell.

"Deerhead," I said. "She might be in Deerhead."

And then I remembered — he had said it to the man in the music hall. *I need to get up to Deerhead*.

"Are you serious?" he said.

I had no idea where Deerhead even was.

I started to say something, but an odd, familiar shape on the far side of City Hall caught my eye. A person was standing near a pedestrian corridor that ran between the two City Hall towers. She had her head turned my way, possibly looking at me.

"Who is she, your sister?" the boy said, cautiously interested. "What's her name?"

But I was fixed in space — because the person was definitely a girl of medium height with dark blond hair. "Krista?" I said out loud. She was definitely watching me. "Oh my god, Krista!" My arm reached instinctively towards her, and then I was running.

Advocates and onlookers streamed in and out, picketing my way, my view. The girl was still too far away for me to be sure of anything. I called out as I ran — "Krista! Wait!" The girl didn't react, just kept her head turned my way.

The circle dancers looped across the square and formed a wall between us. People dancing to drum music, whirling in and out of my way. *It was Krista / It wasn't Krista*.

I was forced to dodge left. When I looked again through the crowds for the girl, instead of her face, there was a fan of loose flying hair. *Was it finer and lighter than Krista's?* And then there was the briefest flash of a pink coat. *Wait — was it Dell?*

I had to slow down, had to weave and push through the crowd.

The girl in the distance seemed to morph and split: *one girl / two girls / Krista / Dell / a woman I'd never seen before / a girl I once went to camp with.*

Someone else cut in front of me and I had to dodge around them. By the time I righted my course, the girl — whoever it was — had disappeared. I ran up to the spot where she'd been standing. The girl wasn't there. I scanned the crowd but didn't see her. No pink coat, no one with blond hair running away from me. I got to the pedestrian corridor that split the City Hall towers. The walkway extended for a full block to another street behind the buildings, but there wasn't a single person down the entire length of it.

Who was she? Krista? Dell? Somebody who was nobody?

I ran full-tilt down the walkway. I had to be sure. Had to see it through.

I was running so fast, the passage so narrow, that the other end came at me like a snapped elastic. I burst out onto the back street. And was stopped by a shearing force.

My stomach heaved inwards, my shoulders pitched forward. My body dropped to the ground like a dead weight.

I tried to breathe but my lungs had compressed. Not a wisp of air seeped in. My eyes stared up, then rolled back. The overhead view of the city — nondescript high-rise towers, short rectangle of hazy sky — glinted briefly then faded to black.

I HEARD A VOICE speak very close to my ear. Extremely close. So close I could feel the warm breath of its words.

"She will fall. Only you can save her."

I tried to answer but my lips wouldn't move, my mouth wouldn't open.

Then the same voice again. Neither loud nor soft. Neither female nor male.

"Follow him. He will take you."

The crow.

"You will go where you would not go. You will see what you would not see."

And then I flew away. Soared into deepest dark.

WHEN I CAME TO, I was looking down the length of my body. Lying on concrete, surrounded by concrete.

"Hey," a quiet male voice said from above.

I broke into a cold sweat and surged to escape, but my gut heaved with agonizing pain. I buckled and clutched my stomach.

"You okay?" the voice said.

I managed to look up. It was *him.* He was kneeling on the pavement. My head was on his lap. He looked so different as he gazed down at me. Like all his guards were down and I was seeing the truer version of him. The him who had once lain on a chair while an artist inked a precise tattoo of a feather on the skin under his ear. The him who had once pushed aside hanger after hanger of hooded sweatshirts in some clothing shop before he landed on this one, the one with the crow on the back.

I started to say something but winced and gasped instead.

He said, "We gotta get you to a hospital."

I tried to protest but only a pathetic whimper came out. I shook my head hard, staring at him to make my point: *no hospital.*

"Home?" he said.

I flinched and shook my head: *no home.*

The boy's eyes scanned across mine as if he were reading subtitles. Then he reached down and took my wrist.

He wound his hand lightly around my wrist.

I was extremely conscious of the light pressure of his fingers on my wrist.

"Your pulse is okay," he said.

I almost smiled, even though I felt like one giant, weltering bruise.

"Can you get up?"

There was no clear thought process, only pain ripping from the center of my body and outward to all my edges. But I was becoming too aware of my head on his knees, of the warmth of his body underneath mine. I jerked to get up, then winged back in pain. He put his hand on my shoulder to support me, but I jerked forward and grabbed my backpack to avoid his touch. That's when I noticed that my bag was unzipped and bits of fluff and spent wrappers were sticking out.

I heard a high-pitched screech and was horrified to realize it was me. Because I could see — my wallet was gone.

I think I began to cry as I checked and rechecked. Nothing else was taken — my bus pass was still there, my water bottle, the newly purchased toothbrush, underwear, socks, and sweatshirts were all still there, even the phone had been left behind.

"Did someone jump you?" he said.

I scanned the area. We were in a narrow back street. There was no traffic, no people walking around, no random girl, no Dell, no Krista.

"My money," was all I could say, a hoarse, gaspy whisper.

"They stole your money?"

I pressed my palms against my eyes and nodded.

My head was so fuzzy. But a clear thought was dropping in: It couldn't have been Krista in the plaza. Krista didn't need my money. There was Clio and her sumptuous princess castle. Money for days. But *someone* was trying to stop me. *Who was it?*

Only six days left.

"Do you need to get somewhere safe?" he said.

I did need to get somewhere safe. Away from attackers. Away from Krista. Away from anyone who knew me, who might be looking for me. Somewhere where I could think. Yes, somewhere safe.

I nodded.

"Okay, come on." He carefully looped my arm around his neck and lifted me gently off the ground. He waited patiently for me to take some weight on my feet, and because my arm was linked over his shoulder, I managed to stay upright. My breath was bursting in and out, a hyperventilating mess.

The memory of the crow's voice reassured me. *He will take you where you need to go.*

Somehow we made it to the main street with its bustle of drivers and pedestrians. Somehow we made it to a bus stop. I didn't ask him where we were going. Every step was excruciating, and the more we walked, the more I relied on him to support me. He never complained. Didn't even groan. He made it easy.

We waited for a bus to pull up — I didn't pay attention to which one. We showed the driver our passes — a good thing I never kept my bus pass in my wallet — and the boy helped me on and eased me into a seat. I collapsed against the window and focused on breathing, and he sat down beside me, pulling off the blank mask that had been dangling around his neck and stuffing it into his backpack.

I didn't want to look at him. The way his chin tucked into the tied collar of his hoodie. How his skinny legs curved over his backpack on the floor and his knees pressed against the seat in front of him. His free hand lying on and protecting the Jocelyn poster that he'd rolled over his lap.

After a few minutes, he took out his cellphone and made a call. It was obvious there was no answer, so he made another call. When that didn't connect, he dialed another number. I pretended not to notice how his jaw clenched, his shoulders squeezed, as he waited for it to connect. This time they answered.

The boy cupped his hand over the phone. "Hey, Lily, it's Gray." Then he added quickly, "Sorry, I mean *Gordon* ... Are you still at the march?" He listened for a bit then said, "No. But I need your help." He listened for a bit more then said, "I have a girl with me. She's hurt." I closed my eyes. "It's a long story — but I'm bringing her to your place." He listened, then said, "Because there might be a connection between her and Jocelyn." There was another listening-pause, then he said, "Yeah, we're on our way right now." He hung up.

It went quiet around us like we were in a bubble. We didn't speak again as the bus drove us to the other side of the city, to another place I didn't know.

5

WE GOT OFF THE bus in a quiet neighborhood packed with low apartment buildings and brick rowhouses. I was woozy and dazed and he offered to brace me, but I was okay enough to walk and basically hobbled after him for the next few blocks.

When he turned us down one of the walkways that led to one of
the rowhouses, I was breathlessly relieved.

The windows of the house were already projecting artificial light. I realized it was getting dark out. The front window
revealed the living room, and it looked warm and inviting.
High shelves against the back wall were crammed with books. A
faded, overstuffed couch was on one side of the room, a well-
worn recliner on the other.

The boy helped me up the stairs to the landing and rang the
doorbell.

"What's your name? I need a name," he said to me. He was
lightly sarcastic when he added, "And not Messenger 93."

I hesitated and the door opened before I could answer. A
stern-faced, solid-bodied older man nodded at the boy. "Hey,
Gordon. Been a while."

He hung his head. "Yeah. I'm sorry. It's Gray now."

"*Gray?*" the man repeated.

"Yeah, I'm going by Gray now." The boy — Gray or Gordon or
whoever he was — nudged his chin in my direction. "And this
is M." Then he nudged his chin from me to the man. "M, this is
Walter."

I tried to wave at him but it came out a pain-wince. The man
stepped back to invite us in and Gray guided me up and over the
stoop.

M.

My new name sent a small shiver through me and I smiled
despite everything.

THE HOUSE SMELLED DELICIOUS, like sauce and cinnamon.
But I didn't want to be hungry — I never wanted to eat food again.

Just thinking of my stomach made me buckle at the knees.

Walter led us down a narrow hall and into the living room that I'd seen from outside. There were pamphlets and placards for the march piled in a corner on the floor. Gray showed me to the overstuffed couch and I collapsed onto it. A striking woman, older and warm-featured like Walter, stepped into the doorway and observed me from a distance. I clutched my stomach and hoped that would buy me some mute-time.

Gray turned to her expectantly. Guiltily. "Hey, Lily."

Lily kept her expression neutral. "Four years since we saw you," she said.

Gray gave a grim nod. "Yeah, I know."

"Your birth community. They were waiting for you."

Gray slumped. "Yeah, I know."

Lily crossed her arms. "We were at the march today."

"Yeah."

"And you didn't find us? Didn't come by to say hello?"

"There was too much going on. It wasn't my place."

"Of course it's your place, Gordon."

"*Gray*," he said. "I'm Gray now."

Lily bristled, then nudged her chin in my direction. "What happened here?"

Gray said, "I don't know. I found her lying on one of those small streets behind City Hall. I think she got jumped."

"You think?"

"I didn't see it. We were talking and she ran off and I followed her. When I came around the corner, she was out."

I tried not to get too caught up in visualizations of him following me.

Lily looked at me. "Did you get jumped?"

I nodded.

"They stole her money," Gray said.

"And why not go to the police? Or a hospital?"

Gray's head dipped guiltily. "She said no."

My eyes shifted over to Lily. I couldn't unhook from her penetrating gaze. My story — whatever it was going to be — would have to be exceptional.

Gray said, "Her sister is missing. That's why we met."

My sister. Even though it was my fault — I'd been the one to own Krista — it made bile crawl up the back of my mouth. Still, I was grateful he didn't mention Messenger 93 and my terrible accusations.

Walter gave me a serious look. "Your sister is missing?"

I nodded.

Gray said, "Last seen in Deerhead."

Had I told him that? I remembered almost nothing of anything that had come out of my mouth. Lily and Walter looked at me, instantly astonished.

Gray said, "Missing for two days. Right, M?" Then he checked with me. He looked so trusting, and I was a liar lying on a couch that wasn't mine. I clutched my stomach and nodded.

Lily noticed my hands on my belly. "They hit you in the stomach?"

I nodded.

"And you passed out?"

I nodded again.

"That's a pretty nifty trick," she said, approaching me. "Hitting you in the exact spot to stop you breathing." She crouched at my feet. "Taking you out like that. They either knew what they were doing, or it was a lucky strike." She grabbed my legs and lifted them onto the couch so I was lying down. "You nauseous at all?"

I shook my head.

She laid her hands on my stomach and pressed down ever so slightly. She looked up to check with me. It felt okay, so I nodded. She moved her hands and palpated softly. "Does it hurt worse when I press?"

I shook my head. The truth was, it was already feeling better.

"Your stomach isn't hard," she said. "Which is good."

She moved her hands up and felt around my ribs. I tried not to read anything into her touch. You know, like maternal attention.

"Does this hurt?" she said.

I shook my head.

"So your ribs are okay. That's good ... Okay. You'll live." She sat back. "You have family we can call?"

A jolt of regret went through me, but I shook my head. *No family*.

She registered that, took a hard look at Gray, glanced at Walter, then looked back at me. It was impossible to read her expression. "Okay," she said. "Lie here. Rest up." She extended her hand in Gray's direction. "You. Come with me." Gray bowed his head and followed her down the hall.

Lily's voice came at me as they retreated, hushed as if she didn't want me to hear, but also gentler, "You can't save every girl who crosses your path, Gordon." And then they were in another room and I couldn't hear them anymore.

I listened for the crow, for another message — *this was its chance to speak*. But nothing came. It was utterly quiet the way peaceful homes are quiet.

I settled into the cushions and wondered what I was supposed to do next.

I WAS STARTLED AWAKE to find Gray in the doorway, holding a glass of water and looking at me. I pulled my legs off the couch and sat up.

"You okay?" he said.

"Yeah. Much better. Thank you." Beads of shame-sweat pricked up over my body, and I tried to cover by smoothing the wrinkles in my top.

We stayed like that for a few awkward moments, him holding the glass of water and me stupidly primping. Finally, he stepped closer and put the glass on the coffee table in front of me and then he sat on the opposite end of the couch. I picked up the glass and took a long haul. It actually felt good to drink. I hadn't realized how thirsty I was.

We sat in awkward silence again. Gray pulled off his tweed cap and ran his hand over the short stubbles of hair on the back of his neck. His hair looked velvety soft. I swirled the glass and focused on the leftover drops at the bottom.

"Why did you run away from me at City Hall?" he said. "What did you see?"

"I thought it was her." I tried to make sense of it. The girl, or girls, the flash of pink, getting knocked out. "Wishful thinking, I guess. You know when you want something so badly?" Gray gave a somber, thoughtful nod. I put the glass down. "I think someone is trying to stop me."

"Who would do that?"

If preaching crows existed, did its counterpart? Some kind of evil, violent thing?

"I don't know," I said. "Someone who doesn't want me to find her?"

"Huh ..." He glanced over at his backpack. "And how do you

know Jocelyn?" He stared at the poster board that was balanced on top, the picture of Jocelyn's face rolled inside.

"I don't know her."

"Does your sister know her?"

Did Krista know Jocelyn? Were they somehow connected?

It was too complicated, too weird, to explain. "I don't know."

"I'm just trying to figure out," he said, "if it's possible they both went to Deerhead for the same reason."

"Yeah, I'm trying to figure that out too."

We both thought for a minute. I noticed how his hands played nervous beats on his knees. How they looked like musician's hands.

I said, "How do they know Jocelyn went to Deerhead?"

"Somebody saw her hitchhiking up there a few weeks ago."

I didn't know anything about Deerhead. Didn't even know where it was. "There's not much around there, right?" My lame/obvious attempt to get more information.

"Middle of nowhere. North of everything." Gray pulled out his cellphone and clicked into a map. He widened it so the city became a speck within the world around it. He tapped north of the city and zoomed in a little. "This is where she lives." He pointed to a blank area off the grid, far from the closest highway. "And this is where she used to live. Where I —" He scrolled and zoomed into a spot farther away. This time to a small town: *Nipewin.* He'd stopped talking.

"Where you ...?" I prompted, keeping my voice quiet.

"Where I was born."

Your birth community, Lily had said to him when we'd arrived. *They were waiting for you.* I wondered how long Gray and Jocelyn had known each other. Been together.

"My birth mom died when I was two," he said, not looking at me, keeping his thumb on that one tiny spot on the map. "I was adopted out, and my parents live down here. So I don't know anything about what it's like up there." He scrolled east of his birth town, then east of the home Jocelyn had run away from, to another spot. "And this is Deerhead."

It was also in the middle of nowhere, also small, surrounded by a few other small communities and lots of undulating green blobs that represented uninhabited woods. One of the towns near Deerhead caught my eye: *Betthurry*. Wasn't that, according to the news on the TV that morning, the place where they'd found the human remains? *Female. Unidentified.* My hands went cold.

Gray said, "So her picture doesn't look familiar to you? You never saw her and your sister together?"

"I don't think so," I said. "I don't actually know if Krista and Jocelyn know each other."

"The picture on the poster is a scan from a screencap. Maybe if you saw a better image ..." He clicked into his photo stream. "Maybe if you see the whole thing ..." He found what he was looking for and angled his phone towards me.

It was a close-up of Jocelyn's face — the same one he'd printed out and glued to his poster. He double-clicked the image to open it up, then showed me the whole photo.

Jocelyn was kneeling on a rumpled unmade bed. She was wearing a small baby blue tank top. The lacy ruffles of a dark blue push-up bra peeked out from underneath. She had on tight denim shorts and her legs were bare. She was beautiful. Sending beautiful shots of her beauty to her boyfriend. Didn't everyone in love do that?

"I'm sorry," I said softly. "She doesn't look familiar."

Gray turned the screen back to himself. "I've looked at this picture a million times."

A million times. Of course he had. Who wouldn't?

"Keep thinking there might be a clue in it or something. Like, in here ..." He zoomed into a corner behind her, and Jocelyn's face disappeared out of frame. There was a corkboard on the wall and it was crowded with tokens: jokey pins and badges; earrings and necklaces tacked together in sparkling clumps; printed photos of an older smiling man.

Gray and I tilted into each other by mistake. The weight of his shoulder against mine was shocking. *Reassuring.*

He was the first to pull away. "She's run off before," he said. "But she usually comes down to the city. They say she's never been gone this long without calling her mom." He hovered his finger over the corner of the corkboard hidden by her head. "What if there's something on there that fills in the blanks? Like, why did she run? And why to Deerhead?"

And then it hit me: Gray and I were on the same mission. Taking the same *leap of faith.* Sometimes you had to look everywhere, at everything, to save people, didn't you? And if your guide was a crow that only you could hear, or a small hidden corner of a corkboard that only you were looking at, was that so wrong?

He will take you where you need to go.

Because wasn't Krista's text to Boyd showing the way to Deerhead? *Only you*: Should follow me. *Single eye*: Don't stop searching. *Finger-pointing-up*: I'm up north. *Scissors*: Cut off from everything we know. *Stars*: Where the stars shine bright and true.

Krista could've meant she was in Deerhead, couldn't she? She could've been pointing the way to some remote place that was cut off from the world.

She will fall.

Gray drummed his hands on his knees. "Damn." He shook his head. "It's bad. I mean — what if they — you know —"

"What?"

"If they —"

"What? Say it."

"Stole them ... For trafficking."

"Trafficking?" I fought a wave of nausea. I hadn't imagined *that* possibility.

Krista materialized in my mind. Imagined video-loops of her, terrified and pleading. Girls crammed bare shoulder to bare shoulder in steel containers, spectral ships crossing the ocean.

My body went cold. *If someone had taken them, could it be the same person who'd attacked me at City Hall? Had Gray saved me from that fate?*

"Can't they just be gone by choice?" I blinked away some rogue tears. "Someplace good?"

"Like where *good*?"

"I don't know." I conjured it up. Krista and Jocelyn together with a bunch of other runaway girls in some beautiful place where everyone took care of each other. "A den of empowered girls?"

Gray gave one choked laugh. "Right." He tapped beats on his knees. "Except they don't usually end up someplace good."

Unearthed human remains. Serial killer.

"They just found a body," I blurted. "Up near there."

"In Betthurry. Yeah, I know." Gray clicked into his browser and showed me the screen. It was a pinned article about the human remains. They still hadn't identified who she was.

I fought a fresh scrim of tears. *Had I wished for this? Brought it on with the force of my vengeful fury?*

Gray turned the screen back so he could consider the article on his own. "When I was eight, a girl in our neighborhood went missing." He lowered his voice, kept his eyes on his phone. "I didn't know her — she was older than me. Ten, I think. They found her body a few weeks later. Some psycho had taken her." He stroked his thumb along the screen. "And I never thought about her again until I heard about Jocelyn ... Never realized till then that a little girl being dead was just a story to me. An *anecdote*. Something we joked about."

Everything he said hit me. I couldn't speak.

But Gray wasn't waiting for my opinion. He shoved his phone back into his pocket, squinted his eyes, and said in a softer voice, "Lily and Walter asked if we want to stay for dinner. Do you want to stay?"

It was too much, expecting the wrong kind of help, accepting the wrong attention.

"Sure, thanks," I blurted.

Because the alternative was leaving. Not knowing where to go. Letting her and everyone fall.

WALTER LADLED STEW INTO bowls and Lily passed them around while Gray and I slumped, anxious and miserable, over the table. When Walter picked up his spoon and started to eat, we ate too. It was so good: hearty vegetables, roasted tomatoes, fresh dill, a side of warm buns slathered with melting butter. Gray and I had two bowls each.

When Gray was done, he pushed his empty bowl away and said, "I'm sorry about ditching the big reunion four years ago."

Lily and Walter stopped eating and looked up at him. I stopped and looked too. "It was my mom who stopped me from going," he said. "She was freaking out about it."

"Freaking out," Lily said, her tone flat. "White woman's hell."

Walter dropped his head to hide a quick grin.

"I know you guys want to connect me to my birth community and everything — and I appreciate that. But my mom — my *white* mom," Gray said, emphasizing it for Lily, "is right. I don't belong there." He drummed his hands on the table. "I guess I don't belong anywhere."

"How do you know you don't belong there?" Walter said. "You won't know until you meet them."

Gray standing outside the circle dancers at the march. Not saying hi to Lily and Walter. Not talking to anyone. Wearing the dollar store mask. The mask not only a statement — but something to hide behind.

"My birth mom is dead," he said evenly. "Their community isn't mine. I never saw the point."

Gray's birth mother was dead. He'd been adopted by a white family.

"And now?" Lily said.

"It's different."

Jocelyn, I thought. *Jocelyn makes it different.*

Gray met Lily's gaze. "I know what's happening out there. I've read the numbers. Even if I don't belong — It's still — I want to do something to help."

"Go on."

I noticed for the first time how Lily's eyes lit up every time she looked at him.

"I want to go to Deerhead. I want to join the search. Please —" Gray prayered his hands. "Take me with you."

"How do your parents feel about you going up?" Walter said.

"My dad bought me all the camping gear." Gray pointed in the general area of the living room, reminding us of his stuffed back-pack. "I'm eighteen now. An adult."

"Okay. Good." Lily smiled without smiling. "We're heading up early tomorrow morning. We're going to spend the weekend helping with the search. I'll call Arthur and ask if we can join the group at Jocelyn's house. That way you can meet them."

"I need to go too." I said it so loud, so fast, it surprised every one of us. But it was true: I had to get up to Deerhead too, and they were the only people who could get me there.

Still, I knew I'd have to convince them. Lily and Walter were already preparing to speak, likely to protest, and so I barged on. "My sister is missing. She ran away, and no one can find her. And my money — the money I need to get up to Deerhead — was stolen today." But it had to be even *bigger* than that. Something bad enough to force me to run after my fake-sister *alone*. "She's my only family." I blocked Trevor from my mind. My mother, my father. It was easy. Easier than you'd think. "She's the only family I have left."

Everyone gave that information some breathing space.

Lily eyed me. "How old are you?"

I couldn't say that I was only sixteen. If I did, my journey would end right there.

I'm eighteen, Gray had said. *An adult.*

I looked into my emptied bowl. "Eighteen."

"So you've aged out of the system," Walter said. "You're on your own?"

I kept my eyes down and nodded. It was everything I could do to fight the incriminating surge of blood to my face.

"How old is your sister?" Walter said.

Ages scrolled through my mind at the speed of light. If Krista was too young, she'd be too vulnerable. Too old, and it wouldn't be as urgent. But I had to say something. "Eighteen."

"I see." Walter said. "Twins."

Twins?! It served me right.

"A powerful loss," he said. "She ran off without telling you?"

I couldn't look at any of them. I nodded again.

Gray said, "Like Jocelyn."

"Surely you don't need us," Lily said. "Have you gone to the police? They'll help you."

Walter said, "The authorities claim there's nothing they can do if the girls go of their own accord. They don't even need consent to leave after age sixteen."

Krista was sixteen. She had gone of her own accord. But there was still a posse of uniforms and detectives helping Clio. They'd set up a *task force*. Gone to our school. Looked through Krista's phone, her locker, her computer, her room. *They downloaded all our data. They have everything we ever did or said. They searched my house*, Boyd had said. *They've been here for hours*. Clio's despairing voice. *No expense spared. They took her toothbrush for DNA evidence!*

Lily got up from the table. "They're supposed to look for all of them. No matter who they are. They're not taking Jocelyn's case seriously. They haven't even bothered to trace her phone."

They'd found Krista's phone before the rest of us even knew she was gone.

"Why can't her mom track it?" Gray said.

"It's too remote up there. They're not getting a signal. But the police could if they tried."

"They *are* looking for Krista," I said, guilty, ashamed. "It's just that — They don't have any leads. No one can find her." I gave Lily a pleading look. "I have to do *something*."

Lily ran her hands through her hair. "Okay, we'll figure it out."

"We'll do what we can to support you," Walter said.

Gray gave me a cautious smile, and I tried to smile back.

SATURDAY, APRIL 14

FIVE DAYS UNTIL THE FALL

THERE WAS A TREMENDOUS thump and I jerked out of a deep sleep and tried to focus through the dark. Dawn light was filtering in through a window and shapes began to appear. Unfamiliar shapes. I bolted up. *Where was I?*

And then I recognized the crammed bookshelves — spines of hardcovers squeezed together, piles of paperbacks balanced on top. Me lying on a too-soft couch and covered with flannel blankets. A worn recliner across the way. Walter and Lily's living room. I couldn't see which of them had made the thump that woke me, but I remembered our trip up north and knew they must be getting ready.

Gray and I had organized our bags for the trip the night before. Charged our phones. I was relieved I'd bought those fresh clothes from the drugstore. Something clean to change into if we were going to be gone for a couple of days. Walter and Lily were packing me a sleeping bag and some extra-warm blankets and clothes because I would probably have to overnight in Gray's tent.

Gray's mask and poster were reflecting luminous blue-white at me from the depths of the living room's darkest corner. He'd decided against bringing the Jocelyn poster with him — it was meant for here, for city people to pay attention — so he'd set it aside, along with the thrift store plastic mask.

I glanced around for Gray and found him asleep on the floor in his sleeping bag. I breathed relief in and held it, then settled back into the couch, into the pillow, and watched him slowly appear through the shadows. His head was tilted to one side, his mouth slightly open and purring, the lines of the feather tattoo on his neck emerging through the dark.

A voice whispered in my ear. "She will fall in five days."

I jolted and checked to make sure the voice hadn't woken Gray. He was sound asleep.

"Hey." I whispered so quietly to the crow that it was practically just exhalations of breath. "I'm supposed to go with them, right?" It was peaceful in the room, only the rhythmic hum of Gray's deep sleep. "Please tell me," I whispered a little louder. "I want to be sure."

But the crow wouldn't answer me, and then I knew it was gone.

I got up, slipping out from under the blankets and off the couch, careful not to wake Gray. I crept over to that one dark corner that held his Jocelyn poster and the mask. Something told me — not a crow, not a noticeable voice, but something farther and fainter inside me — that I would need them at some important point in the future. I had plenty of room in my backpack, and they weighed almost nothing.

I folded the poster, quietly creasing the cardboard into a flat, manageable square, and tucked it and the mask deep into my bag. Underneath the last new sweatshirt. Under Krista's phone. Then I zipped my bag shut and crept back to the couch.

Okay, Crow, I thought as I snuggled back underneath the blankets and waited for morning, *Message received*.

WE DROVE FOR HOURS. First out of the city; then through the suburban sprawl that surrounded it; then past farmland, wide swaths of dormant fields; then into the wild. Bare boughs climbed into the sky, setting a filigree of branches, thick and thin, against the matted clouds.

Walter and Lily chatted from time to time. They explained what they did. That they were both Anishinaabe. That they worked for an organization in the city that advocated for Indigenous rights. That they'd met Gray years before when his birth community was trying to reconnect with him. Gray listened intently, drawing his finger over condensation on the window beside him.

Walter and Lily took turns driving, most of the time holding hands over the center console. I found myself staring from the back seat at their braided hands. It was as if their open affection was an artifact and I was pressing my nose to museum glass.

Instead of stopping for food, we ate sandwiches that Lily had packed, and oranges. When I bit into the sections, juice dribbled down my hand and I made sure Gray wasn't watching as I licked my fingers, and he wasn't. We poured hot tea from thermoses into small plastic cups and blew the steam that rose and carefully sipped without spilling. I spent a lot of energy trying to avoid touching Gray every time we stretched our legs or reached our hands.

At one point when Lily was driving, she glanced back over her shoulder at Gray. "So how did you hear about Jocelyn running away?"

"I watch the online community board. Everything is on there."

"Hm." She nodded. "That's true."

Gray pitched forward, leaning on the back of Walter's seat. "She was last seen hitchhiking around Deerhead after she left, right?"

Lily said, "That's what they told us."

"But why the big search this weekend?"

I was surprised he didn't know.

"They've been going out pretty steady every day," Walter said. "But we just got a report from a driver in those parts that there was a girl matching her description in the passenger seat of a car. They weren't able to get the license plate."

Gray looked a bit nauseous. "That wasn't on the community board. That is — Whoa — I don't know ..."

Lily put up a cautionary hand. "We don't know for sure that it was her."

Gray leaned forward again. "Do they know why she keeps running?"

Again, I was surprised he had to ask.

"It's hard to say for sure," Walter said. "We don't work that closely with her community. But we do know her father died a few years ago. It's been difficult on her and her mom. Jocelyn's uncle Arthur invited them to move near to him and his family so they could support and watch over each other. But apparently Jocelyn isn't happy living there. I mean, it's beautiful, but her dad is gone and nothing's going to make that better." Walter looked back and gave Gray a sad smile.

"When you're told your whole life that there are certain rules," Lily said thoughtfully, watching the road, "and you follow them because you think you have to, but those rules don't work — don't protect you, don't give you comfort — you start looking for something different. A way out. A new way. An old one." She glanced through the rearview. "That's where we are now."

Gray gave a serious nod. "True." He put the tip of his finger against the window. "And that's what Jocelyn is doing?"

"It's my guess," Lily said. Then she said with a quiet smile, "And you too, Gray." She glanced over her shoulder at him. "Okay, so tell me — why *Gray*?"

Gray sort of laughed and slumped back in his seat. "It's my birth mom's last name."

"I know it's her last name. She also named you Gordon."

He didn't say anything, but drew his finger along the glass, outlining a shape I couldn't make out.

"Too cool for Gordon?" Lily said, teasing.

Gray shrugged.

"He had to give up his last name when his parents adopted him," Walter said. "What if this is his way of honoring his birth mom?"

Gray looked down and went very still, and we all knew that was it.

It was quiet for a while. When Lily spoke again, she eyed both of us through the rearview. "When we get to Arthur's, remember: be respectful. It's not our place. We can't forget that." She glanced through the mirror at Gray then at me, and we murmured our agreement. "Their priority is Jocelyn," she said more seriously, looking ahead at the road. "They'll tell us what they need."

It was an easy promise for me to make. In my mind, I was only going along so I could get my next message, the one that would lead me to Krista, that would maybe lead them to Jocelyn.

THE DRIVE CONTINUED ON and Lily and Walter went back to their jazz and podcasts, to their comfortable hand-holding. I kept my eyes on the landscape. Daydreams about my parents and Trevor at home played across the window, projected on the passing trees.

At first I felt sorry for myself and imagined no one cared that I was gone. One less ego to feed and all. I remembered once when I was five and following Mom through the grocery store. Trevor was caged in the cart, his little legs dangling. Mom was *sh-sh*ing him mindlessly while she picked items from the shelves. I decided it would be hilarious if I hid from her. So I tucked myself behind the frozen meat fridge, peeking out from time to time to watch her push Trevor and the cart farther and farther away. It was nothing, just a moment in a childhood full of moments, but she never noticed that I was gone. It was me who was the frantic one, searching one aisle after another for her. Lost and running. It felt like hours before I found her standing in the dairy aisle in front of the eggs, trying to choose between organic free run and the usual. I didn't want to make a big deal of it, and so I stopped crying and slipped in beside her and secretly wiped my tears on the cotton hip of her dress.

I wondered if a *task force* had been set up for me too. Police taking my data, tracing my SIM card to some zigzagging bus, checking my non-existent social media, interviewing people who had no idea who I was, cataloguing my DNA. *Money no object*.

Maybe Dad was a suspect. Maybe they were taking a sledge-hammer to the concrete in our basement right now, on the lookout for bones.

I pictured them at home, waiting for me, gathered at the kitchen table. Dad stoic but compulsively clearing his throat. Mom with a tissue in her hand, dabbing her nose. Trevor pretending to read one of his comic books, pretending he didn't care about any of it.

My body shuddered reflexively and I wondered if I was cruel.

THE FINAL ROAD LEADING to Jocelyn's uncle's house was long and unpaved. Dust kicked up and swirled around the car. I couldn't remember the last time we'd passed a town or a store or even a gas station.

Gray was leaning forward in his seat, watching over Lily's shoulder as Walter drove us in. Tension fanned off him. I wished I had mind-reading abilities. Like Infinity Girl but the opposite — not reflecting him, but absorbing and knowing his deepest thoughts.

Soon he was going to meet the people from his birth community. For the first time. For the worst possible reason. That's what he was afraid of.

Eventually we pulled into a driveway that took us to a neat farmhouse. There was a barn not far away with an enclosed pen full of chickens, and a pasture with two grazing goats. It looked peaceful. Across from the house, a row of cars and pickups lined a cropped field. A few tents were set up, scattered around the field. Walter turned the car into the gravel lot.

"Looks like they have a good turnout," Lily said.

There were a dozen or more kids on the driveway, toddlers to teens, playing soccer with a large silver-and-black husky. They stopped playing when they saw us. A heavy-set teenaged boy picked up the youngest kid and tucked him under one arm. The dog sat back and dropped its ears and stared at us with silver eyes. Lily opened her window and waved and some of the kids waved back, but not in a way like they knew her.

"Wait here," Lily said to us. "We need a minute to figure out how they want to handle this." She and Walter got out of the car and slammed the doors behind them.

Gray sat back in his seat. He followed the kids outside with his eyes, maybe hoping for some kind of acknowledgement. Lily and Walter laid hands on a few small heads as they made their way to the farmhouse, greeting everyone and saying things to them that we couldn't hear. The kids followed on their heels, curious. All except one. A little girl about seven or eight, who stayed back, flanked by the silver husky.

The girl stood on my side of the car and stared at me through the window. Her hands were clenched into fists, her small brow knotted, her feet apart like she was standing her ground. She was wearing a too-big white-sequined vest, and the sequins glinted like they were part of her arsenal. She didn't look like a child, but like a miniature leader of dissidents. A renegade. I was a threat, I realized before she and the dog ran off, following the others into the house.

Gray craned around to look through the rear window. I turned to look too. There was a small mobile home behind the farmhouse, pressed against the wall of trees that skirted the property.

He powered up his phone and scrolled until he landed on a photo. I snuck a look and saw that it was a shot of the same mobile home, but taken in winter so it was locked in a hold of snow.

Gray caught me staring. "That's Jocelyn's place," he said.

"The one she keeps running away from?"

"Yeah." He contemplated the photo. "She posted it a couple of years ago." He read the caption — "*New chapter. New digs.*"

Footsteps in the snow led from the front door to where the unseen photographer was standing, and I imagined Jocelyn making them. Her boots testing then sinking one at a time as she tried to get the best angle to show her friends where she lived now. Maybe retracing those steps twenty-seven — no, twenty-*eight* days ago as she snuck away from home.

Like the map had shown us before we came, we were far from everything here. I wondered how she got to school, or who she hung out with. Definitely not the kids playing soccer, who were all much younger than her.

"I read that when she ran away, she usually went to the city," Gray said as if he were reading my thoughts. Again, I was surprised he didn't know for sure. If she'd gone to the city, wouldn't Gray be her favorite destination? "But she always comes back here. So a part of her must really want to be here too."

"You *read* that she went to the city?" I said. "You don't see each other?"

He turned to me. "What do you mean?"

I tried again. "I just thought — you know — because you're together — you guys would, you know — see each other."

Gray blinked at me. "Jocelyn isn't my girlfriend."

I remembered the photo on his phone of Jocelyn on her bed. He'd stared at that beautiful, kneeling pose *a million times*.

Oh no, I thought. *Unrequited* love. The worst kind.

"I'm sorry," I said, fumbling with my coat zipper. "I thought — because — the photo — the one she sent you —"

"No," he said. He was so easy about it. "I pulled that from her feed."

"Her feed?"

"Yeah." He clicked out of the photo of her home and showed me. And then I saw it was Jocelyn's Ittch stream. And it was full of shots, including the one of her kneeling on the bed. "That one was the best angle of her face."

"Right," I said.

"I don't even know her."

I started. "You don't know her?"

"No." He turned his intensely honest gaze on me. "We were born in the same town. We're the same age. We would've grown up as family. We're practically cousins. I'm not looking for Jocelyn because we're together, or because I want us to be. I'm looking for her because — Because I care what happens to her. Because —" He shook his head. "What if she doesn't turn up and — And I never did anything?"

"Oh," I said, letting it sink in. I remembered his story about a little girl whose disappearance and death had once been turned into a joke.

He craned around to scrutinize Jocelyn's house again. "I need to get in there. I need to check her stuff. See if there's anything they missed."

I was about to say something — I don't know what — when Walter interrupted us by opening the rear passenger door and leaning in. "They want to talk to you, Gray."

Gray sat up. "Did they find her?"

Walter's face turned somber. "They just got back from today's search. Nothing yet."

"Is her mother around?" Nervous energy radiated off Gray.

Walter said gently, "She's inside with the others."

Gray collected himself and stepped out of the car. I started to follow, but Walter angled for me. "Not you," he said. "I'm sorry. They respectfully ask that you wait here until we've had a chance to speak."

"Okay, no problem." I reared back into stillness. Before Gray could slam the door, I said to him, "Will you keep me posted?"

He turned. His expression had changed. I wondered for a second if he felt sorry for me. "Yeah," he said. "For sure."

2

ANOTHER HOUR PASSED, MAYBE two. I didn't know what to do with myself. I didn't have my playlists to distract me. Didn't have my sketchpad or binder or loose-leaf scraps. It was a dangerous lull. I kept thinking of Gray. Wondering what he was learning. How it made him feel. How the planes of his face might shift with each new piece of information, with each new thought. His fingers tapping on his knees. His hand brushing his hair.

No no no no. Stop, I told myself. *Stop now*.

Lily and Walter had brought along a newspaper for the ride, and out of desperation I reached for it and rifled for a page they wouldn't need — a full-page ad for some kitchen design store. The oversized-white-whatever island in the center would make a perfect frame for some Infinity Girl doodles.

Establishing shot: *Infinity Girl hides in the shadows, spying on the impenetrable fortress of Double Kross's evil lair. The only way to escape her nemesis — without destroying her — is to infiltrate the lair and find out what villainous treachery Double Kross is up to. She uses her mirrors to disappear and finds the servants' entrance* because of course Double Kross has servants and luxuries too many to count.

Infinity Girl camouflages herself during an emergency delivery of French pastries. Then scrambles to hide inside a pantry in the kitchen. Because of the optical effect of her mirrors, no one sees her.

But there are other ways she can be discovered: an accidental brush of an elbow, or a miscalculated turn down a hall. Because Infinity Girl still has body mass. She's still a person.

She wiggles her way into some ductwork (okay, it was too cliché —
and do evil lairs even have ductwork?) *and explores the cavernous*
estate. She comes upon the room where Double Kross is holding her
Nefarious Plans meeting. She listens in. Double Kross is in the middle
of schooling her minions.

Speech-bubbles: *"First of all, Infinity Girl is weak. Second: she*
believes everything you tell her. And third: she can't resist showing
up to the game. But — here's the catch —" Double Kross threatens her
minions with her scarlet saber. "She is so desperate to matter that she
will disappear of her own accord." Double Kross uses her saber to stab
a chocolate éclair. "And that's what makes her so hard to find."

I checked the farmhouse again. Nothing had changed. The
tents in the distant field rippled in a short gust of wind. No one
was coming or going. Everyone was inside the house discussing
Jocelyn. My bladder was getting the better of me.

I slipped out of the car and stood behind the open door. I
was sure the husky was going to come charging, or the renegade
girl. When nothing happened and no one came, I stepped out.
Everything was static and still. The woods that lined the property weren't that far away. I jogged for them. I was afraid to
make a sound, to rouse a mysterious something out of hiber-
nation. I tried not to look at anything as I passed. Just wanted to
be done and get back to the car as quickly and inconspicuously
as possible.

The tree trunks were thin and the pine trees sparse, but it was
enough to make me feel hidden. Protected even. The mat of spring
growth had turned the ground into something soft and yielding.
Old leaves cracked under my feet. The fresh air hit me too. It was
new but also sort of familiar. Thousands of years of evolution
forgotten as you find yourself back at the beginning.

I picked a spot behind a pine tree, hidden enough from the farmhouse and tents that I had some privacy, not so far that I couldn't see them if I peered through the branches. A low whirring wind kept me company. The relief was intense. Sweet.

A snap of branch made me jump and I rushed to get dressed. I looked around, but couldn't see anything moving. The rustle got louder and closer. Something coming at me over the matted ground. I found a loose branch and picked it up. The branch was so rotted it almost disintegrated in my hands.

The rustling stopped, advanced again, and stopped. And then I saw it landing on a moss-covered rock not too far away. A crow. It settled and cocked its head to stare at me.

I let out an embarrassed laugh. "Well, hello."

It looked a lot like the crow from my vision. Glossy black feathers. Thin overbite beak. Gray-black claws. But much smaller, and real. When I looked closer, there were also unexpected details. Its legs were textured like snakeskin. The black feathers along its chest were faintly speckled with cream and red. Unlike my dream-crow, but like the crow on Gray's back, its eyes were outlined with yellow.

Very slowly, I squatted and laid the branch down. "Are you here to give me another message?" I didn't expect it to answer; I was just playing. "Because so far, your clues have sucked."

The crow tilted one of its eyes at me.

"No offense." I let my weight down until my butt rested on a cracked tree stump.

The crow flared its wings, but then folded them back in again.

"Wait —" I said, looking closer at it. "Are you hurt?"

But it didn't look hurt. It looked curious.

"Or learning to fly?"

It didn't look young either. Didn't have those scruffy, downy feathers baby birds usually have. It nudged its beak at me and I almost held my breath, almost *did* expect it to say something. But then it settled again and seemed to wait. Its claws flexed and dug into the padding of moss on the rock.

I remembered that thing about crows liking shiny objects. I'd seen a video once about a friendship between a family of crows and a little girl, how every day they'd leave each other tiny gifts. Crows are smart, everyone says. They recognize you. They judge you.

I needed an ally. I checked myself for something shiny, but everything was denim or cotton or leather or nylon. I couldn't rip off zipper-tassels or my clothes would be useless. I couldn't pull off a button or my jeans would fall down.

The crow cocked its head — it was watching my calculations very closely. And then I saw my hand as it fumbled over my jacket, and couldn't help noticing the silver ring on my middle finger. It was a simple band, not fancy, not overly shiny. It represented my one pathetic act of subversion.

When we were in grade seven, before the Krista-days, Boyd's nanny would take us to the mall so we could hang out and pretend we were super-sophisticated. We'd buy junk and wear it for a few weeks, and then replace it with more junk, and on and on. I was the thriftiest of the bunch, and usually just trolled bins and racks without actually committing to anything. Anusha and Boyd were the worst. Bags and bags of cool this-or-thats.

The ring had cost about twenty bucks, bought from one of those pretend-exotic shops loaded with crystals and incense and painted silk. Anusha had convinced Boyd that his style needed to go edgy, that he had to wear jewelry — jangly silver and turquoise — and all-black clothes. Boyd was always up for anything and he bought everything she endorsed. But his new look only lasted a week, maybe not even, before he was back to wearing his usual elite running shoes, track pants, basketball jerseys.

I'd found the ring in a pile of junk on his desk when we were hanging out, and I tried it on, and it had fit. I guess I stole it. Not that he or anyone had ever noticed. And pretty soon even I forgot I was wearing it.

I played with the ring. Twisted it around my finger.

It was off without me consciously pulling it off and I cradled it in the palm of my hand. The crow, from its perch on the rock, took notice. The ring really was pretty.

What would the crow do with it? Would she add it to a nest? Or give it to her beloved? Or find a little girl in the woods and ask to be her friend? Whatever she chose, it would be better than what I was doing with it. Hanging on. Holding it hostage.

I reached my hand towards the crow, the ring a miniature silver lifebuoy for her to catch. She hesitated. "Take it," I said. I kept my voice steady and gentle. She blinked at me. "It's okay." She raised her wings and hopped a tentative step forward. "Come on," I said. I was beginning to feel giddy. "Take it."

She was staring at the ring. I turned it so it would catch a glint of light flashing through the trees. "Take it." She flapped her wings once more and hopped closer, landing on the leaves inches from my knees. "Please take it."

And then she sprang forward. I screeched and recoiled and she grabbed the ring with her beak just as I dropped it. In one fluid motion, she swooped up and into the air above me.

It was such a relief to watch the ring fly away with her. Like it had weighed a thousand pounds.

It was a sign, I told myself. Gray and I would get the answers we needed and we would find our girls and I'd go home and the meaning of my life would be forever etched in history. *M of Arc.*

I followed the crow's rise to the sky, the dappled late afternoon light landing on my face, and pushed myself off the rock. That's when I saw it. Probably the only reason the crow had stuck around for so long. A dead bird at my feet, on its back, head turned to the side, beak open, tongue out, rigid claws sticking up.

A murder of crows.

I bolted away so fast, I practically flew.

I landed in the open area that made up the yard, desperate to keep going, except the little renegade girl and her silver husky stepped in front of me. She was gripping the lapels of her white-sequined vest, eying me like she knew I was up to no good. I aimed for the refuge of Walter and Lily's car.

"*Witiko*," she said when I passed her. I didn't acknowledge her greeting — it was pretty clear it was an insult. "Witiko!" she said to my fleeing back.

Four other little girls came out from behind the car. They stepped in front of it to block my way. They were super-relaxed, super-easy about it. I stopped, not sure where to go, or what would happen next. The oldest must've been about twelve/ thirteen, skinny and tall, and she coddled the smaller ones, stroking their hair and pulling up drooping sweater-arms. The next oldest — maybe eleven — had a shaved head that she bopped like a rapper. The next two were younger — about nine or so, identically round-cheeked and giggling and whispering into each other's ears.

But the renegade girl in the white-sequined vest was the

youngest of all. She came around and stood between me and the others. Her husky padded in and stood sentry beside her.

"My dog Kimi says you want something." Her voice was surprisingly deep for such a little kid. "Kimi says we need to ask you what it is." She seemed to wait for me to say something. Her dog blinked its silver eyes at me. "What do you want?" she said.

I didn't know what to do. It was obviously a trick. Or a test.

The girl looked at her dog. "She doesn't know, Kimi. What do we do now?" She made a show of listening to the dog. "Huh. You think so?" She looked back at me. "Kimi says you think you're right." All five girls stared at me like they were waiting for my response. "But you're not right. You don't know the way."

I didn't answer. I was too busy melting. Melting in front of them while invisibly trying to scoop myself together. I was older than them by years. Trying to keep the upper hand. Holding onto the idea that inside me, the inside me that no one could see, it was strong and surging. That I was bigger than you. Smarter.

I wanted to hang onto that feeling. Grow it. Own it.

I didn't want to be humble. I wanted to *pretend* to be humble.

But I couldn't hide any of that from those girls. The littlest one burst into laughter and then the other girls started laughing too.

"Don't be so scared," the renegade said. She made a show of wiping her hands. "You're allowed to use Jocelyn's house to wash up." She pointed to the mobile home. "They say to tell you it won't be long. They say don't worry, dinner is coming."

Then she reeled away, and the dog went next, and the four other girls followed. The sequins on the renegade's vest flashed and sparkled. I wondered where she'd bought it.

I DIDN'T KNOW ANYONE who lived in a home like Jocelyn's. It was old and run down. So, so small. Jocelyn had been forced to move here from the town she'd grown up in. Gray's birthplace. *Because her father had died.*

The little girl had said I was allowed to go inside to wash up. It would be nice to wash up.

The front stairs were made of cinder block. The door was metal, slightly warped. It stuck when I pulled on the latch-handle, and then it burst free and almost knocked me over. I checked behind me. The yard was empty again, the farmhouse blank, its windows not yet reflecting light or revealing what was happening inside. I turned back to Jocelyn's house.

I was allowed to go inside.

Every corner of the trailer was jammed. Pots and utensils — clean and stacked into each other — were rim to rim on open shelves and across every inch of the short L-shaped kitchen counter. Too much stuff and not enough place to put it. Unopened packing boxes improvised as furniture — coffee table, side tables, plant stand. Blue marker scrawled on the sides: *Henry's clothes, Henry's books, Henry's instruments.* Framed photos and paintings, collected documents, folded blankets, winter coats and boots, were piled in every remaining spot.

I imagined Jocelyn here. Maybe folding her life into a tiny parcel and stacking it inside everything else.

There was a short narrow hall that held the bathroom. I soaped and washed my hands at the sink. Checked my face in the mirror. My hair was scrunched up on one side and I scrabbled my fingers through the knots to smooth it down.

I was a wreck. No one would look at my photo a million times.

I should've left her home then. I hadn't been given permission to do anything except wash up. But curiosity drew me the opposite way, towards the open doors that led to the two bedrooms. The first room I came to I recognized right away from the photo Gray had shown me of Jocelyn on her bed. It was tiny compared to what it had seemed. The bed, with its rumpled sheets and blanket, took up practically the whole space, and the walls were almost like a box around it. Wire hangers draped with clothing — slinky dresses, sparkly shirts, faded sweatshirts — were hooked to thumbtacks stuck in the wood paneling.

I leaned on the bed to check the corkboard, especially interested in the corner that had been hidden in the photo behind Jocelyn's head. Gray had been anxious to fill in that blank. If I found something interesting, I could be the bearer-of-news.

There was the pinned paper-photo of the older man. Handsome, smiling. Leaning against a vintage pickup truck. It had to be her father. Her dead father.

I glanced back at the cardboard boxes in the other room. *Henry's clothes, Henry's books, Henry's instruments.* Portable gravestones.

The corner of the corkboard that you couldn't see in Jocelyn's Ittch photo held two items. First, a postcard-sized flyer for a concert by the Tandem Acorns. My favorite band of all time. *Jocelyn and I liked the same music.* When the Acorns had been scheduled to come to the city the year before, I'd begged my parents to let me go.

Beside the postcard was a beautiful black ink drawing of a word.

truth

Underneath was another word.

nohtuwi

Both were written in spiraling calligraphy, each letter decorated with elegant ink curlicues and streamers and hearts. I wondered if Jocelyn ever dreamed of being an artist.

I didn't know what *nohtawi* meant — I assumed it was a Cree
word — but *truth* repeated in my head. *The truth is hidden inside
the fallacy. The truth is the way*, painted on the city mural. Then the
message the birds had created in the photos. *Messenger 93. Follow
him. He is the fall. He is the way*. Then there was the little renegade's
warning. *You think you're right. But you're not right. You don't know
the way*.

Was it all coming together to warn me I was on the wrong path?

That it wasn't Krista I was supposed to be searching for — but
Jocelyn?

Don't be so scared, the renegade had warned me.

I checked the details of Jocelyn's room one more time, in
case we'd missed anything. Her clothes, her jewelry, her pictures.
Nohtawi. Her longing. Her pain.

Her bed was so tempting. My body yearned to curl up under
her blankets and have a long nap. But it was too Goldilocks.
Who got away lucky that the bears didn't kill her for squatting in
their lives.

I WENT BACK TO the car and shut myself inside. The question
of what I was supposed to do next dissolved. I'd been offered a
better, more noble mission. Not Krista. *Jocelyn*. I was supposed
to help find Jocelyn.

As she falls.

The softly swaying grasses in the field were mesmerizing.
Pretty soon I dozed off.

There was a loud tap and I started awake. It was twilight-
gloomy out. The sun had dropped in the west, its sunset-halo
cloaking the clouds in pink and blue. There was another tap. It
was one of the older kids at the car window. I'd seen him when

we arrived, playing soccer and handling toddlers. He motioned for me to come with him.

I rubbed my eyes and climbed out of the car. The air was chilly. I pulled up the hood of my coat.

"Get your stuff," he said as he opened the trunk and pulled out Gray's backpack. I glanced at the farmhouse. Lights had been turned on inside, making silhouettes of some of the people moving around. Still no Gray.

"C'mon," the boy said. He led the way to a fire pit not far off. I grabbed my bag and followed him. He rooted inside Gray's backpack and found the tent. "Not enough room in the house for everyone." He emptied the small case and began connecting poles and laying out pegs. "Most of us gotta sleep outside. You down for that?"

"Yeah, sure." I'd never slept in a tent. Our family trips had been all hotels and resorts. I dropped my backpack and went over to help — even though I had no idea what I was doing. I smiled at him. "I'm M."

"Charlie." He slid a linked rod into a tent seam.

"Where's Gray?" I said. Very casual.

"*Gray*? Oh, you mean Gordon, right." He sat back on his haunches and measured me. He looked about fourteen. Around Trevor's age. "He's getting caught up."

I wondered if Gray was feeling better about being here. If he was getting what he needed.

Charlie said, "Did the girls tell you that you can use Jocelyn's place to wash up?"

"Yeah, thanks," I said. None of my rod-pieces were fitting together. "What does *Witiko* mean?"

Charlie grunt-laughed. "Why?"

"One of them called me that."

He raised an eyebrow. "What did you do?"

"Walked past her."

He burst out laughing. "Nothing like Witiko stories to mess with a white person's head." He laughed harder. "Witiko is a cannibal. Haunts the woods. Has a heart made of ice. If it eats you, you turn into a Witiko. Sort of like with zombies. Only way to kill it is by melting its heart."

I slumped. "Great."

Charlie had to clamp his fist over his mouth because he was laughing so hard. "Which kid said it?"

I was almost laughing too. "She's about eight? White-sequined vest? Super-tough?"

"Oh yeah." He nodded, his fist stifling more laughter. "Vivvie. She *is* super-tough. She'd lay down her life for any one of us."

Vivvie. She was just a kid.

I fumbled with tent rods. "Do you know Jocelyn?"

"We grew up together. But I haven't seen her since she moved over here with her mom."

"Is there any more news about her?"

"The only thing we got is someone knows someone who saw her thumbing outside Deerhead four weeks back. Another dude thought he saw her two days ago in some random car. But the dude was driving the other way. By the time he turned around and went back to check it out, the car was gone. We can't say for sure it was her. That's all we have."

"Do you know why she would go to Deerhead?"

"Pretty obvious."

"Is it?"

"Yeah. Her dad died near Deerhead."

"Really? What happened?"

"Murder. That's what happened."

"He was *murdered*?"

"Three years now." All Charlie's tent pieces were assembled, so he picked through the collection of parts in front of me. "Her dad was in Deerhead waiting for a ride home 'cause of a snowstorm. But when his ride showed up, her dad was gone. When he didn't show up at home, they sent out the search party. They found his body on the side of the highway, miles from everything, frozen. Someone had picked him up — and left him out on the road. So yeah: murder."

Made-up pictures circled my mind of Jocelyn's father being abandoned and dying on a winter road. I said, "So Jocelyn went down there to look for answers ..."

"You sleuthed that out by yourself?" He gave me the sarcastic-eyebrow-lift.

Jocelyn's father had been murdered. Of course Jocelyn wanted answers.

Charlie shook out the nylon tarp and laid it over the ground. "Damn, this is a fine spread. Gordo's got some serious dough. He got out of the boonies and got rich." He pushed a peg through a loop and into the ground, and added sarcastically, "Lucky him."

I helped him with the pegs, and in a minute he had the tent raised. We stood and admired it together. "Thank you," I said and he nodded. I wondered how terrified I would be sleeping out here.

Charlie went to the fire pit and quickly assembled kindling and logs and lit a fire. I sat on one of the nearby stumps and, despite the coolness of the air and the coldness inside me, I was warmer already. He poked the flames with a stripped stick. "Got bad news for you."

My stomach churned. "Oh?"

"You're not going with them tomorrow. They're gonna take you to the bus stop at Earl's Diner over on Route 8 and send you back to the city."

The urge to cry came over me so quickly I had to flick my fingers over my eyes to hide it. "Why?"

"This ain't your search, man. They've got too much going on without worrying about your ass." He smiled to show he was making light, but another rush of tears threatened and I coughed and tilted my head away. He saw through me and hurried to add, "Hey, it's not so bad. The cops will find your sister. They'll be all over a lost white girl. Don't worry. You'll be okay."

"Was it Gray's idea?" I said. Anger was stronger to cling to than tears. "Did he convince them to send me back?"

Charlie laughed a bit. "No, it wasn't him. He was pulling for you. It was the adults who said no." In an instant, my anger was gone and tears were pressing again. "They say there's no connection between your girl and ours. Jocelyn is on her own out there."

He reached over and patted my shoulder. Like a middle-aged dad. "I know it doesn't feel like it right now, but they're looking out for you. Just like they hope someone's looking out for our Joce. Trust me — you're gonna do more good in the city." He gave me another reassuring smile. "The whole world's got your back, girl. But we —" He circled his hand to encompass the farmhouse and everyone in it. "We only have each other."

I wanted to resist — to say that of course they had more than each other, they had all of us too. But where did Jocelyn and her father fit in with that? There were no *investigations* happening here. They hadn't even traced Jocelyn's phone.

For a second, I considered begging Charlie to convince the adults to change their minds. I considered rushing the farmhouse myself and arguing with my deniers face-to-face. But I knew in my gut, in my heart, that I had no right. This was not my place, and I was not their problem, and my conviction that I needed to help Jocelyn because of some cryptic message from a magical crow would probably not go over.

Charlie smiled at me, then raised an eyebrow. "You good?" A regular old high school guidance counselor.

I blinked at the flames. The urge to cry was gone, the tears crystalized in my chest. I nodded.

"Cool," he said and stood up. "I'm gonna set up Lily and Walter's tent, and then I'll get you some chow." And he walked off like a man with a mission.

Boys with more problems than me taking care of me.

I slumped again. What was I going to do tomorrow when they left me at the bus stop? How was I ever going to find missing girls if I was back in the city? I picked up Charlie's stick and poked the burning logs. I poked them hard enough to launch tiny missile-sparks into the purple sky.

3

A FEW PEOPLE CAME out of the farmhouse and headed to the other tents. The campsites were lined up in a wide semi-circle around the yard. More fires sparked and roared up. I could hear the quiet murmur of voices. Charlie was setting up Lily and Walter's tent near an unlit fire pit between my spot and the rest. I hadn't seen Lily and Walter since they'd left me in the car. Still no sign of Gray.

I pulled out my new Infinity Girl storyboard and smoothed the crumpled newspaper ad against my knee. It was getting dark and I angled the page to the fire so I could see what I was doing.

Where was I? Infinity Girl is spying on Double Kross. Double Kross is planning her demise. Infinity Girl has to come up with a plan. *But what?*

I waited for inspiration. Waited some more. Dusk pressed over the sky. The fire got bigger. I was getting hot. Wishing for Gray to come. Infinity Girl was still hiding in the dark.

"What's that?"

I looked over my shoulder. Vivvie and her crew were standing behind me. She was holding a mug of steaming-something in one hand and pointing at my scribbles with the other. "What is it?" she said again. The other four girls, even the silver husky, looked at me expectantly.

I checked with my drawings. A chaotic jumble of scrawl, stick figures and speech-bubbles barely recognizable. I could have said it was anything.

"It's a storyboard."

"What's that?"

"Like a map for making a movie."

"You're making a movie?"

"Nah, I don't think so."

"Why not?"

I checked on Infinity Girl. Hopelessly stuck in some improbable ductwork. "Because it sucks."

"What's happening?" she said, tapping her finger on the panel where Double Kross was raving at her minions.

"That's the bad guy. She's plotting to kill the hero." I pointed at Infinity Girl. "And the hero is figuring out how to stop her."

"But they don't even know the hero is there. Why doesn't she just zoom down and kill them?"

"Because she can't destroy anyone."

"No killing?"

"No killing."

"Not even bad guys?"

"Not even bad guys."

The oldest girl, the mothering one, whispered in her ear. Vivvie listened then said, "What's her skill?"

I said, "She reflects back to people what they really are."

"But what does she *do*?"

"That's what she does."

"No. That's a power. She's gotta have a skill. She's gotta *do* something."

My pen scratched aimlessly at a corner of the newspaper. That was always my problem. No idea what to do.

The girl with the shaved head whispered in Vivvie's ear. Vivvie said, "They like it. They made a movie once. On their phone, with their friends. It was good. You could do that."

"I don't think so ..."

Vivvie reached inside the lining of her white-sequined vest and pulled something out of a hidden pocket. "She could star in your movie." It was a little folded paper person. Origami. She handed it to me. "But only if you give her a skill."

I reached for it. It was the cutest thing. A small pink-paper figure with an angled head and pointy feet and arms. "You made this?"

"Yup. It's my hobby."

I turned it over, admiring all the precise folds. "You ever hear of a show called *Star Trek*?"

"Yeah?"

"You know the Transporter? How they beamed people from the spaceship to, like, the surface of a planet or something?"

"Yeah?"

"They're dematerializing then rematerializing, right? Well, back in the old days when they shot it, they didn't have money for special effects, so they faked it by shaking sparkles in front of a black backdrop and filming it upside down in slow motion."

Vivvie smiled. "Whoa."

"I always thought it would be cool to try that."

Her brow furrowed. "Me too. I wanna push a button and get someplace fast."

I'd meant filming the upside-down sparkles. But I said, "Yeah, same."

"Where would you go?"

I didn't have an answer. I wasn't ready to go back to the city. I didn't want to save Krista. I wanted to be here.

"I'd beam over to Jocelyn," Vivvie said. "I'd bring her home."

That made me smile in the deepest way. "I wish you could do that too." I gave her back her little figure.

"No, I'm serious. Keep it," Vivvie said. "She wants to be in your movie." She handed me the steaming cup. "They said to give this to you. Sweetgrass tea."

"Thank you." I tucked the paper mini-human in my coat pocket and cradled my hands around the warm ceramic. The scent wafting up through the steam was heavenly.

"Her skill can be slow motion," Vivvie said, stroking the husky's head. "She can mess with the bad guy. The bad guy won't even know it. The bad guy can hurt *herself*." And then she and the husky broke off in a run. Her friends tagged after them. Their high-pitched, happy shrieks made me long for the easiness of being a kid.

4

GRAY FINALLY CAME OUT of the house. I watched him the whole way as he walked towards me, carrying two plates of dinner. It wasn't until he was almost at the fire that I realized I was smiling. I sucked in my lips, chewed on the insides.

"They're sorry about keeping you out here," he said as he approached. "There's a lot to talk about in there. It's pretty crowded."

"I get it. It's okay. I'm fine."

He handed me a plate. Roasted potatoes, squash, grilled sausage. We both inhaled our meals without talking. I was even hungrier than I'd realized. When we finished eating, Gray stoked the fire and caught me up on everything that had happened in the hours since we'd last seen each other. Mostly a recap of what Charlie had already told me: that Jocelyn's father had been mur-

dered, that her family assumed she'd gone to Deerhead to see
the place of his death, either searching for answers or to mourn
him.

"You know that corkboard in her room?" I said. "The part you
can't see in the photo?"

Gray straightened. "Yeah?"

"When I went into her place to wash up, I saw what was on it.
A drawing that I think she made. It's the words *truth* and *nohtawi*."
I spelled the last word out.

"*Nohtawi* ..." Gray said thoughtfully. "They post daily words
on the online community board for people to learn the language.
I think it means 'my father.'" He contemplated the flames. "Yeah,
that's what everyone is saying. That she's out there looking for
the truth about her dad." His jaw muscles contracted — that
tension when you have to accept a legitimate but dangerous possibility. "She could be trying to find the guy who did it. And putting
herself on the line to find him ..."

It made sense. Total, terrifying, infuriating sense. Because no
one else was investigating her father's death. Jocelyn probably
felt she had no choice.

"The cops still haven't put a trace on her phone," Gray said,
his voice rising. "If she still has it on her, this could be over
like that." He jabbed a finger. "Twenty-eight days gone. A whole
month — nothing."

We gnawed on the injustice, on our helplessness. Eventually
Gray came back from his faraway thoughts to fill me in on the
rest. He confirmed that I would be banished the next day to the
bus that went down to the city. That I needed to go back because
I'd stand out among them in Deerhead, and maybe bring unnec-
essary, unwanted attention. He seemed sincerely sorry that I

wouldn't be staying with them, but he promised to share any information they discovered. I made a big show of accepting all of the developments and reassuring him I was fine.

I told myself that I *was* fine. I was being *guided*, which must mean I would receive another clue and get where I needed to go. There was still a chance the messages would help me find Jocelyn and bring her back to her community. What an epic triumph that would be.

I watched Gray tease the fire with the end of the stick. I said, "How was it in there?"

"Sad. Worried."

I could imagine it. How else could it be? I remembered Clio's pressing desperation when I'd sat with her. Her fear. And that was with Krista gone only a couple of days.

I leaned into the warmth of the fire. "What about being here with them — is it okay?"

He met my question with a lingering gaze. "They're being really — I don't know — really nice to me."

I smiled. "That's good. Isn't it?"

"Yeah. Totally."

"But ...?"

"I don't know ... Is this my place? ... I keep thinking that something will happen and I'll know for sure. But —" He lifted another log from the pile and positioned it over the embers. "Nah — I can't tell."

There were so many things I could have said to him. Lines from books and shows and movies. *It's only the beginning. You'll find a way. Give it time.* Characters always had the most poetic answers.

But I said, "Do you like it here?"

He jostled the new log with the stick, and the log smoked then grabbed some flames. "Not *why* I'm here … But the *here* here? … Yeah, I like it."

That made me glad for him.

I wanted so badly to reach out and touch the velvety nape of his neck. To run my finger along the delicate feather tattooed under his right ear.

I said, "I'm sorry about your birth mom."

He checked the ground between his knees. "It's not like I remember her or anything." His voice caught a bit when he said, "I'm sorry about your parents too."

I started, then realized. *My dead parents*. I had told him I was on my own. *It was just me and my twin sister Krista*.

I pretended to search the shadows of the trees. I only had a few more hours with him. I didn't want to fill it with lies.

But was it a lie if I was trying to help find missing girls — not just Krista, but now Jocelyn too? Because I was there for a reason, wasn't I? The crow had led me to him. It had *lured* me. It was helping me *save* people.

I was still trying to figure out how to fix all the fractures that were trailing from the epicenter of my story when Lily and Walter walked by.

"Time to settle in," Lily said. Kind but firm. "It'll be another early morning tomorrow."

Walter set down a sack. "Could rain tonight. You kids should get out of those jeans and sweaters. Cotton is like a sponge for cold and wet. There's some wool underwear in there, and rain pants. Anything of yours you need to keep dry, you should store in that bag."

"Thanks, Walter." Gray sounded a bit sheepish, but he grabbed the sack and began to root inside, passing me the smaller of the tops and long johns and nylon pants. I bundled the comfortably worn clothes in my arms and thanked Walter too.

We exchanged goodnights and Lily and Walter went over to their own camp-spot. They didn't bother to light a fire, just crawled into their tent and zipped themselves inside.

Gray hopped up and grabbed the sleeping bags and blankets that Charlie had left in a pile and headed to the tent.

"Oh," I said. "You're staying out here too?"

"Yeah," he said. "I hope that's okay."

"Totally." I tried to cover my utter relief. "It's your tent."

I was still blushing and awkward when I went off to change in Jocelyn's trailer. The nylon pants were way too big, but there was a draw-cord and I could cinch them around my waist. By the time I got back, two sleeping bags were laid out side by side, and Gray was in one of them. Sound asleep.

I crawled in. It was cold, but not too bad. Walter's wool under-wear was soft and warm. The tent was insulated, and the sleeping bag was like a bundle of cozy. Outside-sounds became hyper-distinct. The whoosh of wind swirling through the woods and over the clear-cut field. The hiss of logs breaking apart and smoldering in the fire pit. The crack of a dead branch breaking under something's weight.

Fire shadow danced across the nylon walls of the tent. Gray's profile was illuminated against it. I measured the lines of his nose and chin. The curve of his relaxed and resting lips. He was so close that if I stretched my fingers, their tips would have brushed his side. It was hard to believe that I'd only met him the day before.

I sighed and rolled over so I wouldn't have to look at him.

A kind of chant started droning in my head. It helped numb out everything that I didn't understand or couldn't have.

Save Krista. Save Jocelyn. Save someone. Isn't that what Joan of Arc would do?

The words droned over and over until I slipped under to the other side.

SUNDAY, APRIL 15

FOUR DAYS UNTIL THE FALL

1

"MESSENGER 93," THE SMALLEST, sweetest voice whispered in my ear. "Wake up." My eyes fluttered open and it was pitch dark and I forgot — again — where I was. It was the smell of new nylon and the sound of wind whirling over the field outside that reminded me.

I blinked my eyes until they adjusted and then I saw a little girl kneeling beside me, neatly set under the sloped roof of the tent, her little body folded quietly on itself like she was an origami sculpture and not a real person.

She motioned for me to follow her and I got out of my sleeping bag and poked out of the flaps. The brisk night air instantly cooled me. I stood up and wobbled and tried to hold my balance.

The origami girl was gone, but I planted my feet on the grass anyway. The blades were cool under my socks. My body began to sway and slowly circle. There was a sizzle and pop and sparks burst in front of me and floated away like a spray of fireflies.

I turned to the fire. It was still smoldering. Its crimson and charcoal glow lit a small group of people approaching through the dark. A group of small people. The renegade and her friends — the mom-teen, the two goofballs, the girl/boy. They were hunched together, walking from the farmhouse, passing my fire. They all stopped and turned to me in unison — surprised to see me.

Curious as to what I was going to do. The silver husky came out of the shadows and padded into position next to her leader.

I wanted to keep watching the girls, but my eyes were blinking closed and I had to fight to stay awake. I thought it was a dream, but I couldn't tell for sure.

"Where are you going?" I said.

"The upside-down sparkles will take us there," Vivvie said. There was a flatness to her voice that reminded me a little of Trevor's. I wanted to cry, I missed him so much.

"Am I going with you?"

"No." She put a finger to her lips. "Don't tell anyone — but we can slow down time."

"I won't tell anyone." I swayed gently. Almost asleep again. "Where are you going?"

"We're going to find her. We have the skills. We have the power."

I forced my eyes to stay open. "You can't look for Jocelyn alone. You're just kids."

"Yes," she said, not because it was fact, but because it was the reason. "I'll give you a present if you let us go."

She reached under her coat and plucked something out. My heart was beating with anticipation. She offered her hand to me. Poised on her palm was one tiny gleaming white disc. A sequin from her vest.

I was incredibly honored.

"Keep it somewhere safe," she said.

"I will," I said.

Her dog was staring at me. It curled its lip and began to growl.

"Is your dog going to hurt me?" I said.

"Yes," Vivvie said. She was turning away. "But only a small hurt." She was walking to the woods and the other girls followed.

It was eerie how they hardly made a sound. The dog's growl got more threatening so I didn't move.

"I don't want it to hurt me," I said to the girls as they picked their way over the clear-cut grass. "I have no tolerance for pain." But they didn't react, only walked into the woods and wound their way among the thin trees.

The husky stayed. It bared its teeth and growled at me. Its canines were long and pointed, as sharp and shining as crescent moons. I could feel myself shaking but I wasn't able to move. My body was still rooted and swaying. The dog reared back and its muscles flexed and then it torqued into a pounce. Its jaw opened as it jumped at me, the full set of sharp teeth more menacing than anything I'd ever seen. I couldn't move as its gaping mouth flew towards my face.

I remembered my father reading me *Little Red Riding Hood*. We were in my bed. I was on his lap. I was full of wonder. There was a wolf in that story. It pretended to be the grandmother, then devoured everyone, even the girl.

The husky's icy silver eyes stared me down as it pounced, ferociously glaring. Starved for everything inside me. My mouth opened in an involuntary scream and the husky's mouth arrived so that we were mouth to mouth, teeth to teeth.

I remembered my dog Pepper and how he used to run circles around me in the park, how he would push his furry weight against my leg when he wanted me to scratch his throat.

The husky's teeth penetrated my head as I sank deep inside her.

A little girl's voice whispered in my ear, "She will fall in four days."

A SHORT SQUAWK WOKE me and my eyes fluttered open. A glossy crow was standing on my thigh, something hard clasped inside its beak, its black claws flexing into the borrowed rain pants. I started up and the crow dropped its treasure and flew away. Was it the same crow I'd met the day before in the woods?

I looked around, dazed from a deep sleep. I was damp and chilled through, sitting on the grass. An orange sun was low behind the trees, so it was day but still early. Everything was normal. The tent beside me, the fire — now out — the quiet clearing, the woods.

The crow's gift had landed in the grass by my feet and I picked it up. It was a small metal coil. Minimally shiny. Like the spring from inside a ballpoint pen. I turned it over in my hands.

"M? Are you okay?" It was Gray's voice. I glanced over my shoulder. He was crawling out of the tent.

I fumbled with the spring. It reminded me vaguely of the gold rings that Remy wrapped around her braids. For some reason I didn't want to lose it, so I pulled at my hair and twisted the spring around a strand and tucked it behind my ear.

Gray arrived and crouched next to me. "Are you okay?"

Was I okay? I remembered the dream about the girls and the husky and how it had eaten me. I ran my hand over my face, checking for injuries or blood, but didn't feel any wounds. My fingers came away damp but clean. The only thing wrong was an intensity of cold.

I said, "I think I was sleepwalking or something."

"Do you sleepwalk?" His brow furrowed. He seemed genuinely concerned.

"Not usually," I said. "But I had the weirdest dream." I tried to piece together the odd bits that I could remember. "It was those girls — they came to tell me they were leaving to look for Jocelyn."

"Which girls?"

"The ones, you know, who were playing ball when we arrived? The little ones. Vivvie."

"Vivvie? Sequined vest?"

"Yes, her. She told me that only she could find Jocelyn. Then she led four girls into the woods to search for her." I pointed in the direction they'd gone. "But before I could do anything, her dog ate me."

"The silver husky?"

"Yeah."

"Random." He got up and urged me up too.

I started to shiver. Gray put his hand on my arm. His skin was much warmer than mine. "You're soaked. You should change before we take the tent down," he said.

"Right." I hesitated, started to say something, started to go to him, then whirled away and crawled into the tent.

But I was uneasy. The certainty that I'd somehow said or done something wrong nagged at me while I changed out of Walter's wool hiking clothes and into my jeans and a new drugstore sweatshirt. Worry flushed through me, burned me up. Irritated the underside of my skin like a rash.

I finished dressing — tying my boots on, zipping up my rain-coat — and was about to crawl out again when I felt something inside my mouth, lodged between my gums and cheek. It was small and sharp, almost like a chipped piece of glass.

I shuddered a little as I reached into my mouth and probed for whatever it was. I wished and wished that it was nothing too hideous — I'd been sleeping outside for who-knows-how-long and any kind of bug could have crawled inside me.

But even before I saw it, as I was pulling it out, I recognized the tiny, shining disc.

A white sequin from Vivvie's too-big vest.

At the exact moment that I balanced the sequin on the tip of my finger, a terrible, heart-shattering cry rang out. Then another and another. Many voices yelling and streaking through space as if no one could move quickly enough.

I bolted out of the tent. Three women — their faces wrenched with distress — were racing past me and into the woods. More people ran behind them — everyone leaping over fallen tree trunks and moss-covered rocks. Two dogs I hadn't seen before barked and sniffed the ground. I noticed the husky wasn't with them. Their footfalls on the rotting groundcover echoed from the forest as the trackers went deeper and deeper inside.

Other people ran out of the house, throwing on coats, and climbed into cars and trucks. Walter's car was pulling out too and that's when I saw that Gray was inside it, sitting in the passenger seat. Gravel roared and dust tornadoed as one vehicle after another raced away down the drive.

Lily was among a few people who stayed behind at the house, all of them watching the exodus with tense expressions.

It all started to make sense — the girls, Vivvie, her silver husky, they *had* left in the middle of the night. It hadn't been a dream. Or it had, and it had showed me what was going to come.

And maybe I had caused it. Telling Vivvie about beaming to another place, wishing with her that she could materialize to where Jocelyn was so she could bring her home.

I hadn't stopped them. I had let them get away. I had lost them.

I rushed to pack everything up. Because I had room in my backpack, I shoved Walter's waterproof sack of clothes and the sleeping bag in with my stuff. It took ages longer than it should have to collapse the tent and squeeze it into its too-small pouch. Nothing fit the way it was supposed to, too much was distracting me from getting it right on first tries. When I was finally done, I hauled Gray's and my backpacks to the parking strip and waited for the cars to return.

Lily came out of the farmhouse with another woman who'd stayed behind. The woman was tiny and frail with a dark face, drawn and deeply lined. Something about her reminded me of the Jocelyn photo. I wondered if this was her mother. A woman too sick to run with the others, needing Lily to keep her company. She pulled out a cigarette and Lily lit it for her and they huddled a little against the cold breeze.

I paced in a circle, not sure what to do. I couldn't sit still and do nothing.

It was my fault that Vivvie and the girls had left. Stupid Infinity Girl and our dreams of empowerment. Believing we could change the way things are.

I aimed for Lily and the woman. Lily noticed me coming and left the woman on the stoop to head me off. Her expression was softer already. She reached her hands out as we approached each other and I thought for a minute that she was going to hug me — I almost reached out my own hands because, in that moment, there was maybe nothing I wanted more. But she placed them on my shoulders and used them to hold me back. "I'm sorry, M. You've been really patient. You just have to wait a while longer. We'll get you to the bus as soon as we can."

"But I don't want to go."

No one was bursting through the wilds looking for Krista. Other people ran the show — *experts, professionals, authorities.* I wanted to be like Lily and Walter, Arthur and the others. *Out there. Seeing with my own eyes.* "Please let me help. I'll do anything. Search the woods, hand out flyers, make coffee, whatever —"

"I know, and we appreciate it, but we don't need your help." The way she said it was kind. But final.

I was about to make another plea, but was cut off by the crunch of wheels on gravel. We both turned to watch Walter's car pull into the yard. Walter and Gray both looked somber behind the windshield and my heart dropped. Lily groaned. "Oh no."

Walter must have known we'd think the worst, so he got out quickly and waved his hands. "It's not the girls," he said. "Everyone's working their way down to the community hall. More help is coming."

Lily let out a breath. "Okay. I'll let the others know." She was about to turn away when Walter stopped her.

"But we have another problem." He crossed his arms and shot a look over at Gray who was still sitting in the car, eyelids drooping. Lily glanced at Gray and crossed her arms too.

"Just got a call from his dad," Walter said. "Gray wasn't answering his phone. They had no idea he was with us. That new camping gear? It was for a trip his dad was going to take him on … to make up for the fact that they wouldn't allow him to search for Jocelyn on his own."

Lily let out an epic sigh, walking away to fill the air with it. She wandered the drive, shaking her head, slumping and realigning her back.

Gray slinked out of the car. It was painful to watch.

Lily turned on him. "You see what's going on here, right?"

Gray sunk into himself and stared at his boots.

"I am not going to turn a blind eye to you running away from your family while families here are in pain." Lily jabbed her

finger at him. "You are going home right now, and we —" she
twirled her finger to include herself and Walter — "will talk about
this later."

I was shrinking too and hoped Lily wouldn't see through me
and into my parallel lie.

Even Walter seemed to be shrinking. "Yeah, I told his dad we'd
put him on the bus. We can bring the kids to the stop at Earl's
on our way to the community center."

"Damn straight." Lily shook her head. "I should've called your
parents before we left. I blame myself," she said as she headed
back to the house. "I blame myself."

Gray didn't say a word. He grabbed the backpacks I'd piled on
the drive and loaded them into the trunk.

2

THE DRIVE TO EARL'S was long and uncomfortably devoid of
talk. Gray huddled into his corner of the back seat, practically
pressed against the window. As if he could somehow slip through
the glass and into the landscape. He didn't want to go home, I
knew that. But it was more than that. It was obvious he didn't
want to be cut off from what was happening at the farmhouse.
He looked like someone being banished to wander the desert
forever.

Earl's was a diner on a lonely stretch of highway, bunched
together with a few other shops — a couple of gas stations, a con-
venience store, a canoe and kayak market. It was also one of

many stops along the way for a bus service that connected people
to busier areas.

Lily got out of the car without saying anything and headed to
the diner. It looked like she'd lost some of her steam. Walter
glanced back at us, then gave the ground a guilty kick. Gray had
nothing to say, so he climbed out of the car, and I got out too.

We grabbed our backpacks from the trunk and slung them
over our shoulders. Walter got out and shuffled along beside us,
not speaking, but not exactly stone-faced either. A cold wind
buffeted and bowled down the highway and we had to turn our
backs against it while we waited. When Lily came back, she had
two slips of paper in her hand. She gave us each one.

"Here are your tickets," she said. "The bus gets here in an
hour. You'll be back in the city by late afternoon. Gray, your
parents are expecting you. I assume you'll make sure they get
M where she needs to go." Gray steeled himself and I felt myself
flush. "Can I trust you?" She stared him down. The worst kind of
ferocity — the kind you respect. Gray nodded.

"Here's what *you* can trust —" She placed a hand on his arm.
"That we will do everything we can to find the little ones and
everything we can to find Jocelyn. Okay?"

"Yeah, okay." Barely audible.

Lily huffed and blinked her eyes and then turned abruptly
towards the trunk of the car. "Let me get you some food for the
trip." A cooler was in there, packed with essentials.

"Lily." Gray stopped her. "It's okay. You've done enough. Too
much. My backpack is full of food." He indicated his bag. "And I
have some money." He fluttered the bus ticket at her. "I will pay
you back for this the next time I see you."

"Me too," I said, feeling stupid that I hadn't even considered the expense to Lily and Walter. Also stupidly excited for an excuse to see them again at some future point.

Lily softened and put a hand on Gray's cheek. "Are you going to work it out, my boy?"

Gray nodded.

"Soon?" she said.

He managed a smile. "I promise."

She bowed her head and gave him a tight hug. Walter stepped in and grabbed Gray. "You'll speak with your parents, right?" He squeezed Gray's arms. "You'll come back here." Gray nodded and Walter pulled him close and gave him three strong pats on the back.

I felt my throat constrict and stepped out of the way, not expecting anything for myself. But Lily pulled me into a hug too and I sank against her.

"I am so sorry about your sister," she said in my ear. "I pray that you find her."

Then she released me and marched to the car and got into it. She started it up while Walter climbed into the passenger side. Gray and I watched them take off down the road, the car speeding away to its nobler, higher purpose, us aching and diminished at being left behind.

THE DINER WAS HALF-FULL of truckers and road-trippers slurping on coffees and shoving toast and scrambled eggs into their mouths. A TV flashed from behind the cash, tuned to the same twenty-four-hour news channel that had been on at the coffee shop in the city.

Gray and I found a table. I didn't have money — because it had been stolen. I remembered the girl I'd seen at City Hall and how

I'd tried to run after her. The flash of pink. I thought of Dell. The Ittch star. I fiddled with my sleeve. Without a shower to wash it off, the address Dell had penned on the inside of my wrist was still there. *You should come to the party next week. It'll be off the hook.* Had she been the one to hit me and steal my wallet? But that didn't make sense either. Dell would have even less reason to need my money than Krista.

So ... who had it been?

Serial killer. Sex trafficker.

Gray pulled scraps of cash from his jeans' pocket and counted it out. $8.60. All he had left after paying for his knife two days before.

"I left my cards at home," Gray said guiltily. As if he was responsible for feeding me. "Didn't want to take anything else from my parents."

But I knew leaving cards behind also gave parents one less way to track you. "It's okay," I said.

The TV screen flashed to the next news report. Subtitles scrolled along the bottom of the screen — *human remains, routine maintenance work, Betthurry. Body has been identified.* I grabbed Gray's forearm and he looked over his shoulder. I could feel the muscles in his arm tense as the shot panned over a weedy patch of construction off a country highway. *Where the body was found.* The screen cut to a photo of a young woman. White, brunette, pretty, smiling. It wasn't Jocelyn or Krista. A law student who'd gone missing from the city a year ago. *Killer has not yet been caught.*

As she falls, so do we all.

I shuddered and let go of Gray's arm and we didn't look at each other.

Find Jocelyn.

Find Krista.

Find all the missing girls.

I fought nausea as Gray ordered one breakfast for us to split. We didn't talk much as we rationed out the eggs and toast. I kept secretly checking on him. He looked distracted and nauseous too, and pretty soon he pushed his half-eaten breakfast away, and then so did I.

Behind Gray, the door chimed open and two uniformed officers walked in — a man and a woman. They headed for a table at the other end of the diner and settled in. A server handed them menus and poured coffee.

The TV flashed to another report. Krista stared out at me from her glamorous Missing Teen shot. Subtitles scrolled along the bottom. She was still gone. No new developments. There were lingering shots of our neighborhood, our school, of Clio's house, patrol vehicles, cops coming and going. I wondered how Clio was doing. Little Eddie.

Gray tapped his fork against his plate. A high-pitched porcelain beat.

Jocelyn had been missing a lot longer than Krista. Where was the news report for her? And what about Vivvie and her friends had they begun an official search for them yet?

The *ping-ping* of Gray tapping his fork against the plate was epically loud. I jerked forward. My hand clamped over his to stop the sound. He froze and stared at me. I froze too. Shocked by the smoothness and warmth of his skin, of my own against it. Locked in his gaze.

Gray's phone buzzed with a text and we were both startled. He checked the screen.

I checked on the cops behind him. The server had come back to take their orders.

"It's a group text from Arthur," Gray said, reading his screen. "One of the girls took a phone with them and they have a trace on it." I almost whooped with surprised relief — but then Gray read on. "Bad news is, they have to track it through cell triangulation. Because we're in the middle of nowhere, the transmission radius is thirty miles." Gray flashed his phone at me. It showed a screen capture of a gridded map, various roads crisscrossing it, small points indicating towns. "Thirty square miles is huge," he said. "They could be anywhere in there. Tracking every inch on foot could take forever."

Behind him, the TV flashed to another story. Me this time. My terrible photo. *Missing for three days*.

The officers were staring out the window, sipping coffee.

I pulled my coat hood over my head and shrank down. They would drag me home. Gray would find out who I really was.

Another text buzzed on Gray's phone. "Arthur says he's sending everyone out to look for the girls." He gave me a grim smile. "So the search for Jocelyn has to wait."

If Messenger 93 was a real thing, then maybe only I could find Krista. She was going to fall in *four days*. And if I believed in destiny or fate, maybe it meant I was supposed to be with Gray, and that Jocelyn would also be found. And if we found Jocelyn, then Vivvie and the other little girls would never have to run after her again, and they would go back home and grow up safe.

Gray was the one to say it out loud. "I can't wait. I need to get to Deerhead."

A jolt of excitement stirred me up. "We're supposed to be on our way home," I whispered. "We promised Lily."

"I came all the way out here," he said. "I want to search."

Me too, I thought. *I want to search with you.*

I lowered my voice even more. "There are two cops behind you."

Gray checked very casually behind him. Then he looked back and pointed to a narrow hallway at the back of the diner. It led to the restrooms and also to a service exit.

We packed the bus tickets Lily gave us into our bags and spun away from the table towards the back of the diner. We ducked down the hall and pushed our way through the service door, bursting out of warm, bustling, familiar reality — through a wardrobe wall, down a rabbit hole — and landing in the chill northern scrub.

I was smiling despite everything, but Gray got serious right away. "Deerhead is far. We have no car, and no bus goes there."

"Right." I slumped and racked my brain for ideas. Then I pointed through the trees to the two-lane highway that ran alongside Earl's. "What if we hitchhike? I know it's sketchy — but we have each other."

"Lily and Walter can't see me," Gray said. "If they catch me, I'm back at square one."

"True."

We considered more options.

"What if we walk to the next major turnoff?" Gray said. "Through the woods so we aren't seen, but following the highway so we don't get lost."

"That could work."

Gray consulted the map on his phone. "If we walk north through the woods, we can get to Highway 6 in maybe three hours. Then we can hitch the 6." He looked closer at the map. "We take the 6 all the way to County Road 5. Then it's not far to

Deerhead — we could walk that part. Once we're in the area, we can ask around, look for Jocelyn and your sister."

"Sounds good." I adjusted my backpack and stepped towards the woods. "Let's go."

We headed into the trees together and waded into the brush. Then we tripped over the same hidden stump, stumbled into each other, reeled apart, and burst out laughing.

THE GOING WAS HARD. Surprisingly hard. One minute we'd be hiking up crumbling hills, the next sinking to our knees in a ditch of mushy underbrush. We pushed through the tangled boughs of evergreens, then passed easily through open stands of spring-budding trees. Sometimes we had to cross private property. We scaled wire-and-wood-post fences that marked the limits and prayed we wouldn't cut ourselves.

We tried to stay parallel to the road so we wouldn't lose our way. The hiss of tires on pavement as the occasional car traveled by made us feel somewhat less alone. But it also reminded us that we were pretty much alone.

The fragrance of green lifted me in a way I hadn't expected, binding me to where I was in each moment. This footfall, this cedar copse, this leafless branch, this patch of sky.

"So what's your message?" Gray said after an hour of hike-focused silence.

"What do you mean?"

"*Messenger 93*. What's your message?"

The idea of telling him about the crow intrigued me. What would he say about it?

"You want to know how it happened?"

"Hell yeah."

I geared myself up. *Gray wasn't Boyd or Remy or Anusha or Trevor.*

"It started in a dream — this crow flying to me," I said. "But when I woke up, there was a real crow in my room. Or it *looked* real. It talked to me. I heard it clearly. It called me Messenger 93. Said I have seven days to find Krista. If I don't find her, she's going to fall."

"Seven days?" Gray repeated ominously.

"And every night it comes back and counts down the days. *She will fall in six days. She will fall in five days. She will fall in four days.*"

"Hold up —" Gray said, kind of bouncing his steps as we walked on. "What does *fall* mean?"

"I don't know. I thought, you know, like, *fall*. Like —" I didn't want to say the word, but this was Gray and I had to. "*Die*."

"But *fall* can mean a lot of things."

I couldn't think of a single other meaning.

"Fall *asleep*," he said, bouncing along, playing. "Fall down. Fall out with someone. Fall prey to something."

"Fall under a spell," I said, wanting to play too. Wanting it to be a fun and easy answer.

He leaned dramatically towards me. "You can fall for someone."

That made me laugh out loud. I wanted to pull him to me, to wonder together about that meaning.

I said, "I know it sounds crazy." Maybe I'd be repeating that line for the rest of my life. "But I swear that's how it happened. The crow came to me *before* I knew Krista had run away. That's why I started looking into how they were handling her case — the searches and all that. And when I went to the police station to talk to Detective Stanzi — *you* showed up." Gray looked slightly amazed. "You were searching for a missing girl too. And you had that crow on your back." I pointed at the hoodie he was wearing under his raincoat. "And that tattoo on your neck."

He gave a small astonished laugh. "That is — whoa — that is weird."

"I know, right?"

We were walking hard, but he watched me too, and his look was so intent, so interested, it made me lightheaded.

"Do you have a message for me?" he said. My answer was a dorky laugh, and he pushed my arm lightly. "Come on, with a name like that you gotta hand out some kind of message."

I pretended to think, but his message came to me right away. I psyched myself up to say it, to not care if it got me into trouble. "I think you're really talented and you could be a big star."

"You mean my music? How do you know about that?"

I cringed. I hadn't told him about being with him when he was trying to sell his song.

"Ah," he said, calculating it on his own. "You followed me from the police station that day. That's how you knew about the knife." He patted his left forearm.

"Yeah."

"But I don't want to be a star." He turned to observe me. It was like he was analyzing my deepest self. "Maybe *you* want to be a star. Maybe that's what this is about."

He didn't say it to hurt me, but it was a slap. I tried to walk ahead, but he stuck to my side, sidestepping roots and rocks.

"I mean," he said, "everyone wants to be special."

"Do they?" I stared ahead into the woods, hoping he wouldn't notice my glowing cheeks. *I didn't want to be a star.* That was the last thing I wanted to be.

He started playing drumbeats on the front of his raincoat.

"You wanna matter. Wanna be here.

You carve scars here.

Scars, they persist.

I wanna live life.

Wanna be here.

Don't need a star here, to prove I exist."

I smiled despite myself. "Ow," I said, miming a shot to the heart.

"No, no, that's not about you," he said, super-casual. "Just try-ing out some new lyrics. I'm so talented, right?" He grinned at me and it made me warm.

"Message Girl, she a fly girl.

The crow fly by and speak.

Message Bird, catch her eye, bird.

Share the prophecy."

"You see?" I said, smiling wide. "You're so good!"

He laughed. Then turned to me and got serious again. "I mean — What if it works? What if the messages actually show you the way?"

A hum started up in my chest. "It would be incredible."

"Yeah. No kidding."

As we walked on, I marveled at the possibility. Gray seemed to marvel too.

IT TOOK FIVE-AND-A-HALF HOURS to arrive at the inter-section of the 6. We burst out of the woods in the same way we'd entered them, blinking against the change of light and feeling suddenly out of place.

We stopped to drink from our water bottles. Gray pulled granola bars and mixed nuts from his backpack. I was so lucky he'd pre-pared to camp. Hunger was a bear.

When we were done eating, we made our way to the eastbound shoulder of the two-lane highway and began the next leg of the hike, this time hoping for a ride. The road was mostly straight so if a car or truck passed, we'd have plenty of time to face oncoming traffic and wave them down. But it was deserted, and so we kept walking.

Each bone in my feet was scrunched and pleading. The pain traveled relentlessly up. My calves burned next. Then my thighs. Soon every one of my muscles cramped and screamed at me. My body begged me to stop moving, to lie down, anywhere, even right on the pavement.

I hadn't trained for this. Had never walked so long or so hard. Had never spent so much time carrying a backpack. But I couldn't say a word about it. I didn't want Gray to know what a lightweight I was.

Gray trudged ahead of me, his shoulders pressed forward, his head bowed. He'd changed out of the raincoat he'd been wearing earlier and into his hoodie and tweed cap. His backpack was strapped over the luminescent crow. Exactly like when I first followed him.

Except this time he knew I was there, close behind him. This time, I wasn't scared.

3

WE WALKED THE HIGHWAY for another half hour — an ever-expanding sponge of grueling time — when a semi rolled into view over the horizon. Gray and I shared a half-smile before we turned to it and held out our thumbs.

The truck trundled through the distance and towards us, slightly dipping and rising over the contours of the road. I tried to shake a growing sense of dread as it neared, tried not to read anything ominous in the way dust swirled up around it and clouded the front grille. I told myself that it was just my usual nerves at anything outside my usual boring experience. Gray didn't seem worried — he was behind me, mumbling a stream of wishes, "Come on, man, stop for us. Stop. All you gotta do is slow down, pull over, let us in. Come on, buddy. Take us where we need to go."

As the truck passed by, we waved and called out, cheering, begging, even while the long trailer shook the asphalt and roared in our ears, even as dust and gravel lashed up at our faces. It took us a few seconds to understand that he *was* slowing down and easing over to the side and rolling to a stop. The rear lights blinked into hazard-mode, and we took it as a personal greeting. Gray and I whooped and high-fived and ran to the passenger side of the cab.

But when we got there, we didn't know what to do. Was a hitchhiker supposed to go ahead and open the door, or were we supposed to wait for the door to be opened? Wasn't there a possibility that he hadn't stopped for us? We checked with each other and hesitated, pacing the narrow space between the truck and the scrub, nudging each other to make the first move. Finally, the passenger door opened from the inside and a soft white face peered out. "You girls gonna stand out there all day?"

Gray and I laughed. I was the first to jump on the running board and hop into the cab. "Hey sir," I said in as friendly a voice as I could offer. "Thank you so much for stopping."

The trucker wasn't wearing a coat and his arms were bare and sticking out of a worn tee that didn't cover his belly. A few exposed, hairy inches cleaved the space between his clothed parts. He grinned at me and his cheeks crowded out his eyes. His lips were wet and cherry red. "Pleasure is mine," he said. His tone was jovial and welcoming, and that was a relief.

I settled onto the bench and dumped my backpack at my feet, and Gray hopped up beside me and did the same. "Thanks, mister," Gray said. "Appreciate it."

The trucker's smile faltered. "Hey," he said, "I thought you two was both girls." He looked from one to the other of us and jutted his chin.

"Nope," Gray said, trying to match the guy's jovial tone. The lowness of his voice made the mistake almost funny.

The trucker sized us up. "Where y'all headed?" It sounded like he was going to change his mind. "'Cause we'll see how far I can take ya." He put the truck into gear and rolled forward.

"We're only going as far as County Road 5, if that works for you." Gray gave him a friendly, easy smile.

"County Road 5," the trucker said, looking ahead as he gained the road and pulled up to speed. "County Road 5," he repeated.

Gray took out his phone and pulled up the map. He angled it into the trucker's line of sight. "Don't know if you can see this," he said, drawing a line across the screen. "This is where we want to go."

"Oh, the exit to Deerhead. Gotcha." The trucker thumped the steering wheel. "That's not too far. An hour and a half, give or take." He threw us a knowing grin. "You kids headed down to the national park? Gonna do it under the stars?"

"Yeah," Gray said, settling back. "We're camping in the park."

I refused to get sucked into visions of us *doing it* under the stars. I could almost feel the warmth of Gray's mouth on mine, the tingle of our lips connecting.

Gray crossed his arms over his chest and closed his eyes.

Sleep — it was a tempting possibility. The cab was warm and the gentle jostling was already lulling me. The weight of my exhausted limbs released into the upholstered bench. Was it safe to fall under? I glanced at the man beside me, so close we could have bumped thighs. He caught me checking him out and threw me a grin, as if to say we were on the same page or something. I smiled back, then quickly copied Gray's pose — settled in, arms crossed, eyes closed. I had no intention of falling asleep, but maybe I would pretend and it would give me a place to hide for a few minutes.

"HEY, YOU WANT A beer?" His voice was alarmingly loud in my ear. I jolted out of deep sleep and opened my eyes. The trucker's arm was knocking against mine, and the neck of an uncapped bottle was gripped in his hand. I noticed there was an empty rolling around at his feet. The yeasty smell filled my nose.

"No thanks," I said. The clock on the dashboard indicated we'd been driving for over an hour. My head felt woozy. Why had he let us sleep for so long? I noticed a slight splay in my legs and instinctively rammed my legs together and laid my hand over my thighs. I nudged Gray to wake him and he was startled and looked around, blinking his eyes.

"What about you, kid?" The trucker reached the bottle across me and I had to lean into Gray so the guy's arm wouldn't brush my chest.

Gray looked at the beer. "You sure that's a good idea?"

"You judging me?" The trucker's face collapsed, his grinning mouth and soft cheeks melting into an exaggerated frown. "I offer you a ride and you sandbag the whole way and then you judge me?"

"Sorry," Gray said, holding his hands up in surrender. He checked through the windshield. Twilight was setting in. Clouds with no beginning or end covered the sky. "You're making good time though, hey?"

The trucker harrumphed and brought the beer to his lips and took a long swig. When he pulled the bottle away, he was still scowling. "Thumbers never say no to a drink when I pick 'em up."

My arm was aligned against Gray's and I could feel him tense. Gray said, "You pick up a lot of girls out here?"

"Some." The trucker drew his bottle in a circle. "The pavement princesses, the ones hustling for cash, I stay away from those." He nudged me and I tried not to shrink back. "But the Alice in Wonderlands, those I pick up."

"Alice in Wonderlands?" I said.

"The sweet ones," he said like it was obvious. "Like you." He winked at me and thumped my thigh with the bottom of his beer.

Gray said, "Runaways?"

"Sure." The trucker nodded. "Trying to get someplace nice."

Gray and I exchanged a glance. "And where's nice around here?"

The trucker eyed us. "You two running away?"

"Maybe," Gray said. He was mesmerizingly calm. "If we were, where would we go?"

The trucker grunt-laughed and shook his head. "Most of 'em wanna get to a city. North, south, east, west, pick one." He took another long slug of beer and contemplated the road ahead. "Just don't get an Alice crying though. Because if you do, man, she don't stop." He grinned at us, unfurling the red, wet inside of his bottom lip. "But they're eye candy," he shrugged, "so who am I to say shut up?" He let out a howl of laughter and Gray and I pretended to laugh along.

I waited until our merriment dropped off. "Do any of them ever go to Deerhead?"

The trucker frowned. "Nothing in Deerhead as far as I know."

I glanced at Gray to warn him I was about to show my hand, and he blinked in agreement. I tried to keep my voice steady. "You pick up a girl in the last few days? A bit taller than me. White. Dark blond hair."

He looked me over. "You lose someone?"

"Her name is Krista. She's young, pretty." I hesitated, almost gave him the wrong information, then said, "She's my sister."

"You got a pretty sister?" He grinned at me. His pupils dilated, his tongue darted over his lips. I tried not to recoil. "*That* I'd like to see."

"So you never ran into her?"

He raised his beer-holding hand. "Think I'd remember."

I was unreasonably disappointed. Because it *was* possible that Krista had hitchhiked from one city to another. It was *infinitesimally* possible that I was following her escape route and had stumbled into her mode of transport. Messenger 93 and all.

"I guess you wanna find her?" he said, turning to me again, grinning again. I tried to keep my expression innocent. "You really do. I can see it." He was grinning so hard his eyes almost disappeared into the pods of his cheeks.

Gray searched through his phone until he found the picture of Jocelyn. He made sure to zoom in on her face to avoid showing her frilly top or her bare legs on the bed. "What about her?" he said, angling the screen so the trucker could see it.

The trucker slammed his back against his seat. "Bingo!" He pointed his beer bottle at Jocelyn's face. "That's bingo right there!"

Gray pulled his phone back so quickly it was like a recoil button. I could feel him shudder, like he'd shown something he shouldn't have. "So you've seen her?"

"I'm saying I'd *pay* to see her." He thumped the steering wheel with his beer-less hand.

"So, you haven't?" Gray said, barely masking the anger in his voice.

"I'll tell ya something, if a bunch of pretty girls are partying in the woods right now, that'd be worth a late slip." He took a slurp of beer, then wiped his mouth. "For the right price, I'd help you look for 'em."

"That's okay," Gray said, playing nice again, speaking as if we were just having an ordinary conversation. "But thank you."

The trucker pointed his bottle at the remote landscape outside the windshield. "Get 'em where they wanna go. Take care of 'em. That's what I do."

"Yeah?" I said, trying to keep it friendly.

"No one protects 'em," he said. Fumes of his beery breath wafted over me. A snare I couldn't get out of. "That's the lie they tell Alice." He was serious now, getting worked up. "That Daddy is gonna protect 'em." He shook his head mournfully. "Daddy never does. He turns his back is what he does." He thumped his beer against his chest. "But I do. I protect 'em."

A buzz of apprehension jolted through me. "Nice," I said, trying to ignore it.

The trucker tapped his bottle against my thigh again. This

time it was a slight tap, just the edge of the rim. "And you know what the little Alices do?" he said.

And then I knew for sure that he wasn't giving us a lift out of the goodness of his heart, or because he was bored, or because he wanted to protect us.

"They show gratitude," he said.

"Yeah?" I said, pretending to smile, playing dumb.

"They pay their way," he said.

"Oh, okay," I said too quickly, bending over to get my backpack. "How much do you want?" Except there was no money inside my bag, and Gray had no money either.

The trucker put his hand on my shoulder to stop me. "That's not how they pay."

Of course I knew that's what he meant. He had to play his game in the middle of nowhere, hurtling down a lonely road.

A loaded hush squashed the air in the cab.

Out of the corner of my eye, I could see Gray's right hand reaching into his left sleeve.

The knife.

Pictures of a *Psycho*-type stabbing strobed through my mind. Spurting blood, agonizing screams, anguished expressions. The truck veering off the road into trees. A fatal crash.

Another possibility cut in too. A way to survive maybe. To not kill anyone. To get away.

I put my hand on Gray's forearm, the one closest to me with the knife strapped to it, and gave it a sharp squeeze. *Get ready*, I wanted the gesture to say to him, *trust me*. Immediately Gray's hand stopped reaching.

I arranged the muscles of my face into a docile smile and turned to the trucker. I remembered Gray's mask — it felt like I was wearing it. An anonymous somebody else talking through holes in thin plastic. "I'll pay our way," I said.

"Good girl," the trucker said. He began to fumble under his gut for his belt buckle.

"No, wait," I said. My hand went to his arm — it was much less soft than it looked. I tried not to gag. I said, "You can't be driving. It won't be good."

"Yeah, right," he said. His face had melted again and his bottom lip was hanging open, the tip of his tongue sticking against it. All the parts of his mouth were so red. His breath had started to wheeze in and out in shallow bursts. It smelled like puke.

He checked the rearview mirror and began to slow the truck down, easing it to the shoulder. The cab joggled and vibrated as we landed on the gravel shoulder. Gray felt for my hand and pulled it into the space where our legs were touching. He laced his fingers with mine and we held hands, the veins in our wrists pulsing together, for the several seconds it took the truck to roll to a stop.

The trucker locked the brake and flopped back and fumbled with his belt buckle again. "Wait," I said. "This is no good. There's not enough room. Let's just hop out on the side. For privacy." I tipped my head to indicate Gray. "It'll be much better outside." I smiled at the trucker. "For both of us." I didn't recognize the voice I was using.

"Sure, sure," he said, now fumbling with the handle of the driver's door. "Let's go for it." He opened the door and leaned out, then grabbed my wrist and pulled me after him. I was a doll, weightless and nothing.

I glanced back at Gray and he looked like ash. But he was

reaching for the passenger door and slinging our two backpacks over his arm.

I let the trucker pull me to the side of the road, behind the truck and out of view of any oncoming traffic, which there wasn't. He was fixated on me, either groping his hands through my hair or rooting for his belt buckle. I locked eyes on what I was doing, but I was intensely aware of Gray slipping out the passenger side with our bags, of him edging towards the woods.

"Let me," I said to the trucker. I let him fondle my hair and the top of my head as I crouched to undo his belt buckle. I tried to crowd out the devastating thought that this was the first time I'd ever done anything like this.

My gag reflex kicked in and I made sure not to look up and show him my face. I reached for his zipper. His gut pressed into my shaking, fumbling hands. His rough fingers pushed at my head, poking and prodding at me, until his jeans were down.

Hate coursed through me. I had no idea what I was supposed to do, or how I was supposed to do it. But I knew — *I wasn't going to do it.*

A flash of movement caught my eye. I didn't have to look to know it was Gray and his knife, charging towards us, coming to avenge. But that's not how this was going down. With Gray summoning blood and then going to jail for it. I was going to stop it.

Rolls of white skin, soft and hard mixed together, thatches of overlapping coarse dark hair. Hands on my head, on my face, a thumb pushed into my mouth. Salt and grime on my tongue. I couldn't see what was happening, couldn't breathe it in.

In a movement so quick and sharp even I had no time to register it, I drew my arm back and punched with all my strength

into the void. I heard him yelp-scream before he started to
crumple over, his head and chest caving in towards me like a
human tsunami.

I ducked out of the way. I spent only a second, a frozen, drawn-
out second, reveling in his stooped and groveling pain. But then
he had his own explosion of rage. Moaning and grunting, he
flung his hand out. His fingers caught the pocket of my coat and
he yanked hard. I yanked hard the other way. There was a screech
of ripping fabric. High on adrenaline, I rolled my hand into a
fist and punched him across the face. There was a spurt of blood.
He yelled out and reared back, holding his hand to his nose. But
I was free.

I wheeled away and grabbed Gray's knife-wielding hand and
pulled him towards our backpacks that he'd left on the side of
the road. I grabbed mine and checked to make sure that Gray was
with me and that he grabbed his too, and together we leapt off the
road and over the brush and into the woods.

Anguished muffled yelps echoed after us, and it amazed me
that I'd had enough strength, or that the trucker's body was weak
enough, that I could momentarily crush him.

4

WE RAN FOR A long time without looking back, crashing
through the obstacle-course forest like hunted animals. We
slowed only when it started to rain. Gray pulled out his raincoat,
a plastic poncho, and a garbage bag. He slipped the poncho over

my head, covering my coat and backpack. He zipped on his rain-coat, then tore holes in the garbage bag and slipped it over his head and arms. I helped yank the plastic bag over his backpack. He noticed the rain stinging my eyes, and took off his cap and slid it under my hood and over my head. The tweed brim kept the rain off my face. The whole thing took a minute, no more, then we were on the move again, leaning against the weather.

The rain didn't stay low-key — the kind where we could've put up the tent — but unleashed with a vengeance. It was so forceful, it hissed as it fell, lashing through the tree cover. It wasn't long before we were sopping, first our jeans soaking through, then the damp leaching up under our coats and down through our socks. Walter had tried to warn us. He'd even given us proper clothes. But I'd taken the warm wool underwear off when I'd dressed for a day I thought would be spent on a bus.

Deep cold began to sink in, bitter and sharp as winter. The teeth chatter of shivering and the mushy squelch of our footfalls were the only sounds we had the energy to make.

The sun was setting behind us and for a while there was a cer-tain amount of ambient light, but heavy rainclouds kept rolling in and soon it was total black. Gray stopped to root around in the outside pockets of his backpack, and he pulled out two small flash-lights. He gave one to me and we proceeded by flashlight, aiming the beams ahead of us and continuing on without speaking. We hiked for another hour before the rain let up to almost nothing. We climbed a small hill and reached higher, dryer ground.

"I need to stop." My words slurred. My teeth chattered. My bones felt like they'd been carved out of ice.

Gray was shivering and panting to catch his breath. "Yeah, me too."

Suddenly I realized that we could die. If we didn't warm up soon, our bodies would literally shut down. Gray seemed to know it too. He fell to his knees and worked on pulling the tent out. I took off the poncho and used it to cover anything that came out of our bags. Spattering drops echoed around us like gunshot. Together, we spread the tent and raised it, part by part. Then we dug a trench around it using thick greenwood branches.

My hands were so cold, I couldn't feel them anymore. The rest of me, I wished I couldn't feel. Every muscle ached.

We had no choice but to crawl inside the tent with our soaking clothes and backpacks. We set the flashlights at angles on the ground so we could see what we were doing, then pulled off our boots and coats and laid them at the entrance.

Gray didn't waste a second — he stripped off his jeans and sweatshirt. I tried not to notice the flashlight glow on his skin, his long limbs and slim back, the curved scapulas arcing out. He fumbled with the leather holster that was wrapped around his forearm, unstrapped the knife, and laid it on the ground. He covered up just as fast, pulling on long underwear from Walter's waterproof bag.

The wool underwear I'd worn the night before was still damp from my time on the dew-covered grass that morning. So I got a sweatshirt from my backpack. Luckily it was dry. I had no second pair of pants.

Gray, still shivering, unrolled his sleeping bag and burrowed inside it, and I turned away from him and changed quickly, swapping one sweatshirt for another, stripping off my jeans. The wet denim stuck to my skin. It took forever to peel them off.

I couldn't help checking out my own flashlight-revealed body — the new white cotton drugstore sweatshirt and undies, coldsplotched skin, too many awkward angles. I was so relieved when I could finally crawl, bare-legged, into my sleeping bag — Walter's sleeping bag actually. Lucky chance that I had it.

Except for the mound of wet clothes by the front flap, it was dry in the tent. I could almost cry from the relief of it. From the relief of not running. Of letting my body lie down and rest. But I was chilled through and, like Gray, was kneading and rubbing at my icy parts.

"I'm frozen," I said after a while.

"Me too." Gray's teeth were chattering so hard, he could hardly speak.

"Maybe we should do that thing ... where we share body heat?"

"Yeah, right." His voice was subdued. "If you're okay with it."

"I'm okay," I said.

I unzipped the side of my sleeping bag and Gray did the same and we paired them together. We crawled back in and checked with each other. I don't know who was the first to reach out, but then we had our arms wrapped around each other and our legs extended and intertwined. So cold, I could feel his cold. We pressed together, my cheek against his neck, against the skin with the feather tattoo.

And then I started to cry. I tried to stop the tears, but I couldn't. He stroked his hands along my back. It was possible he was crying too.

After a while, our body heat began to rise. Its warm ribbon passed through our chests where they pressed together, and down to our twined feet and grasping hands. It looped through us, from one to the other and back into ourselves. Soon I stopped crying, and I could feel Gray's tensed body soften and relax against me.

I was afraid to fall asleep, not sure if it would mean the end of me. I was afraid of Gray falling asleep for the same reason. We stared at each other. Keeping each other awake. Alive. His eyes — interstellar planets — searched mine, and mine — bleary and sore — searched his. It was disorienting and strange and I didn't want it to stop.

He took a breath to say something and there was so much feeling in his expression that I almost worried what it would be. "I'm sorry," he said.

It took me by surprise. "For what?" I even managed a smile. "I'm, like, ten thousand times warmer."

But his expression stayed serious. "For what happened back there. For not stopping it."

"I didn't want you to use the knife."

"I know, but —"

But I didn't want to talk about the trucker. Didn't want to think about him ever again.

"I knew what I was doing, Gray. And it worked."

"What if it *didn't* work?"

We were still holding hands, our fingers laced together in the slender space between us.

"You were right there," I said. He flinched and closed his eyes. "Gray, I knew you were there. That's what mattered."

He opened his eyes and gave me a pleading look. "How am I going to help Jocelyn if I cave every time it gets real?"

"You won't cave," I said. "You haven't caved once."

It looked like he wanted to argue, but he stopped himself and his eyes searched mine.

I said, "You haven't given up on finding her. You got us here. Because of you we're in this tent. It was you showing everyone her face at City Hall, making sure they saw her. It was you asking questions at the police station. Every time they try to shut you down, you go around them."

His jaw clenched a bit. His fingers squeezed mine. Like an involuntary beat of a heart.

"Do you love her?" I said.

He blinked a few times. His lips twitched then softened.

Warmth drew through me as I waited for him to answer. I wanted so badly to hear him talk about it. If anyone could make me believe in love, it was Gray.

He thought a while longer. Long enough that it burned me up from the inside out.

"I don't really know anything about it," he said. "But I know I don't feel that way about Jocelyn."

I was very aware of how my body relaxed. "She's practically your cousin," I said, gently mimicking his earlier words, making fun of my question.

"Yeah," he said, softly smiling. "She's family."

It went quiet between us again. Our fingers were laced together. Our toes were touching. Small points of soothing weight.

I said, "I don't know anything about it either."

"No?" he said.

I shook my head, watching him the whole time.

He leaned closer, gazed intently at all the aspects of my face. He was so close I could taste his breath. I reached for him too, and then our lips came together. Our mouths, our bodies, equally pressing and urgent. Equally yearning.

Oh this. This is what it means.

MONDAY, APRIL 16

THREE DAYS UNTIL THE FALL

I ROUSED BUT DIDN'T wake all the way up when Gray reached for his flashlight in the middle of the night. He turned it off, then reached for mine and turned it off too. This time I knew exactly where I was. Where I wanted to be. Beside Gray in the shimmering dark.

I floated in warmth as he lay down again, as he draped his arm across my stomach. It was a dream to feel him there, and I didn't ever want to lose that feeling, that knowing. Didn't ever want to forget it.

I laid my arm across his side. Didn't question that I was allowed to put parts of myself on him. I released myself to the hypnotic rise and fall of his breath, his mouth against my shoulder, the softness of his hair against my cheek. He steadied my body and my mind. I was full of wonder. *Wonder full.*

Before long, I fell back into deepest sleep.

"SHE WILL FALL IN three days." In my ear, as usual. Not dramatic, not loud or quiet. Not male, not female. The tent was lit from outside. A gossamer blue. The air felt crystalized with cool.

There was a squawk in the distance. *Caw!* A crow flying by overhead.

Fall can mean a lot of things. You can fall for someone.

I said his name in my mind. *Gray*.

I looked beside me. He was gone and his sleeping bag had been unzipped from mine and already rolled up. The smell of cooking drifted over and I inhaled.

I sat up and rubbed sleep from my eyes. My backpack was gone, and so were all the other wet things. My raincoat was still there, and I pulled it on. It was dry and warm. The smell of simmering food and budding trees and moldering groundcover made me lightheaded.

My stomach rumbled. I remembered that I'd dreamt of eating — my father's pancakes, Lily's stew, sharing an ice cream cone with Trevor when we were kids.

I combed my fingers through my hair before unzipping the flap and crawling out of the tent. Our backpacks and boots and any clothing that had gotten wet were hung on low branches or laid out to dry on the plastic garbage bag Gray had worn the day before. Gray was crouched on a deadwood log not far off, stirring a small pot that was set over the low blue burn of a portable cookstove.

He looked so good. He was wearing his tweed cap, and I remembered the feel of it on my head, how it had kept the rain from clipping my face.

He smiled and passed me my socks and the woolen long johns Walter had lent me, stiff but dry now. I tried hard not to beam like a fool while I pulled them over my bare legs.

It was a good morning. Lavender clouds lay in fuzzy strips across the sky. The sun was low and rising and burnished gold. It looked like a celestial being caught in the treetops. The whole world was different today. Snug and safe and buzzing.

I found a dead stump and rolled it close to Gray, close to the grill.

"What do you want for breakfast?" he said. "Instant oatmeal or chicken cacciatore?"

"Chicken cacciatore?" I laughed.

"For real. I brought these freeze-dried meals with me. I'm so hungry, I could eat them all right now." He shrugged. "But you have your pick."

"Oh, man," I said. My stomach rumbled again. "Bring on the chicken cacciatore." A hot meal sounded too good to be true.

"I don't have any coffee, if that's your thing," he said, pointing to his bag. "But there might be some cocoa in there."

"Oh my god, hot chocolate? I love you!" My skin flushed and I clamped my mouth.

"Whoa." Gray made a show of being blown away, then he gave me a lopsided grin. "So I guess you want some?"

I had to force my voice to sound as normal as possible. "Cocoa sounds amazing."

"Cool. I'll put water on to boil after we eat. Cocoa's over there." He smiled and pointed to where he'd laid out all our stuff to dry. His blank mask was there, found at the bottom of my backpack, and so was the Jocelyn poster I'd folded up and brought along.

I was so giddy that I picked up the mask and held it against my face. "Better?" I peered at him through the eyeholes. But I could hardly see him. The mask felt uncomfortable against my skin. My voice sounded hollow. I remembered why he'd had to buy it — *For the invisible girls who disappear off our streets every day. If they're nobody, I'm nobody* — and felt stupid. I didn't have to check with him to know it wasn't a joke.

"Sorry," I said, hiding the mask and the Jocelyn poster back inside my bag. "I don't know why I brought them."

He swirled the pot. "It's okay — it sort of feels like they should be here."

I picked up a pouch of cocoa and a thermal cup and joined him again. I yanked at the packaging, but it wouldn't tear and he took it from me without making a big deal and pulled out his knife and used it to slice into the foil.

"Thanks," I said as he poured the cocoa powder into the cup.

He turned the knife over in his hands and considered the sharp-angled blade. "I guess I didn't actually buy it for camping ... for food ..." I remembered our encounter at City Hall. How I'd made him justify himself. "I guess I bought it for, you know ... wild bears and psychos ..." His lips twitched into a wry smile. A private smile. "But Arthur told me carrying a knife for protection is a 'naïve game.' Only works for people who know how to use one."

"I get it," I said. "Probably seemed like a good idea at the time." He looked up and we shared his smile, and it warmed me all the way through.

Gray slid the knife back into its holster and reached into his pocket and handed me a small sewing kit. "Didn't know this was in my supplies until this morning. Not sure if you care, but if you do —" He pointed to my coat and I saw that the left-hand pocket was flapping open. Torn from the day before. I blocked out the reason why it was torn.

A white card-edge poked out of the ripped hole. I realized it was the photo I'd found in Krista's locker. The one of her kissing my cheek.

I thanked Gray and pulled off my coat.

There was a tiny pair of scissors in the sewing kit, and their tininess was so adorable they made me want to laugh again. They made me *want to* want to laugh. But the giddiness was gone.

Manipulating the almost-invisible needle and a half-spool of black thread, I sewed the photo back inside my pocket. I remembered how only a few days before, I'd started looking for Krista with that strange and certain feeling that I was onto something. But that feeling was gone. Instead there was a weird queasiness that didn't make sense. I used the tiny scissors to snip the thread, and couldn't stop thinking of Krista's last text. *The scissors, the stars*.

I showed Gray my terrible sewing job and laughed too loudly and said something that probably made no sense. Anything to crowd out the unthinkable thought, anything to crush it down. *That I was in the wrong place. For the wrong reason.*

2

THIS TIME I WORE the right clothes to walk. Walter's borrowed wool underwear, his rain pants cinched tight around my waist, my raincoat zipped over it. We used the GPS on Gray's phone to orient ourselves and saw that we were still a few hours walk from Deerhead.

"Shouldn't we look for the girls as we go?" I said. "Places they could be hiding out. Or ..." I didn't want to mention any dire possibility.

"I thought we'd ask in Deerhead and go from there," Gray said, leading the way through the woods.

"But Deerhead is just a starting point. What if it *was* Jocelyn in that car they saw a few days ago? Maybe they were driving to or from someplace around here. Wouldn't it make sense to search the area?"

"You mean, like, spy on people?"

"Did anyone say what kind of car it was?"

"A blue Chevy sedan. Older model."

"So we can look for one of those."

"One small problem with that," he said, teasing it out like a joke. "It might not be the best idea for me to lurk around on private property. You heard what happens out here to kids who look like me, right?"

I cringed. How could I dispute him?

But what if the girls were actually somewhere close by?

As if he were reading my mind, Gray said, "Do you really think there's a chance Jocelyn and your sister are together?"

Everything felt very fragile, like the world could collapse at the slightest touch.

Did I really think it was possible?

I said, "It would be weird if they're together, wouldn't it?"

"If your messages take us to them and they're together, that would be —" He shook his head, trying to imagine it. Then he mimed bowing down to me.

I shoved his arm. It felt good to touch him, to have the right. Like we belonged to each other somehow. The only thing I wanted was to keep walking with him. No, what I wanted more than anything was for him to touch me like he had the night before. To feel the wonder again of him looking only at me.

"It could go either way," I said, giving him a smile despite all the problems. "Either it's true. Or I'm crazy."

"My dad once told me this theory that every person is just a projection of ourselves."

"You mean, like, we're all the same underneath?"

"No. He meant, everyone you see is *you*. Good, bad, random. You are *everyone*."

"Whoa." I let it blow my mind. "Do you believe that?"

He laughed. "I don't even *understand* it."

I laughed with him and it felt so good. So *light*.

"Honestly," he said, glancing at me, grinning, "I think it's cool to have something nice to believe in."

That made me feel even lighter. *Yes, me too*.

"The messages you're getting — They're positive, right?" he said. "They're not telling you to burn shit down." He gave me a grave look. "Are they?"

"No!" The thought that I could burn something down was mildly terrifying. "Ever hear of Joan of Arc? She thought God spoke to her. That she was supposed to bring messages to help win the war. She was super-revered. But then the enemy caught her — and they burned her alive at the stake."

Gray clutched his chest. "That is disgusting."

"I know! It's like everyone who thinks they have some special gift and then tries to help ends up dying this gruesome death. Like, what does that mean?"

"White savior," Gray said under his breath.

"What?"

"Nothing."

"No, what? Tell me."

"There's this thing. It's, like, you feel good helping people, so you keep up a system where people need to be helped. Instead of fixing the problem and taking on whatever or whoever is in power, you go around saving victims. Usually those victims aren't white, which keeps the system going. You decide you always know best, that your way is always right. So really — you're part of the reason nothing changes."

"Is that what you think I'm doing?"

He brushed a strand of hair from my cheek. "There are girls missing, so ..." He got quiet and walked on and I stumbled to keep up.

I thought about Jocelyn and how I didn't know anything about her. I thought about Krista. She was invisible to me. *An enemy*. And what about the hundreds of other mysterious people who crossed my path, who I was afraid of seeing? More *ideas* than human beings.

Then there was me. What did I really know about her?

"Okay," Gray said, startling me out of my thoughts. "Let's look for the girls on the way. Eliminate possibilities."

WE STARTED TO SPY on people's properties. Instead of using the roads, we walked along back boundaries, following whatever fencing they had, on the lookout for any sign of the girls, for an old blue Chevy.

I wanted badly to hold Gray's hand, but we were walking too fast and our backpacks were too heavy. I stared a lot at the back of his head as he led the way.

We spied on tiny bungalows with swing sets on clear-cut lawns. We spied on working farms with vast planted fields and stalled animals. We spied on boarded-up vacation homes. We spied on expensive, expansive retreats and broken-down, abandoned shacks. Sometimes we had to trespass and crawl through scrub and bush until we got close enough to investigate. If there was no vehicle in the driveway, we'd watch anyway, and then eliminate them for no other reason than we *had a feeling* the

girls weren't there. We wished out loud that we had proper sur-
veillance equipment. Binoculars, for instance. It would've made
things so much faster and easier. Safer. One property at a time,
we made our way, somehow unnoticed, unheeded.

There was never any sign of Krista or Jocelyn or Vivvie or her
cousins. And no sign of any old blue Chevy.

We saw only one actual person — a middle-aged white guy in
a bathrobe and slippers shoving a sagging bag of garbage into
a bin outside his house. His house was a long, narrow mobile
home propped on concrete blocks surrounded by forest. His
car was an ancient minivan, the kind soccer moms used to drive.
We settled in to spy on him just in case.

What did he do all day, I wondered after he went back inside
his house. There was nothing here but wilderness and sky. How
did he fill the time? The loneliness?

Gray and I were hiding in a maze of trees, crouched on top of
a thick mat of pine needles. Our shoulders were touching. It
was a warm day and birds chirped around us, so many different
songs I'd never heard before. It was easy to forget the serious-
ness of why we were there. To slip out of the big picture and into
the extreme close-up of those moments. Maybe Gray felt it too
because he turned to me and we stared at each other. I didn't
know what was supposed to happen next. Even that bewildering
dizziness was better than everything else.

Then something huge and dark burst from the mobile home
like a bear from a cave. It was yowling and grunting like a bear.

Gray and I jerked to our feet.

It was the man, still in his bathrobe and slippers, shouting
without words, lumbering towards us. Holding a shotgun.

I stumbled away. My legs gave out. Wobbled and caved under

my body. I staggered to the nearest tree. Gray was stumbling too. Both of us too shocked to move properly. Too scared.

There was an epic howl behind us. It burst and echoed like a cannon.

Somehow we both managed to push upright. We grabbed hands and push-pulled each other through the woods. We could hear him behind us crashing over the brush. We urged our bodies on, winding through the forest, bashing past trees, aiming for imaginary paths.

There was a loud pop and then a crack and shatter of bark over our heads.

I stumbled again, muscles melting from fear, almost useless. The lurching huff of Gray's breath over my shoulder kept me going.

There was another pop, and another. Bark cracked and splintered. Scattered like fireworks.

The ground sloped downwards into a valley. We slipped and stumbled along a narrowing track. By the time the path dipped into an even narrower gulley, it was too late. Gray and I were stuck running between two sharp rises of moss-covered rock.

"Help us," I begged the crow under my heaving breath, my arms and legs urging and pumping. "Please help us." There was no answer. Only an indifferent gulley of shadows and rock. Nowhere to go but forward.

Then a ridge of light opened up through the rocky path ahead of us.

We ran hard, harder, until we burst out of the shade and almost stepped right onto a two-lane highway. On the other side of the road was a sheer wall of rock rising up like a warehouse.

We checked east. There was a car approaching along the west-bound lane. Gray elbowed me and we both stopped. There was something about the way it drove that made us not want to run out and hail it. It was moving way too slowly, braking almost to a stop, driving a bit farther on, then slowing down again. It was quite far off, but there was definitely a glint of a siren on its roof. A patrol vehicle on the lookout for something or someone.

Maybe Krista was up north and they were close to finding her. Or maybe they were finally looking for Jocelyn. Or Vivvie and her cousins. Or a serial killer on the run and on the verge of being caught.

We checked the other way. A pickup was approaching on the eastbound.

Gray pulled me away from the mouth of the gulley so we could hide in the scrub on the shoulder. We couldn't cross the road and keep running — the rock-face on the other side was too steep. We couldn't hail either vehicle — we weren't ready to be found. We couldn't turn back into the gulley — trigger-happy sniper might still be chasing us. Might turn us in. Might shoot us in front of the law.

Time clicked into slow motion as the eastbound pickup neared us. We took in the driver — a skinny youngish guy with long loose hair and an easy grin on his face. No one beside him in the passenger seat.

His expression shifted as he registered the patrol vehicle coming towards him. His pickup decelerated abruptly as it passed us — so close I could have thrown a rock in the bed. But the bed was already occupied. A silver-and-black husky with silver eyes. Five dark heads beside her, five small faces peering out, one girl wearing a white-sequined vest.

Gray shot up, and just as quickly I yanked him down.

Vivvie's face lit up and she craned over the side of the truck.

She had seen us. She flung out her hand — about to bang on the window of the cab.

In the other direction, the patrol vehicle was closing in. Slowing, rolling to speed, slowing again. Heading straight for us.

Gray and I shook our heads at Vivvie: *Don't give us up.*

The pickup was traveling away from us now, closing in on the patrol car. Vivvie saw it. She understood why we were hiding: in a few short moments we were going to get caught, dragged home, rescue mission aborted.

She stood up in the bed. Her husky stood up beside her. Her cousins were waving their hands, saying things we couldn't hear.

There was a split-second when the truck was parallel with the patrol car. And just as they passed each other, the husky leapt out of the back of the truck and onto the hood of the cruiser.

We could hear the thud even from where we were. The patrol car squealed to a stop and the husky slumped against the windshield, slid down the hood, and landed on the pavement.

She will fall.

The sound of the girls screaming pierced the air.

The pickup immediately braked and then pulled to a crooked stop on the shoulder.

Gray scuttled through the scrub towards them, ducking down so he'd stay hidden. I jumped up and followed, crouching as low as I could too, taking a few glances over my shoulder to make sure the gunslinger wasn't on our heels.

The troopers got out of the car. Two uniformed men wearing black aviator sunglasses.

There was a lot of yelling. The officers, the girls, the pickup driver who'd gotten out of his cab. He was holding his hair tight

off his face in agonized surprise. One officer went to the husky —
Kimi — and bent over her and put his hands on her chest.

Vivvie jumped out of the bed of the truck. She was yelling and
tried to push the officer away. He didn't budge, but focused his
attention on Kimi while the other officer went over to talk to the
pickup driver.

Gray and I scooted closer so we could hear their voices.

"I was just taking the kids to Deerhead," the pickup driver was
saying, his voice loud and plaintive. "They said they were lost and
needed to get back to their families."

The officer said something, but his voice was so low I couldn't
make it out. The driver responded with his loud, despairing voice,
"But I couldn't leave them on the side of the road, could I? Is that
what you're saying I shoulda done?"

The officer responded, again too low. He motioned down the
road the way the driver had come. Vivvie and her cousins were
crouched in a circle around the dog, laying gentle hands on her
belly, crying and swiping at their eyes and noses.

"No, no, let me help!" the driver was saying. "I'll drive back
your way. We can put the dog in my bed. I can take a coupla girls."

The officer who'd been crouched with Kimi stood up and he
and the other officer conferred for a bit. Then they turned to
the driver and said something we couldn't hear. There was an
immediate flurry of activity. The door to the pickup bed was
popped down and an emergency blanket was pulled from the
patrol vehicle. All three men went to Kimi and all five girls
stood and gave them room. The men very gently, very quickly,
wrapped Kimi in the blanket and hoisted her up off the ground.
The dog's eyes were open, her tongue was out. She was panting.
Quick, shallow breaths. She was alive.

The bed door was slammed shut. Then three girls — the twins and the child-mom — were ushered into the back of the patrol vehicle. The two other kids — the girl/boy and Vivvie — ran to the passenger side of the pickup while the driver got into the driver's seat. The officers got back into their vehicle and waited while the pickup driver started up and slowly pulled a U-turn on the highway, then headed west the way he'd come. The officers pulled out after him and both vehicles drove off down the west-bound lane.

When the pickup passed, Vivvie was staring at us out the back window of the cab. She pressed a finger against the window and her mouth circled into a pleading O. *Go!*

Go! Don't stop until you find Jocelyn.

At least the girls had been found, I thought as I watched them drive away. Saved by Kimi. Who had saved us too.

3

WE FOLLOWED THE ROAD, sheltered inside the woods, in the direction of Deerhead. After about two hours of steady hiking, we stumbled into town. It was a small town — there was a diner, a family restaurant, a gas station, a motel, and a few other store-fronts. I was so exhausted. I was ready to break into one of the motel's rooms so I could fall into a bed.

There was a sad used-up pall over the town. Charlie's story about Jocelyn's dad echoed back. *He was in Deerhead waiting for a ride home. Found his body, side of the highway, frozen to death.*

Murder. I pictured Jocelyn following her father's broken trail, retracing his final steps, looking for her own clues. Grief-stricken, but maybe not alone. Maybe a walking target for someone pretending to help her.

I shuddered and followed Gray out of the protection of the woods. We were about to step onto the main street when I stopped and grabbed Gray. He followed my gaze. Several people had converged in the parking lot of the motel and were chatting over their cars and pointing in various directions. "Lily," Gray said, as if she was the one to fear.

We scrambled for a stand of trees and hid in the shadows to watch the group of ten or so. Walter was there too, and so was the woman I'd decided was Jocelyn's mother. Lily and Walter looked strong, ready to take on dragons and trolls.

"The cops must've brought the little girls back to their families," Gray said in low voice. "None of their parents are here." He peered at them for a few more seconds, then said, "The search for Jocelyn must be back on."

He pulled out his phone and contemplated his list of recent calls. I could see the numbers — *home, Dad,* and also *Lily* from the phone-call he'd made two days ago asking if he could bring me to their house.

"You want to talk to Lily?" I said gently. "It's not like she'll know we're right across the street."

"If anyone would know we're right across the street, it's Lily." He watched the group at the motel make decisions. A few got into cars and drove off, Lily and Walter and the rest stayed behind, talking, checking around.

Gray twitched and groaned under his breath. I could feel him starting to move forward, then flinching back, and it reminded me a little of when I'd followed him at City Hall, how my muscles had surged and slumped, how I'd accused him. How I was wrong about so many things.

Neither of us saw the two patrol vehicles until they pulled into the motel parking lot and steered close to Lily and her group. So much law enforcement in such a remote area.

A shot went off inside me. I stumbled for cover.

Even though they couldn't have known I was there, even if it wasn't me they were looking for, I kept rushing away, escaping the cops and Jocelyn's search party, ducking back and back, until I was submerged in the forest again. I was about to turn and run when something caught my arm and pulled me to a stop.

"Hey, whoa," Gray said. "You leaving without me?" He offered a small smile to keep it light. But there was a lump in my stomach and it was swelling.

"No," I said, panting. "I just ... wanted to get to cover." I gathered my breath, my will, then looked up at him again. "You should go to them, Gray. Tell them I went back to the city and that you stayed. It's okay."

"No —"

"You should be with them."

"They'll just send me home again. They don't want me here."

"That's not true. They'll understand — because you stayed for the right reason." *Not like you*, a hidden voice hounded me from the darkness.

I backed away from him and his eyes focused intently as he measured his choices.

Hyper-telescopic eyes. *The memory of his touch on my skin.*

"You should go to them, Gray. I'll be okay." I tried to smile at him. Because I knew this was the right thing to do — I had to give him up, had to let him go. I had to look for Krista, had to let him look for Jocelyn.

Our eyes were locked, both of us listening so hard to the preaching inside our own heads that you couldn't even call it looking at each other.

I knew then that I'd do anything for him. That I'd done it already. I had changed my mind so I could be with him.

I didn't look back once as I walked away. Didn't even glance over my shoulder.

But soon I heard the steady dead-leaf crunch of his boots on the trail behind me.

Then his hand slipped into mine.

And the wholeness of my relief was epic.

FATIGUE AND HUNGER RADIATED off us like illness. We didn't really look for Jocelyn or Krista, but trudged through the forest with no clear direction or plan. We didn't spy on properties — I can't remember if we passed one — and didn't see a single person that we could investigate or watch. We needed rest and a place to camp before it got dark. But neither one of us had the energy to make the decision to stop.

We walked another two hours without break when Gray froze and crouched down behind a thicket. He put his finger to his lips and I crouched too and followed his pointed gaze.

Silent movement deep inside the woods seemed to gather like smoke. As it wound around the trees, shaking off the barred shadows of the setting sun, I saw that it was a person. A tiny man wearing an oversized, drooping parka and an enormous, faded, knit cap on his head. He walked perfectly erect and poised, almost like a ballerina, picking his way around moss-covered rocks, pointing soft boots over fallen branches. He was carrying an old wicker basket in one arm, and every now and then he'd bend over and pull a fresh clump out of the ground and add it to the basket. I looked down and noticed for the first time how many shoots of green were pushing up.

The man was leaning over, inspecting a patch of soil, when his head snapped up and he looked at us. "Good evening, good evening."

Gray and I shrank back, but the man waved his hand like he was expecting us, or like he ran into strangers in the woods all the time. Gray stood up and stepped out of the thicket. "Hello."

The man lifted his basket. "Dandelion and chickweed arrived on time for dinner."

Gray took a cautious step towards him. "I hope we're not trespassing."

"No, no. The land belongs to all of us."

Gray approached him warily. "Sorry if we took you by surprise." He extended his hand. "My name is Gray." The man shook his hand. The top of his wool cap barely came to Gray's chest.

"And I'm M," I said.

"Welcome, Gray. Welcome, M," he said, shaking my hand too. "My name is Dusty." He beamed up at us. "What's the given occasion? Hiking through the park?"

I remembered the trucker asking if Gray and I were headed for the national park. Hideous memory-flashes edged in of what had happened the day before. I had to hold my breath to block them out.

"You live around here?" Gray said. Wondering, I could tell, if this man had anything to do with Jocelyn or her disappearance.

It seemed unlikely. He had that radiant calm of someone too high for meanness or evil.

"I live everywhere, and nowhere," Dusty said. "I live in the universe." He grinned mysteriously. "Or maybe I only live in the minds and hearts of the people who meet me."

Gray and I snuck a look at each other.

Clutching his basket to his chest, Dusty ambled off. He beckoned with his finger. "Come. Come for dinner."

Gray and I exchanged another glance. He was pale and drawn and his eyes were drooped with exhaustion. I imagined I looked about the same. We needed food and water and sleep. And maybe this strange little monk would know something about Krista or Jocelyn.

HE LED US ON a maze-like trail, changing direction, either left or right, at seemingly random trees. Every now and then he'd stop so he could pluck out another fresh shoot and add it to his basket, or he'd pick up a stone or leaf or insignificant piece of forest, stand erect, examine it closely, and then toss it back to the ground. I had to suppress an urge to hurry him. I had no right to be impatient, but the word "dinner" played on repeat in my head.

We arrived at a small stream and, even though the sun was setting fast, the light was brighter because of the clearing around it. Dusty led us along the shore of river rocks, and soon he stopped again to comb up a handful of tiny pebbles. He examined them minutely, then plucked one from the rest and presented it to me. "You see, my lady?" he said. "A diamond leaves its mark."

I reached for the pebble and searched the spot he wanted me

to see. Even by the dim light, I could see a crystal glistening in its stone belly.

"An ancient sea washed over it," he said. "A gift to you, my lady."

"Thank you," I said, folding my hand around it.

We continued on until we came to an impenetrable copse of evergreens. Dusty kept advancing towards it, and then I saw there was a narrow passage between neatly trimmed branches. We followed until we came out into a clearing.

We were in a yard with a small cabin. Gray and I both stopped. Inspecting for anything suspicious or telling.

The cabin was made the old-fashioned way — glazed logs stacked on top of each other, a vaulted roof over a front porch, a wood door flanked by two windows, trim painted green. On the far side, there was a garage with an overgrown gravel lane winding away through the woods, probably to one of the country roads that crisscrossed the area. The garage looked newer than the cabin, aluminum-sided and ordinary. Its door was rolled up and inside was a small, beat-up car. Not a blue Chevy sedan, but something moss-green and rust.

There was no garden in front of the cabin, but a circle of trampled grass around it. The thing that made it remarkable was that there were five large sculptures — the kind you see some-times where misshapen rocks are balanced on top of each other. The sculptures stood like star-points around the perimeter of the yard.

No sign of any lost or hiding girls.

Gray was obviously measuring that too, because he said abruptly, "We're on the lookout for some missing people."

Dusty stopped and turned. "Missing?" He looked genuinely concerned.

"Yeah. One is a girl from my hometown — Here, I'll show you." He rifled for his phone and found the Jocelyn picture and showed it. Dusty went over and examined the screen with grave attention.

I stepped in too. "The other is a girl from the city," I said. "My age. Dark blond hair, blue eyes, medium height ... Pretty."

Dusty studied my face with the same solemn expression. His features were fine with high pockmarked cheeks and penny-brown eyes.

Gray pointed to his phone. "Jocelyn's been missing for a month. Maybe you saw her walking around? Or in town?"

Dusty looked back at the screen. "I don't go to town much. When I am here, I am here."

"So no girl came to you asking for help? Or she could've been on the road, hitchhiking?"

Dusty shook his head sadly. "I never saw any girl on the road. And no one has come by since before winter. Not even hikers from the park."

Gray considered him for a moment, then said, "We've been walking all day. Is it okay if we crash in your yard tonight?"

"But I brought you here! I welcome you."

"We have a tent," Gray said. "It's not big. It could fit over there." He pointed at a spot across from the cabin.

"Plenty of room," Dusty said as he walked over to one of his more elaborate balancing sculptures.

"I can set it up so we won't break your —" But Gray didn't finish before Dusty kicked the sculpture over.

We both cried out, and Dusty waved us off. "It's nothing. It is just a *thing*, for crying out loud. It is just a thing that can be made again." He grinned at us. "And now we eat." He did a half-pirouette and led the way to his cabin.

IT WAS SMALLER INSIDE than I expected. There was a room that was half living room, with a fireplace and a ratty couch and chair, and half kitchen, with a butcher-block counter, an old-school freezer-on-top fridge, a small cooktop, and cupboards painted the same forest green as the outside trim. There was a tiny second room with a wrought-iron single bed and an oak dresser, and one more closed door at the back, which I hoped was a bathroom.

Dusty laid his basket of greens on the counter. "You have anything you can spare to eat?"

"Yeah sure." Gray rifled through his backpack and pulled out two cans. "You like baked beans?"

"Whatever you can give is what we're supposed to eat today. Even if it is nothing."

"Well, the beans are good."

Dusty took the cans from Gray, opened them, spilled them into a pot, and set the pot on the cooktop. Then he pulled out two handfuls of greens from his basket and put them into a tub in the sink.

While the beans heated, Gray and I took turns washing up in Dusty's makeshift bathroom — a basic toilet, sink, bathtub, no mirror or doodads.

Back in the kitchen, we drank our fill of water, filled up our water bottles, checked our supplies. Gray pulled out his charger and plugged it into an outlet by the kitchen counter. He plugged his phone in, then collapsed on the couch. I joined him, sinking with relief into the cushiony softness. By now, my stomach was flailing with hunger.

When the beans were hot, Dusty pulled the only bowl from his cupboard and scooped some into it for himself, then divided the rest back into the two cans. He balanced a handful of clean greens on top of each serving, pushing them down into the rims, then handed us each a crooked fork and a warm can. It was everything I could do not to dump the entire portion into my mouth at once.

Cradling his bowl, Dusty plié-ed onto the chair across from us and closed his eyes. He half-mumbled under his breath. "*Spirit of life. Your true light shines. Within and without. Radiant on earth. Brilliant in heaven. Show us our wisdom, so we nurture each day, so we forgive our weakness, and the weakness of others. Free us from routine. Reveal our true purpose. Give us the will and the courage to heal.*"

Gray and I exchanged a ravenous look. But I was so grateful for my warm can, for finding Dusty, for Gray, that I said my own private thank-yous too.

"*The song of the universe sings always and through all of time. I am here.*" Then Dusty opened his eyes, dug into his bowl, and shoved a heaping spoon of beans into his mouth. The fresh greens stuck out from between his lips like soft quills.

Gray and I dug in too. It made me want to laugh and cry at the same time. Nothing had ever tasted so good.

Dusty ate slowly, chewing each bite for several minutes, smacking and licking his lips. Gray and I were completely done eating before he'd taken his third spoonful.

It had gotten dark inside the cabin. I shivered and fought to keep awake.

"Warmth comes from within," Dusty said. "You have to go into your own self. You have to become the warmth, you see what I'm saying?"

I didn't, but nodded anyway.

He set his half-eaten bowl on the fireplace hearth and rooted deep in the pocket of his parka. "It's because you have to understand how to do it." He pulled out a disposable lighter and lit it. "I can't *tell* you how to do it. One has to understand it oneself."

He touched the flame end of the lighter to some kindling in the fireplace and it ignited and blazed. For the first time I saw that he was old. Maybe in his fifties or sixties. "If a person wants to become the warmth, then they can learn it. But it's something that one has to learn. You see?"

We nodded at him and he sat down again. "People, they listen to the sounds of the world — the fire, the wind, the leaves. It's part of them. But they don't understand it. You see? But it is part of them. Because it's *love*." A beatific expression spread over his face as he looked at us. "That's what it is. It is love."

My skin began to tingle. *How had we arrived here?*

Flames wrapped around a pyramid of split logs on the grate and soft smoke sifted upwards. Gray and I nestled into the couch, too tired to do anything more. Our hands were close together on the cushions, but not touching. I wondered if I might move my hand over to his.

A long silence wrapped around us as we all watched the fire, mesmerized by the movement of the flames, by the deepness of our exhaustion, and me by Gray's too-far closeness.

"Who occupies your mind?" Dusty said, and I started and looked over and saw that he was speaking to Gray.

Gray kind of shook out of half-sleep. "You mean Jocelyn?"

"No, the other one."

I caught my breath and watched closely.

Gray became very still. His eyes flicked to the fire. "My birth mother."

"Yes, this one." Dusty bowed his head. "It weighs heavy. She's gone, and it makes you think about the original father."

"No," Gray said as if to end the conversation. I realized that no one had mentioned his birth father. "I don't care about that," he said, staring straight ahead.

I wondered if it was possible that his birth father was part of the group that had congregated at Arthur's.

Dusty came over and crouched beside me to observe Gray more closely. "We all carry your weight," he said. "Throw the weight down."

"I'm not trying to replace my parents," Gray said. He sat forward and drummed his fingers on his knees. "Just trying to figure things out."

"Fire is a clean thing," Dusty said to him. "You light a fire, the thing that is toxic, it leaves. Even the smoke itself, it gets carried away. You see what I'm saying?"

An echo of Gray's voice filled my mind. *It's not telling you to burn shit down, is it?* Lily had said, *You start looking for something different. A way out. A new way. An old one.* The crow had said, *As she falls, so do we all.*

"You must throw the weight on the fire." Dusty mimed throwing something on the flames.

The muscles of Gray's face were getting tighter. "I've made enough trouble. I don't want to make more."

"Throw the weight down and something new will come."

Gray stood up. "If you guys don't mind," he said. "I'm going to crash." He sounded easy, but I could see stress in the clutch of his hands.

"I hear you," Dusty said. He sat back in his chair.

Gray unplugged his phone from the charger. He fumbled the phone in his hands, turning it on and off. He stepped one way, then the other. Distracted, he said, "It's been a long day. I'm beat." Then he picked up both our backpacks and went to the front door. "Thanks for everything." He didn't look at me or Dusty. He opened the door, stepped outside, closed the door behind him.

I didn't know where to go. Should I follow him? Should I crawl inside the tent and lay my body beside his? Was I going to pester him with meaningless questions and awkward condolences?

But how could I trust myself to lie beside him and be still? How could I stop myself from throwing my arms around him like a needy girl?

Dusty offered me a gentle smile. "I'm happy you came."

"Me too." I tried to smile back. But my insides had started to spin. It was chaotic and violent. Everything in me wanted to follow Gray

"I don't know why I'm here," I blurted.

"You don't?" Dusty observed me. "But you are looking for her."

I said, "The other missing girl — Jocelyn — she was last seen in this area."

"Yes, I see." He nodded his head.

"She disappeared a month ago."

"Yes."

"But the girl I'm looking for — Krista ..."

"I hear you." He was waiting for me so patiently, so calmly.

"I don't know if she's here," I said. "No one has seen her in this area. There's no reason for her to be here. There was only one thing in her text — a finger pointing up — that I thought could mean she's up north. I can't remember anymore why I was so sure it meant that." I met his quiet gaze, my thoughts whirling and jamming. Gray, outside, so close, pulled me like a magnet. But Dusty was nodding and waiting for me to continue. So I said, "Is it enough if I *believe* it?"

He considered my question. "If you can be peaceful in your belief, if you can hold certainty in your heart, it means your belief is strong. But if you can't be peaceful in it — if you have to force it, or fight it, or get angry, or hurt a person — it means your belief is weak. You see what I'm saying?"

"I think so," I said. Another lie.

He rubbed his eyes and stood up. "I want to go to sleep now. You have another journey ahead, and I want to see it." He pointed to his temple. "In here. I want to be quiet and still in my bed so I can see it."

My head was pounding. I was confused.

"When you walk," he said, "get yourself ready. You see what I'm saying?"

I nodded. I wished to see everything he was saying, but I couldn't.

He held his fist out to me. "You can only be true. That is all you can be."

I had kept the pebble he'd given me in a crease in my palm. I could feel it as I touched my fist to his. A slight point pressing into my skin.

Dusty's eyes softened and he said, "I love you."

A startling buzz went through me.

"I love you too," I said. The first time I'd said it in forever where it meant what it was supposed to mean.

And the weird thing was — I could feel it too.

4

I CRAWLED INTO THE tent as quietly as I could. I thought I'd waited long enough that there was a pretty good chance Gray was fully asleep.

I was surprised that some ambient light filtered through the
nylon walls, and then realized it was moonlight. It was a clear
night and the moon was high and almost full.

I looked at Gray for a while. How his body in the sleeping bag
was in silhouette, how his chest was rising and falling evenly, how
his profile was like no one else's in the world.

I took off my boots and set them beside his on the ground by
the opening. He'd laid out our stuff in an orderly way. Our backpacks side by side. Extra blanket for if it got too cold. His knife
in its leather holster.

He'd spread out my sleeping bag too, but hadn't connected
ours together. I didn't know how to take that. It wasn't a cold night,
and he was distracted by worries urgent enough to crowd everything else out.

But I wanted to feel him beside me, even if it was just the
accidental press of his thigh.

I slipped into my sleeping bag. The taut angles of the tent
looked like a net suspended over us. A shroud caught in that
moment right before it drops.

The close air smelled of Gray. I inhaled deeply and held my
breath. Maybe that was the only way left for me to hold on to him.

TUESDAY, APRIL 17

TWO DAYS UNTIL THE FALL

1

"SHE WILL FALL IN two days!" A panicked screech in my ear. So loud it jolted me out of my dreams.

My vision cleared and I saw the inside of the tent. Gray was sitting up beside me. *Why was he awake?* It was still dark. But lighter too — closer to dawn than midnight.

"Hey," I said. My voice cut the quiet. "You're up early."

Gray was very still. I noticed he was holding his phone in his lap. The screen was dim, but its muted light was part of the reason I could see him so well.

I sat up and touched his arm. He was wearing the long underwear. The worn wool was soft under my fingers. "Are you okay?"

"I couldn't sleep," he said without looking at me. "I had a bad feeling."

My stomach twisted. *It was Jocelyn. They must've found something.*

"So I checked," he said, lifting his phone slightly to show what he meant. "But no."

Hearing the no should've filled me with relief. Bad news would definitely be worse than no news. But he'd said it with an edge.

"Gray — what is it? You're freaking me out."

"When I searched Missing Persons, someone else came up."

Everything went cold. Maybe the ticking I'd heard was the countdown to this.

He turned his phone to show me the screen. My startled, flashed-out expression. "Missing for five days. Posted by your family. Your *mom*, your *dad*, your *brother*."

The truth had been tapping my shoulder all the way here.

He stared at me. "You're sixteen."

My stomach flipped with such force, I thought I was going to puke.

"Krista isn't even your sister. She's some other runaway."

I could hardly speak. "A girl from my school."

Even in the dark I could see his face crumple. "You *used* Jocelyn?"

Adrenaline shot through my veins.

His voice got louder. "You stole her tragedy so you could come here?"

Is that what I had done?

But I'd understood what I was doing, hadn't I? The whole time, I'd understood it.

"Jocelyn isn't like your friend from school." He spit the words out. "She isn't on some *joyride*. She's not somewhere *safe*."

My legs started to move on their own. They kicked out from under me, wheeling me out of the sleeping bag.

"Jocelyn is *gone*."

Shame exploded inside me like a bomb. It propelled me across the tent.

"You sold me that stuff about Messenger 93?"

If I didn't get out of there, I would die.

"You were using me."

My hands scrambled in the dark to find my boots, to pull them on and knot up the laces.

"You used all of us."

I fumbled for my stuff, bundled one thing after another against my chest. The hyper-wheeze of my breath buzzed in my ears.

"I trusted you," Gray said.

I groped for the tent zipper.

"I believed you." His voice lost its edge. "I wanted to believe you."

I stumbled headfirst into the clearing. The moon had abandoned us. Dusty's cabin was visible in the ebbing light. So were the rocks from his ruined sculpture. Beyond the circle, the trees looked like the blacked-out monsters from nightmares.

Gray crawled out behind me. "You broke it." His face was soft and swollen, like he had melted. "I gave you my trust — and you broke it." His voice was agony.

I did this. This was my fault.

"Who are you?" he said.

I wanted to surrender my hands to him, but they were full. My disgraceful armor.

"Why are you here?" he said.

I took him in. He was everything. Everything I could never be. *HE IS THE FALL.*

"I'm sorry, Gray. I don't know what I'm doing."

"M—" he said.

But the explosive roar of my wrong eclipsed everything. I had to escape.

"M—" His voice chased after me.

I was flying away. Past Dusty's cabin. Through the clearing. Straight into the woods.

The tree-monsters pulled me into their world and ate me up.

2

GRAY YELLED THROUGH THE forest. "*M! M!*" The sound of his feet thrashing across the underbrush echoed. He was coming after me.

It was pitch black, but I was running blind anyway. Gripping my bundle of stuff against my chest, getting knocked around by tree trunks and branches.

Gray's face, agonized and angry, flashed like a projection in front of me. *I believed you. I wanted to believe you. I gave you my trust. You broke it.*

Before long I didn't hear his calls through the dark anymore. Didn't hear the crash and split of his misguided chase.

I stumbled on and on and on and on.

Loneliness shut its gate between me and everything else. How long had it been since I'd felt its steel plate inside my chest? *Five days.*

The sky got lighter above the trees as day dawned. The trees reached up and shredded the light. Still I walked on and on.

My legs gave out when the sun was high. I climbed up onto a large boulder and dropped my things. My unzipped backpack, sweatshirts spilling out, raincoat tangled in the straps. And something else. Crushed and brown. A dead animal.

It was Gray's holster.

I picked it up. The leather was soft.

Gray was gone.

His knife was in the sheath. I pulled it out and held it up. The blade was tarnished. Perforations of rust scabbed the long edge.

But it was sharp. Pointed. Usable.

I raised the handle, pushing the blade against the neck of the world. I wished to end this. Wanted to stab the truth into another realm. Or better — turn the blade against myself.

But I was too tired even for that.

I collapsed onto the rock, lifted the sleeve of my sweatshirt, and strapped Gray's holster to my arm. It was tricky, connecting the short belt and buckle with one hand. But I got it, and then the knife slipped into place easily. As if I'd worn knives against my body my whole life. I zipped on my raincoat and curled into a ball around my backpack.

The shadows of the woods were deep. Every sound was amplified. Chirps and squawks filled the air. I didn't care about animal attacks or threatening humans. I deserved whatever harm came to me. My eyes were blinking closed, but I searched for the crow. Listened for its voice. It didn't come. Because I had not heeded the right call. I hadn't done any of the right things. I'd betrayed Gray and everyone he cared about. *You were using me. You used all of us.* I'd left only sadness and destruction in my wake.

The forest floor was a tapestry of matted leaves from years gone by — faded orange and yellow and red as far as my eyes could see. The branches of trees weren't monstrous anymore, but like dancers' arms winding and waving. Once upon a time, I had wanted to be a dancer.

Then I'd wanted to be a singer.

I'd wanted to be a basketball player.

Wanted to be a leader.

A philanthropist.

A genius.

A filmmaker.

When I was very young, I'd wanted to be a fairy. But that was back when I thought everything was true and good. Including me.

IT STARTED AS A knocking on my chest. *Thwack thwack thwack*. I woke up in a groggy fog and immediately felt for Gray. But then I remembered he was gone, and it was like he was being ripped out of my veins in real time.

Thwack thwack thwack. It knocked against my chest like an outside heartbeat.

I bolted up and looked around. The rock was cold under my body. I wrapped my arms around my chest and tried to orient myself.

I opened my backpack and took a halfhearted glance inside. I had no sleeping bag, no tent, no food. At least I'd refilled my water bottle at Dusty's. I searched for the sun and found it through the branches. It was still pretty high in the sky. Not so late then.

Thwack thwack thwack. It was coming from up there. I focused my attention through the labyrinth of branches. And then I saw it: a helicopter crossing overhead.

"Aaaah!" I called out and jumped up. I scooted down the side of the boulder and ran in the direction it was traveling. "Aaaah!" I screamed at it, believing the pilot could hear me through the mass of trees, above the sound of its rotating blades.

I screamed at it and followed through the woods. *A helicopter out here in the backwoods, searching for something*. Maybe they were closing in on Jocelyn. Maybe Krista was somewhere out here after all. Maybe they'd found the serial killer.

I ran and screamed and jumped and flapped my arms, but the helicopter was too fast and there were too many trees and I was too small. In ten seconds, I lost sight of it. Still, I kept running in the same direction, hoping for a clearing, hoping it might turn around and come back.

I ran until my foot caught on a twist of exposed root. It sent me sprawling to the ground.

Nothing was broken. Everything hurt.

The shock of it unzipped me.

My sobs echoed in the wild. They didn't sound real. They were coming from a place so deep inside my body, they could've been my organs rejecting me.

If a girl falls in the forest and no one is there to see her, does she exist?

But then I remembered: I still had Krista's phone. With the push of a button, I could alert that helicopter, could get it to turn around, come back. In the next moment, I could be sitting in its warm belly, speeding home.

I opened my bag and scrambled through the glut of stuff inside until my hands wrapped around the most obvious and ordinary tool in the world. Krista's phone. I almost laughed, almost kissed it. Classic twist — me running around on a mission, channeling some idea of Joan of Arc, only to have my enemy swoop in at the last second to save me.

I pushed the home button.

Nothing happened.

I pressed it again. Nothing.

I pressed the power button instead. The screen stayed black. I held the button down longer. Nothing.

I shook the phone. I banged it. Knocked it against my knee. Nothing, nothing, nothing.

Of course the battery was dead. It had been sitting in my bag for days.

I hysteria-laughed for five minutes. Then dragged myself off the ground. I was back at the beginning. But if I had learned one thing it was that when you don't know what to do you just have to start.

THERE WERE NO HOUSES, no farms, no shelter of any kind. There were no wire fences that showed that people owned the land. I searched for a road. I could follow a road until I got to a town. Then I'd call my parents and wait for them to come get me. I would go home with them. I would tell them some story. Then I'd crawl into bed and it would all be over.

I walked another few hours without stopping. My pace was slow, steady. I still hadn't crossed a road or fence — and then I remembered Dusty and the trucker both mentioning the national park. I wondered if I'd stumbled into it. Instead of looking for roads and fences, I started looking for park signs, for signs of trails, for hikers.

After another long stretch of nothing, I came to a narrow stream. It was something like the one near Dusty, but narrower, more quiet. It wasn't running fast and the water was clear, its crystalline surface winding over speckled rocks and roots of trees. The clearing for the water-path allowed some sunlight to get through, and I badly needed to feel the sun's warmth. I found a rock on the shore and sat down.

I opened my bag and pulled out my water bottle and took a few sips. The cool liquid felt good going down. Water for lunch. Sunlight bounced off the metal rim and something about it reminded me of Infinity Girl. How I'd always imagined her mirror-panels bouncing all the light away from her.

I rifled in my backpack for a pen and something to write on. There were only two scraps of paper in my bag: the bus ticket that

Lily had bought to send me back to the city, and the newspaper page with the ad I'd already drawn across. I turned the paper over to the side that was covered with print. Stories about wars and corruption.

I scratched a bunch of panels across the newsprint. This would not be the same day as the one with Infinity Girl stuck in Double Kross's mansion. This new scene would be set somewhere else in the story, at some later point, yet to be determined.

Infinity Girl has failed in her mission. She is a sitting target for Double Kross.

Establishing shot: *Infinity Girl arrives at the owl in City Hall Square. She's looking for the person who has the secret code for thwarting Double Kross. It's written on a tablet that he guards night and day. He keeps it because he knows Double Kross has enemies, and also that she is dangerous. But this agent will not kill Double Kross either. He has no idea that Infinity Girl's life depends on his information.*

Infinity Girl stumbles through the square. She will reveal herself to him today. She is ready. But her powers have grown weak and she is steadily losing strength.

Cut to: *A face in the busy crowd. Infinity Girl locks eyes on him.*

Train-effect of people passing in front of the person, obscuring his identity.

Infinity Girl pushes through the anonymous crowd. She gets closer. She's almost there. And then she realizes it's not the person she seeks. She collapses to the ground. One of her superhero mirrors breaks. She picks up two long shards. A moment of hesitation. A decision. She aims the shards at her own body. She smashes all the mirrors that cover her. Naked and broken, she falls in a heap. The crowd continues to mill about her, rushing in both directions.

I drew one last panel and wrote inside it: *The End.*

What a waste.

I'd always promised myself — no love story. There was nothing true about them. They always, in some way, killed the hero in the end.

I shoved the newspaper into my backpack, bunched my clothes on top of it, then pulled myself up and made myself keep going.

I TRIED TO KEEP to one direction, but had the constant, suspicious feeling that I was walking in loopy circles. I couldn't tell if it was late afternoon or early evening by the time I found the first trail. It was marked with a blue rectangle that was painted on the bark of a smooth old tree. Farther down, there was another blue-painted rectangle. When I got to that tree, there was another blue-painted rectangle on a farther-off tree.

The trail was a trail, which means there were well-worn parts where I could go fast — as fast as I could, despite everything — and there were trickier parts where I had to go slowly, scaling narrow passages over rocks and roots.

There was always the pressing urgency of waning light, of being caught in the middle of nowhere with no shelter and a long night ahead. With every next degree of darkness, my senses heightened. I tried to tell myself there was nothing to fear, but fear kept catching up to me.

It started tracking me at true nightfall. It was a simultaneous awareness that I'd lost the light to see the trail, and that a very specific crackling of groundcover in the distance was steady and getting closer.

Witiko. Now it was Vivvie's voice echoing in my memory-chamber. An ice-hearted cannibal-zombie that chased you through the woods.

There was a tremendously loud crack behind me. *Something really big.*

The serial killer.

I froze and didn't breathe as I turned my head around to see if I could see anything. But it was like I was up against a monolithic wall of black. Caught as darkness closed in on me like a giant crushing compactor.

The stalking thing froze too. Or at least I didn't hear it in the next few seconds.

I couldn't run. If it was a creature, it would be faster than me, would have better night vision, would be able to smell me from miles away. If it was the serial killer, he probably knew these woods better than I did. I was standing there like bait on a hook.

Then my body took over. It began to hustle me through the forest.

I succumbed to its primitive decree. *I ran.*

Somehow I slipped past trees and over obstacles on the ground. Somehow I made it to the next step and the next step without falling or breaking my leg. My breathing was too loud in my ears now, and I couldn't hear anymore if the thing/person was still following me. I couldn't stop to take stock.

Soon the light changed again and I could see the forest clearly, and there were long shadows everywhere like in daytime. I saw it was the moon rising above the trees. It was bruise-yellow and its waxing edge was smudged and sloppy. I ran faster now, desperate to escape the penitentiary shadow-bars of tree trunks and silhouettes.

I ran until, by some miracle or mathematical inevitability, I burst out of the labyrinth and landed on a dirt road.

Left or right. I didn't know which was the better choice. But I thought I saw the hard rim of a domed shape above the trees to the left. A building, or a rock-face, I couldn't tell which.

I glanced over my shoulder and checked back the way I'd come. The silence was electric, like an accumulation of a dozen bated breaths. Then something snapped again.

I turned left down the road and ran.

My movement wasn't athletic or smooth. It was always at the edge of disaster, my muscles, wobbly and failing, were spurred only by adrenaline and instinct.

I rounded a curve in the road and the domed shape that rose over the trees was only a few hundred yards away from me, sitting in an otherwise empty clearing, highlighted by the bright and sloppy moon. A rusted old water tower.

3

THE WATER TOWER WAS immensely high, maybe seven stories. Its fat tank was propped on four stilt-legs, and two of the legs were also ladders that led up to a railed walkway that circled the tank. There was no fence to stop me from climbing up. So I kept running and leapt onto the closest ladder and grabbed the rusted metal rails and pulled myself up.

I'd scaled maybe twenty rungs when I finally dared to stop and check behind me again. There was nothing in the clearing. It was a long, rectangular field, mowed or maintained by someone. Nothing was stalking me from it. Even the short blades of grass weren't moving. I checked the woods from where I'd come. They were a ways off, but the moon was so bright, its light shone in like a high-powered lantern.

Something just inside the tree line shuffled and stopped. I could feel its eyes on me.

I launched myself up the ladder.

It was terrifyingly steep and narrow and rickety. I didn't look down anymore. If I did, my legs would give out. I'd never tested my fear of heights, had never been on a rollercoaster or zipline or circus-trapeze, or any of those manufactured tests of courage, but I had a sudden certainty that heights were not my thing. The bottoms of my feet and backs of my legs were numbing out.

There were too many rungs. My breath was fading fast, my muscles had reached the end of their strength. But I kept climbing, hand over hand, step over step. Like I was climbing to the moon.

When I finally pulled myself up onto the ringed walkway, I couldn't even stand. I collapsed onto the rusted-cage flooring and panted. I checked the clearing around the tower, and then the forest beyond it. As far as I could see, no creature or stalker had skulked out. Not yet, anyway.

I stared and stared at the edge of the forest, waiting for whatever it was to come out and find a way to get me. But, despite all my efforts to stop it, my body shut down and my eyes closed.

WHEN I WOKE UP next, the first thing I saw was a thousand stars glimmering in a velvet-black sky. The moon was still alive, but it had spun farther away. For that one moment I was in awe and not imagining some horrific death filled with my screams and hemorrhaging blood.

Then I noticed the swollen belly of the water tank at my side, and I remembered where I was. I didn't want to, but checked the other way and saw that I was on the narrowest precipice of a walkway, only one thin rusted crossbar between me and a seven-story plummet to the ground.

I sat up, but my body was stiff and sore like nothing I'd ever felt before. Violent shivers spasmed my muscles. Then I realized how cold it was. Running had kept me warm for hours, and now there was nothing to hold the cold at bay.

Dusty's words came back to me: *Warmth comes from within. Go into your own self. Become the warmth.*

I tried it. Tried channeling heat. Tried magnetically pulling it to me and forcing it into my cells. But it didn't work. If anything, I was colder than ever.

Very carefully, I took my backpack off and rummaged inside for the extra two sweatshirts and pairs of socks. It was a desperate high-wire act as I stripped off my coat, gingerly trying not to drop anything, and layered on the extra clothes.

When I pulled on the first sweatshirt, I noticed Gray's knife strapped to my left arm. Did it make me feel safer knowing it was there? Or was it more terrifying knowing I could use it?

I put my coat back on over the layers, pulled the hood over my head, and strapped my backpack on again. I zipped every zipper, snapped every snap, then covered my hands with the socks so I was as bundled as could be.

The cold had sunk deep. If possible, I shivered even more.

I scanned the area. I couldn't tell if my stalker was still watching from the forest. There was no stakeout at the bottom of the tower's four stilt-legs. It was so far to the ground, my stomach twisted and my head spun. I couldn't imagine ever making it down again.

She will fall.

That's when I understood. The whole time, the messages had been warning me.

You will go where you would not go. You will see what you would not see.

They'd been trying to open my eyes to what I already knew.

It's not enough. It's never going to be enough.

It wasn't rabid wolves or fairy-tale monsters or fugitive serial killers that were going to get me. It was loneliness.

As she falls, so do we all.

Krista ran away because of it. We were all running away from it.

The truth is the way.

This was how I was going to disappear. Forever lost on the caged walkway of some abandoned water tower. Nothing to remember me by but my rotting flesh and bones. No one ever finding them.

WEDNESDAY, APRIL 18

ONE DAY UNTIL THE FALL

1

IT WAS DAYBREAK WHEN I woke up again, with the sun just appearing at the brink of the world. I was wedged between the tank and the inner edge of the walkway. So cold, my body didn't even bother to shiver. I was still alive, and I wasn't sure how to feel about that.

I listened closely. There was a dull roar of wind in the distance, the flourish of a million leaves. But I didn't hear the countdown. *She will fall in one day.* Where was it?

Had something happened to Krista? Had she fallen already? Was it all over?

Images of her deadly plummet rocketed through my brain — her tumbling backwards into a black abyss, an open-mouth scream ratcheting her face, her falling, falling, falling out of my reach. *All my fault.*

A swirl of movement caught my eye and I looked up. There they were, perched on the guardrail only a few feet away. Six silent crows.

"Say it," I said.

Their six glossy heads twitched left and right. But they didn't caw. Didn't say a word.

"Say it: *She will fall in one day.*"

They didn't seem to care that I was there. They weren't scared of me.

I banged my fist against the rusty grated walkway. "She will fall in one day. Say it!" The metal was still echoing from my punch: *channnnnnngggg*. I noticed the thick layer of socks encasing my hands and wished Gray was there so we could laugh.

"So is that it then?"

The nearest crow twitched its head to look at me. The others kept their attention out towards the woods.

"You're not talking to me? You bring me all this way, and I don't find Krista, and then you leave me up here all by myself?"

Two of the crows took a few steps away along the rail.

I was getting louder, angrier. "I've lost everything, you know." I thumped a socked hand against my chest. "I don't even have *me* anymore." The one crow was still watching me. I jabbed a socked hand at it. "I didn't find Krista. We never found Jocelyn. Gray hates me. I'm made up of lies. What was it for?" I was yelling now. "Tell me! What was it for?"

The closest crow lifted its wings and gained a bit of air and flew-hopped a few feet down the rail to join its buddies.

I jabbed the air again. "Joan of Arc heard a voice that was supposed to help her win a war." My heart was constricting. "But in a war there are two sides, aren't there? Innocent people *die* in wars." In a moment my heart was going to burst. "And all those other prophets and messiahs — the good ones, the selfless and noble ones — they didn't make the world a better place, did they?" My railing voice echoed off empty treetops. The crows ignored it. "You sent me out here for nothing." I pounded the rail and it *channngged* and still the crows didn't care. "*Save her, save us all?* Who has ever ever SAVED THE WORLD?!"

"Nineteen hours."

"What?!" I yelled at nobody.

Nineteen hours.

There it was. Whispering in my ear.

I torqued myself around to look behind me. Of course nothing was there.

HURRY.

This time not a voice, but written on the water tank in tall all-cap letters.

HURRY.

The crow had given me another countdown: *Nineteen hours.*

It was morning, so mathematically speaking, nineteen hours would arrive not long after midnight. Which would make it end the next day. *Tomorrow.* The day of Krista's fall.

HURRY.

I put my hands against the rail — the socks kept me from getting a proper grip, but I was able to pull myself to standing. In the crisp morning light, I could see for miles. There was the dirt road I'd run, and the menacing forest spreading all the way to the horizon. I craned to see in the other direction. The view was blocked by the fat belly of the tank.

The walkway was narrow, built to protect its workers with only one thin rail. I leaned against the tank and clutched my sock-covered hands to its rusted surface. The crows eyed me, but didn't move as I inched my way along until I could see the other side. The water tower was perched on a hill. At the bottom of the hill, maybe half a mile away through the woods at the end of a runway-like clearing, was a small town.

A town.

The closest crow flared its wings and angled itself so it could keep a side-eye on me.

All this time, I had been a short sprint from safety.

In the not-too-far distance, a ways off from the town but closer to me, there was a circular clearing. A bull's-eye within green. Inside the circle stood a small cabin. Shaded front porch, tendrils of smoke drifting out of the chimney, doors and windows closed against the cool invading air. It looked idyllic and innocent. Like a little kid drawing of a home.

The stretch between me and the cabin was short enough that I could see the stacked logs, the dark green paint on the trim, and a couple of sculptures on the perimeter that were made out of balancing rocks.

Dusty.

I *had* walked in a loopy circle.

I searched the clearing for Gray's tent — its comforting, exhilarating blue. But the tent had been set up in a part of the clearing that wasn't visible from up there.

I had to get to him. Had to face what I had done.

One of the crows gave an abrupt caw. *HURRY.*

I started and pulled the layers of socks off my hands. I fished around in my hair behind my left ear. It was tangled so tightly that I had to rip the strands that were holding it in place. *A spring from a pen.* The present the crow had given me near Jocelyn's house. When the small coil was free, I teased off my broken wisps of hair and rubbed it clean against my jeans until it was as shiny as it would ever be.

"Thank you," I said as I extended the old spring towards the nearest crow on the rail.

The crow considered my offer — profile-stare, beak high — but didn't come over to get it. I left my gift anyway, balancing it on top of the rail and making sure it was steady.

By the time I started climbing down the ladder, the crows still hadn't moved to pick it up. By the time I got all the way down to the ground, all six crows were gone.

IT WASN'T *"HURRY"* ON the side of the water tank. The rest of the letters scrolled into view as I climbed off the tower. It was BETTHURRY — the name of the town.

Breaking news — Betthurry, site of unidentified human remains.

Except not unidentified anymore. A law student. Once missing, but now found.

I was as hobbled as an old woman, my muscles atrophied from cold and fatigue. I urged my body on, cutting into the woods, aiming for Dusty's house.

Even though I had no idea what I was going to say to Gray, I couldn't wait to get to him. *I was wrong. I made a mistake. I want to help. I want to do the right thing. Tell me what it is and I will be there for you.* Couldn't wait to see his face again, even if it was torqued with justifiable anger.

"Gray!" My voice ricocheted off bark and stone. He had looked for me the night before. Maybe if he heard me calling now, he would come. "Gray!"

It should've been ten minutes, fifteen at most, to get to Dusty's. But I walked much longer than that. Too long. I kept calling his name, even as I collapsed on a rock and heaved with frustrated breath.

I didn't hear his approach, but felt his light arm wrap around my shoulder.

It was like a pin in a balloon. "Where's Gray?" I said even before I looked up.

"He is gone."

Of course Gray would've left. Of course he had to get on with his life.

"He called his friends," Dusty said in a gentle voice. "They came for him."

I imagined Lily and Walter jumping out of their car and hugging him. Forgiving him. I imagined Gray's happiness at being with the right people. Relief filled me to know he was safe.

Dusty looped his arm under mine and lifted me up. I didn't feel like an old woman anymore, but like a baby.

"Did they find Jocelyn?" I said.

Dusty shook his head. "They are still looking for the young lady. Now they're looking for you too."

"They're looking for me?" Tears sprang to my eyes. *Looking for me was a waste of their time.*

Dusty tugged at my arm and I took my own weight and followed him. He led the way through the woods in silence, this time without stopping to admire the wilderness. It wasn't long before we arrived at the cabin. He settled me on the couch and left the living room. Down the hall, there was a hard rush of water.

I knew I had to contact my parents, or someone who could get me to them. I rooted inside my backpack and found my charger, then pulled out Krista's phone and plugged it into the same outlet Gray had used the night before.

I kept my eyes riveted to the black screen and the empty battery icon. The phone was sluggish — not just dead, but probably damp and half-frozen like me.

It still hadn't powered on by the time Dusty tapped my shoulder a few minutes later. "You are shivering," he said, and it woke me to the fact. I could hear the insistent chatter of my teeth.

"Come." He grabbed my bag for me and led me to the bathroom and showed me the bathtub full of steaming water. I stared at it like it was an alien. He stood my backpack on the floor, then stepped out and closed the door between us. For the first time I noticed my own smell. Musky sweat and musty dust on dirty clothes. I'd never gone so long without washing.

I stripped off my clothes and Walter's life-saving long underwear. Gray's holstered knife was still fastened to my arm, and it surprised me again. A weapon I had no need for. I unclipped the holster and stuffed it into my bag. Then I stepped into the bath.

The hot water melted me. It felt so good to be nestled in its warmth. I picked up the nugget of soap from the ledge and scrubbed it through my hair and down my body. It made me long for Gray and the touch I'd never known before him.

No one would touch me like that again. And if it wasn't him, I didn't want it.

I scrubbed the soap along my arm, underneath it, then over my shoulder and down to my wrist. Black marks laced the inside of my arm like medical stitches.

I saw her clearly as she wrote the letters. Dell in the courtyard of her school, lifting my hand, clicking her pen, the slight tickle as she left the address for her party on my skin. Only a few words were still legible: the date and time. Dell's party was tonight.

I washed the pen marks off and pulled myself out of the tub. At least I had fresh underwear. One of my sweatshirts was clean and still smelled like store. I ran my fingers through the knots in my wet hair. I was grateful there was no mirror to show me my ravaged self.

WHEN I LEFT THE bathroom, I found Dusty sitting in his chair in front of the fire, sieving a small collection of pebbles from one hand to the other. He looked up when I walked out and pointed to a steaming bowl filled with broth, cubed potatoes, and forest greens set on the kitchen counter by Krista's phone. "Please, my lady. You need to eat." It was the same bowl and spoon he'd used when he'd welcomed us two nights ago. A whole identity ago.

"Thank you." But it was hard to eat. Over-hunger, exhaustion, and shame had messed with my system. I had to contact my parents, and that made me nervous too. They would have to drive all the way up north, take me home, and fit me back inside my life.

I tapped into Krista's phone. It was alive now, ready to let me in. *9393.*

My mother had an Ittch account. I could message her there.

I logged into my account, the one Krista had hacked to lure Boyd. Except now there wasn't just the one follower — me — there were thousands of followers. I remembered my mom's social media pleas for my return, how only a few hours after she'd posted, a boggling amount of people had jumped on board.

I didn't have time to consider my sketchy fame. Mostly I didn't care.

I clicked into the *Search Accounts* bar. But instead of searching for my mom, my fingers typed Gray's name. His grid came up: photos of him and his friends, an electric guitar, a fat pug. I zoomed in on one of the shots. Zoomed close on his face. The angles I thought I knew so well. The eyes I'd hoped would keep looking at me.

I hesitated at the message button. What if I just said hello? Let him know I was okay? Told him not to waste any time searching for me?

My fingers hovered over his message box. I began to type: *I'm safe. I'm sorry —*

A veil of tears dropped in so thick I couldn't see anymore. I stopped writing. But my hands were shaking. By mistake I pressed send.

Before I could register any regret, I noticed there was a new message in my inbox. From Boyd. Dated April 15. Three days ago.

Hey. R u still looking for K?

I remembered something about her text.

K used to do that. She had her own code for it.

The eye = I. Like... Imma do this, I wanna go there, whatever.

The finger I don't get. Pointing at what?

The scissors = K said it was like a peace sign but bad.
Like shred the peace, make trouble.

The stars should be where she is or what she's doing.
But sorry don't get it.

It's bad out there. Hope ur ok.

There was a moment of *aw*. Aw, Boyd was checking in on me. Aw, Boyd cared that I was okay. Aw, Boyd thought I had what it took to solve Krista's infuriating code.

But I also couldn't help wondering — was this actually the key to Krista's message?

Only you: Only Boyd can find me. Single eye: *I am* ... Pointing finger: *somewhere* ... Scissors: *making trouble* ... Stars: *something/ somewhere* ...

Her other message was still in my inbox — the one she'd sent to Boyd from my account: Owl emoji, *Fri at 2.*

Except I had never bothered to look for Krista at City Hall on Friday at two, had I? Even when she might've been right there in front of me. *A girl, medium height, dark blond hair, standing near the pedestrian corridor that ran between the City Hall towers, turned my way, possibly looking at me.* A person with a vested interest in stopping me from finding her.

Krista wanted Boyd to find her. She wanted him to chase after her. To prove his undying love.

Krista wouldn't think twice about knocking me out on a back street and stealing my money — not for herself, but to stop me from interfering with her plans. So she could keep planting her riddles and puzzles. So she could achieve her perfect ending.

But I'd been too busy impersonating Messenger 93. Following Gray. *Falling for him.*

Lying to him.

I clicked into Krista's Ittch. There were no new posts in her feed. She was obviously still gone. Still destined to fall, I supposed. In fewer than *nineteen hours*.

A voice floated in. *Seventeen hours.*

And then another voice, or thought, or realization. *Dell was hosting a party tonight.* A party could go late, into the beginning of a new day. Dell was the last person to be seen with Krista.

But I wasn't going to search for Krista anymore. I didn't want to save her. I didn't want to save anyone. As Vivvie would say, *I didn't have the skills.*

Still, something made me click over to Dell's Ittch account. I noticed right away that her follower-count had doubled since the night when Remy had shown it to me. But Dell hadn't added any recent glamor shots or school-taunting thumbs-down posts. The latest images on her grid were black boxes with red-lettered invitations to The Crusade.

The Crusade? That seemed a bit excessive for a beauty product promo party.

Each invite counted down the days. *3 days to The Crusade.*
2 days to The Crusade. 1 day to The Crusade. Tonight! Inviting everyone to *Make a Difference!* She shared the address I'd just washed
from my skin. She shared the password. *Sweet-sweet.* So much for
exclusive entry.

The last actual photo in her stream was from five days ago,
right before the invitation countdowns began. It was a close-up of
two intertwined hands. Soft white fingers with slick manicures.
Baby's first ink, it read underneath.

Both wrists had small tattoos on them. One had a subtle red
rash around it — freshly done. It caught my attention because it
was a black silhouette of a bird. Just like the tattoo on that influ-
encer's ankle in the Ittch photo, the one the waitress in the diner
had noticed when I was trolling Krista's most-liked list. It was
just like the bird silhouette sketched on the paper that was taped
to Krista's locker. The scrap that was now in the pocket of my
raincoat. That I'd stolen as a possible clue.

The tattoo on the other wrist in the photo was ... two tiny
paired stars.

I went back to Dell's feed. And then I saw them everywhere. Star
emojis in her bio, photos of her wearing star earrings or star
pins. Much farther down, a close-up of her face with star-shaped
makeup around one of her eyes.

I remembered Remy telling me about the photo Krista had
taken of Dell in front of our school: *That post went viral. It sent Dell
to a whole new level. Everyone knows her now.*

And Dell in the courtyard after that, saying: *The response to
that post was lit. I owe that girl big-time.*

Dell was the biggest star in our world. Her over-the-top signa-
ture was stars. Krista — Tragically Missing Teen — was making her

an even bigger star. And all of it was happening right out in the open.

The finger emoji wasn't pointing up. It was scratching an: *Ittch*.

Eye, finger, scissors, stars: *I'm on Ittch making trouble with Dell. Only you, Boyd, can save me.*

Krista must have assumed that it would get out that she'd taken that shot of Dell in front of our school. That Boyd would wonder if Krista had gone off with Dell. She assumed he would investigate. Then later, when he didn't solve that riddle, she assumed he would solve the next one — the owl at City Hall — and he would find her there. Krista must've imagined that Boyd would bring her home, both of them aglow with everlasting love, reunited forever and always.

She will fall.

Seventeen hours.

Is it so terrible that I wanted to see it for myself?

I rifled in my backpack for the bus ticket Lily had given me. It was still valid. I turned to Dusty. "My parents aren't answering." One more lie. "I have to get home on my own."

He was still sieving pebbles from hand to hand. "Yes."

"I know it's far, but if you could take me to the depot at Earl's, I can take the bus to the city, and from there I can get back to my family."

He opened his hands over the table and released the cluster of pebbles onto it. "I will take you where you need to go, my lady."

DUSTY DROVE ME THROUGH the countryside, along roads that Gray and I had skirted, and eventually along the highway that had brought the trucker. We didn't talk, but settled into our different silences and watched the way ahead as it came at us and then disappeared into the past.

It didn't take long before we arrived at the traveler's intersection with its kayak shop and gas stations and Earl's Diner. Dusty pulled his car into the lot and stopped.

I grabbed my bag, but turned to him before I got out. "You saved my life. Thank you."

He said, "If a person is going to be, they will be." A peaceful smile spread across his face. "It's magic, you see?"

I let his smile infuse me. "I see."

"It's *magic*, you hear me?"

"It's magic," I said. "I hear you." And we sat there and smiled at each other for a long time, and I let it fill me up.

2

AS THE BUS TRUNDLED back to the city, I slept on and off. The landscape changed in reverse from when I left — wilderness to suburban to city. The light crested then waned as day came and went, as it turned into evening, and then into night.

As we entered the city, I readied myself. Took stock of all the things I'd collected since I'd started. The black feather that had appeared on my floor on the first night. The photo of Krista kissing my face. Her phone. Her doodle of an M-shaped black bird. The single white sequin from Vivvie's vest. Vivvie's origami power-girl. The pebble from Dusty. And three things that belonged to Gray — the Jocelyn poster, the blank plastic mask, and his knife.

I had to face it: I'd stolen most of them. Then I had justified stealing them.

I checked to make sure no one was watching me — the three people nearby were all fast asleep — and strapped the knife back around my forearm. Until I could get it to Gray — maybe through Lily — it would stay with me. Not as a weapon, but as a reminder.

By the time the bus arrived downtown, it was late. Ticking close to eleven.

I got off at the depot, hiding my face inside my coat hood like I'd done on the first couple of days. Just a little while longer, I thought, and this game would be over.

I searched Krista's GPS for a route to Dell's party. It was kind of far from the city center, on the west end, and took a few transfers. As I traveled the route, my fingers played nervously with the browser on her phone. Pretty soon I was logging into my Ittch.

The inbox showed 5 messages. All from Gray.

Some wishes do come true.

I'd sent him my lame, unfinished apology — *I'm safe. I'm sorry* — and he had answered five times:

Where are you?

They're looking for you.

You gotta let them know where you are.

And most amazing of all: *We got a trace on Jocelyn's phone. Vivvie and the girls did it. Convinced those cops who picked them up to look into it.*

Then one last message: *I thought you should know.*

I wrote him back:

Best news ever!

Thanks for telling me!

Then I wrote: *Back in the city. Going home soon. Have one more thing to do.*

Then: *One last Crusade* :)

By the time the bus pulled up to the last stop, I still hadn't heard back from him. It was okay though. He'd done enough already.

IT WAS A SKETCHY part of town, mostly old warehouses and industrial buildings, made sketchier by the nighttime dark. There was nobody wandering the street, no lineup down the block for any party, no sign out front. The moon scrolled onto the horizon. It looked gigantic, like it always does when it's full and low. It tagged the far-off city landmarks like a bruised eye.

I wondered if it was possible that I was too late, that the party had ended already. I stood under the one streetlamp and checked the numbers on the industrial doors. Someone had spray-painted a black-and-white skull on one of them. I took a breath and knocked on it.

No one came. I tried the handle. It was locked. I banged harder, this time with both hands. I banged again and again. I was about to give up when I heard the *thunk* of the bolt unlatching on the other side. The door pushed open against me.

A bulky, bearded guy in black clothes stood on the other side. "Sorry, man, thought it was over down here." He sounded out of breath. "You here for the Crusade? For that girl?"

"That girl?"

"The missing one."

Krista. My heart rate accelerated. *This was about Krista.*

"Yes," I said. "I'm here for her."

The doorman looked me over. "You got the password?"

Dell had put the password in plain sight on her Ittch. I could still hear her baby-voice as she was writing the invite on my arm. "Sweet-sweet," I said to the doorman.

"Cool." He stepped aside so I could go in.

HE LED ME UP three warehouse-flights of stairs, the extra-long kind. After what I'd been through over the last week, it was easy to climb. Thumping techno bass accompanied us up the last flight. It sounded like a party — not a Crusade for a missing girl. I remembered Dell trying to sell me on some beauty product. *Radiant Beam will make your skin super-soft and bright!* Dell was going to save us all by making us more beautiful.

The bouncer presented the only door on the top floor. The music was so loud I couldn't hear what he said. I smiled and watched him leave, then secured the hood of my raincoat over my head — a stealth approach — and walked in.

The room was one of those glamorized warehouse spaces — concrete surfaces dressed up with chandeliers and gold velvet, glitter-balls punching tiny gleaming holes across everything, shabby velvet chairs grouped together.

Even though it was late, there were still a lot of people, all ages but mostly young. It was dark and the music was lit and some kids were dancing — messy-dancing, leaning on each other, lolling heads. Drunk or high. Most were hanging out in groups, talking, laughing.

There were a few people walking around in costumes: black lace half-masks, black bodysuits, black tights, black lace gloves. Donation boxes were looped around their necks. Collecting funds for Krista, I supposed. *That missing girl.*

Maybe this was Krista's ultimate game. Get someone famous to throw her a party. Force people to show up by the hundreds to bow to her. Guilt them into raising money for her cause.

Through the thumping chaos, I spotted my old gang — Anusha, L.J., Hattie. They were sitting cross-legged on the ground, off to

one side. Like everyone else, they looked like they were at a party —
into each other, heads keeping time to the beat. The view cleared
a bit, and then I saw Boyd and Remy sitting with them too.

I don't know why I hadn't expected them all to be there. If this
was a party for Krista, obviously they would have to show up. No
more cryptic clues for Boyd to miss or mess up. *Krista was forcing
him to ride in like a shining knight.*

Anusha said something that made them all burst out laughing.
Hattie and L.J. covered their mouths like it was scandalous. Remy
grabbed Boyd's knee. He threaded his fingers with hers. It was
the briefest connection, and then their hands split apart.

It was strange not to feel that old heart-race when I looked at
Boyd. I remembered Anusha saying once that the best part of
breaking up was that you get to fall in love again.

Fall in love.

Fall could mean so many things.

Something you could do over and over. Something you could
pick yourself up from.

Gray rushed my mind, but I blinked him out. I had to stay
focused.

I scanned the room again. There was no obvious place for a
physical fall. At least not a deadly one. A couple of the donation
box people strolled by. I noticed long black feathers flaring off
their black, body-suited arms and backs. More feathers and a
partial beak on their half-masks.

Were they supposed to be *crows*?

One of them stepped too close to me and I whirled away, right
into a kid on the dance floor. He caught my arm and held me steady.
He was sweating, his pupils were dilated. "You okay?" he said.

I recognized him from school and clutched my hood to my

face. "What time is it?"

His phone was in his hand and he showed me the screen. *11:54*

Today was ending in six minutes. In six minutes, *tomorrow* would begin.

Where was Krista?

But it wasn't Krista who I found next. It was another strange and familiar person. Her startled expression stared out from a giant enlarged photo. *Crusade of Love, Please Help, Donations Welcome.* She was me.

The photo had been shamelessly enhanced. My two different eye colors had been intensified. Ultra-fine, super-long lashes curled around them. My hair was highlighted and golden. My skin flawless. Rose-dabbed lips and cheeks.

I couldn't remember the photo ever having been taken. But then I noticed the collar of my raincoat — the one I'd worn every day that week — and the V of my sweatshirt — the one I'd been wearing the day I met Dell. Dell studying my face in the court-yard of her school. *We'll do a before-and-after.* Pulling out her phone and snapping a picture. *Hey, we can make you famous!* Her dazzling smile.

The poster of me was propped beside a group of standing mon-itors. The screens were all playing the same film. People from my school being interviewed, their voices muted, but subtitles popping across the bottom. Quick-cut footage of different scenes.

A random girl holding a crumpled piece of paper close to the lens, pulling it tight to make up for the creases. The camera zoomed in on my storyboard with stick-figure Superstar, Goddess, and Genius. The panel I'd rejected in the caf. Two speech-bubbles from Superstar's mouth: *Messenger 93! Help me, Messenger 93!*

A random guy in our school, showing a scrap of paper to the

camera, with *Messenger 93* scrawled across it in my handwriting.
I had doodled bird silhouettes and *Messenger 93* on looseleaf
during Ms. Stathakis's History class. He turned the scrap over
and showed the other side: *We have to talk. It's important.* The note
I'd thrown at Anusha in English class. That I'd forgotten to sign.
That she'd crumpled up and tossed.

My brother, Trevor, holding the Infinity Girl storyboard I'd
scribbled outside Clio's house. I must've dropped it while I was
fumbling with Krista's phone. Clio must've found it and given
it to him. The camera zoomed in on the stick-figure crow on
Infinity Girl's shoulder. The speech-bubble: *Messenger 93, face
what most frightens you.*

Remy, standing in Emmett Park, talking to an off-camera interviewer. Subtitles popped in underneath: *She said this crow arrived
from another planet and told her to find Krista. She said the crow told
her that saving Krista would save everyone.*

A close-up of Trevor talking to the interviewer: *She has this
thing for crows.*

One of the guys from Math Lab: *We had no idea. She didn't seem
like that kind of person.*

Mrs. Fariah, my Computer Science teacher: *She's quite the
diligent student. But I did happen upon her researching Joan of Arc.
I imagine that speaks to a certain mind-set.*

Anusha, L.J., and Hattie crammed together on one chair.
Anusha was talking: *She said she was looking for Krista. We were
pretty surprised.*

Remy: *She said Krista's baby brother told her that he could see the
crow too. You know what they say about babies, right? Like, they can
see stuff the rest of us can't.*

Dell: *I was the last person to see her. I remember every single thing* about that day. I had no idea it would be the beginning of all this. When she went missing I just knew I had to help. That's how the Crusade started.

Remy: *I tried to help her, but she didn't want help. I guess she had to do it by herself.*

Random guy holding my *We have to talk* note. His subtitles underneath: *She's telling us we've lost our ability to, like, communicate, right? We have to talk to each other. Connection is really important.*

Dell: *She said a lot of deep stuff. Like how you can love and not even know it. Like if you don't really see someone, it's not even love.*

L.J.: *Yeah, I believe her. Oh my god, we all think in different ways, don't we? And we need that right now. It's, you know* ... She stared off-screen as she chose her next words. Her lips started moving again and new subtitles popped in: *Beautiful thinking. Being brave. That's what's going to save us.*

Remy: *She said the crow called her Messenger 93.*

Random Girl: *I think she's Messenger 93.*

Random Guy: *She's totally Messenger 93.*

Dell smiling her dazzling smile: *Maybe she's my little messenger.*

The screen cut to black with white titles: *Messenger 93.*

Underneath, subtitles popped in for Dell's voiceover: *We're donating every cent towards her search. Thanks to you, we'll be able to send more helicopters and units up north.* Cross-fade to Dell on her fuzzy couch: *We're going to bring her home.* She gave a discreet smile: *Hopefully she'll have Krista with her.*

The screen went black then looped back to the opening titles: *Crusade of Love.*

My mind numbed out. Techno thumped in my ears like my own amplified heartbeat.

You can't be a hero without someone to save.

THURSDAY, APRIL 19

THE FALL

1

"SHE FALLS TODAY!" A voice reverberated through speakers. It jolted me back into the room. I checked through the crowd and found a stage. Barbie-Boy was on it, talking into a microphone.

Had he actually said, *She falls today*? I couldn't tell anymore.

"It's midnight, everyone!" He looked different than I remembered. Not a bored kid playing with his friends, but bold and sharp. Evangelical. "Thanks for coming out to *Crusade of Love*. We raised a ton of money tonight!" He raised his fist and the crowd cheered.

I wanted to feel proud. Excited. Here was the attention I'd been waiting for. *They'd made a film for me. They'd raised money. For more helicopters and units.* I mattered to them.

Instead I felt sick. Anger simmered underneath it deep, deep down.

Jocelyn was still missing. She'd been missing for —

I reached into my backpack and pulled out the poster Gray had made for her. I smoothed the board as flat as I could. Smoothed her face, her gentle, hopeful expression. Smoothed Gray's writing, the blue marker-scrawl haloing her head: *Have you seen Jocelyn? Missing for 27 days*. I found my pen and scratched out the 27 and wrote 33 above it. *Jocelyn. Missing for 33 days*.

"Dell wants to thank you for all your donations!" Barbie-Boy pointed across the room. I followed the direction of his hand until I found Dell at the donation desk. Paper-white hair, gleaming teeth, radiant skin. She waved and gave a dazzling smile, and the crowd cheered her. She was wearing a white silk blouse and white silk wide-leg pants. The fabric rippled around her body as she waved. It made her look like an iridescent sea creature.

I pulled Gray's mask out of my bag. It was slightly crushed from all the traveling. I snapped it over my face. *For the invisible girls who disappear off our streets every day. If they're nobody, I'm nobody.* One of many reasons Gray had wanted to wear a mask that day.

I held the Jocelyn poster above my head and channeled Gray. "Where's Jocelyn? Help us find Jocelyn!" I shouted through the mask, pushing my way past partiers, dancers, Donation-Box Crow People.

No one paid attention. Or if they did, they only glanced at me. Up/down. Disdain. Boredom. They glanced away. So absorbed with whatever else they were doing/thinking.

I jabbed the Jocelyn poster in the air above me. "Help us find Jocelyn!"

Anusha, L.J., Hattie, along with a bunch of other kids, were lined up at the coat-check, getting ready to leave. Not noticing.

I shouted louder through the mask. "Where is Jocelyn? Missing for thirty-three days!"

Remy and Boyd were in a dark corner, taking turns whispering into each other's ears.

I called out to the whole room. "You want a missing girl? Help find Jocelyn!"

My body jerked suddenly around. I looked down. A hand was gripping my wrist. I aimed my masked eyes along the arm —

until I got to her tightly grinning face. Dell. "What are you doing?" she said.

I aimed the Jocelyn poster between us. Showed it to her. "This girl is actually missing."

"I'm sorry," Dell said, babying-up her voice. "This isn't for her."

"You have all this money, Dell. Why don't you spread it around?"

She stared at Jocelyn's photocopied face. "I don't even know her."

"*You don't even know her*? You don't know Messenger 93. And trust me — you don't know Krista." I shook the poster at her. "Or would you rather spend your time posing in front of schools with your thumb down?"

"I deleted all those posts." Dell did look ashamed. "We can't save everyone!"

I didn't know what to do next. It was getting hot under the mask. I could hardly breathe.

Because what was the difference between me and Dell? Was I trying to help Jocelyn and save Krista, or was I riding some mission to fake-glory?

I remembered Gray saying how we were everyone — ourselves, each other, the universe. So who was supposed to figure out how to fit us all together?

I said, "Where are you hiding her?"

Dell said, "I think you should leave."

I sharpened my voice. "Where is Krista?"

Dell's face crumpled like I'd hit her. "We're doing the best we can."

I pulled down the mask. I didn't care anymore if she knew who I was. The seconds were counting down. "I need to find Krista *now*!"

Dell looked right at my real face. She didn't register who I was. Because the girl in front of her didn't bear any resemblance to the one she'd masked with enhancements and filters. The Messenger 93 that Dell had created.

"This was going to be for Krista," she said. "Her big reveal. It would've been *epic*." She waved her hand, implicating everything — dancers, bystanders, the gold velvet, the glitter balls.

I owe that girl big-time. Going viral. More followers. More attention. More love.

Dell said, "But Krista couldn't take the competition."

A small commotion started up behind her. It was Boyd and Remy and one of the Donation-Box Crow People. Boyd stepped between Remy and the Crow. Remy backed away.

"Why do we need so much drama?" Dell asked herself. "It doesn't even stop when we sleep. We dream about some other version of our lives. We fight with people we don't even know. We have annoying problems that are gone when we wake up."

Remy had joined the girls in the coat-check line. Boyd was saying something to the Crow, who approached a side door with a VIP sign taped to it.

Dell said, "Isn't our real-life suffering enough?"

The Crow glanced back at Boyd. Her beaked half-mask was beautiful — made of lace and feathers. She opened the VIP door and stepped through it. Boyd hesitated. He looked back at Remy. Then he turned to the door and went through it too.

"Don't worry." Dell came back into focus. She gave me a truly loving smile. "We're going to save Messenger 93. She's worth more than Krista any day."

On the other side of the coat-check, through the main doors, three uniformed officers walked in. They flanked and blocked the exit and scanned the crowd. A few of the kids noticed and flurried around each other.

It must've come out that I'd stolen Krista's phone. That's how they knew to track me up north. *Helicopters and patrol cars*. It was probably why they were here now: tracking my movements.

There was a flutter of silk as Dell turned and noticed the police too. I hid my face behind the Jocelyn poster and edged away. I did a last check that no one was watching me, then slipped through the VIP door.

THE DOOR DIDN'T OPEN to some inner sanctum like I'd imagined, but led straight outside to a fire escape landing. The rusted metal steps that were anchored to the side of the building reminded me of climbing up the water tower. I looked down between my feet, through the grating. A narrow alley ran between the party warehouse and the warehouse beside it. Only hard pavement at the bottom.

She will fall.

Red velvet cord was wound around the rail that led upwards. Boyd wasn't on the staircase. Neither was the Crow. I climbed up alone. The wind buffeted lightly against the brickwork and swirled into the hood of my coat. It sent shivers down my neck and back. I clung to the velvet cord like it was an umbilical. It took me all the way up to the top landing, which led out onto the roof. The city sparkled far away, beyond the warehouse-infested distance.

There was a large fenced-in patio in the center of the roof, with plush furniture, exotic carpets, potted plants. Sticky, empty glasses and overflowing ashtrays littered the coffee tables. Strings of lights twinkled from the wood-slat walls and along an overhead arbor.

There was another source of light too. White and eerie, like it was coming from a parallel reality. And then I saw what it was. *The moon*. It had orbited into the night sky. It was full and pure in its roundness. A god watching me through its one annoyed, all-seeing eye.

Only you can save her.

There were no VIPs on the roof. No people at all. Just me wandering in the pale and eerie light, the wind gusting in sooty whorls around me.

2

AT FIRST I HEARD it as an indistinct drone. Then I heard them more clearly. Boyd's voice: low, insistent, steady. Krista's voice: high, weepy, on-edge.

"So now you're with that girl?"

"I'm sorry. I can't —"

"No, I know you can't. Because you don't see the big picture. But I see it, Boyd. It's supposed to be you and me —"

"You shouldn't have run off like that, K. Your mom is —"

"My mom is not part of this conversation. My mom is going through her own shit."

"She's really worried, Krista. It's not fair to her —"

"Not fair? You know what's not fair? Is watching your father fucking die of cancer. That's what's not fair. You know what's not fair? Having your boyfriend dump you out of the blue just when you think your life is finally — maybe — okay again."

"Krista, come on — It's time to go home — We can talk about this —"

"I've been waiting for you, Boyd! You know how that looks? Dell must think I'm such a fucking loser. She didn't even *know* me and she's still taking care of me. Because she's a *good* person. She has a *heart*. Not like you, Boyd. Dell can have anyone — she's a *star* — and she chose me. *Me*."

"Wait, Krista — That's not — You never let me — I never get to say the things I want to say!" He stopped. He was staring at me. By accident, I had wandered too close. Drifted around the fencing of the patio, around the brick box of an elevator bulkhead. Drawn to them like the inevitable next tick of a clock.

Krista noticed Boyd shift. She swung around. Her crow mask was pushed up on top of her head. Her eyes were swollen. Tears were streaming down her face.

I didn't know what to do, as surprised that I was there with them as they were to see me. I dropped my backpack and surrendered. The Jocelyn poster fluttered in my left hand like a flag. "Get off the roof, Krista," I said. "You're going to fall —"

But Krista screamed the most crushing scream I've ever heard. There was a split-second where Boyd and I connected. His eyes were glassy with panic.

She will fall.

Then she charged at me.

Literally charged. Crouched over, black-gloved hands clawed out, fresh bird tattoo on her wrist, mouth pried open with rage. Her scream turned into a growl. A growl that came from so deep inside her, it sounded like a storm from the other side of the world.

She was on me before I could stop it. The force of it knocked the Jocelyn poster out of my hand and it spiraled away in the gusting wind, turning end over end like tumbleweed.

Krista and I clasped each other. Reeled together. She stumbled, and then we both went down, me landing hard on my back on the concrete, Krista on top of me. She was growling, digging her nails into my arms, twisting our bodies. The little pointed beak on her half-mask came at my eye. I flinched and rolled us over to one side.

We thrashed and writhed, her coming at me, me trying to get away. Boyd was somewhere in the nighttime air, doing/yelling something.

Krista reared off me and sank into stillness. She was holding a knife. Gray's knife.

She jumped up. She was staring at the knife, marveling at its unexpected arrival.

I jumped up too. My breath turned to ice in my throat.

Krista turned the knife so that light glanced off its blade. She aimed it slowly higher and higher until it was pointed at my neck. I stepped backwards. Boyd was saying her name. "Krista. Krista. Krista. Stop."

She spiraled the knife through the air in front of my face. A choreographed move stolen from some movie bad guy. I was hypnotized by the waving blade. This was the moment I'd been waiting for. The one we'd been counting down to. The part of the infinity loop you can never get out of. I held my breath and inched backwards.

"You came here to kill someone?" Krista said, snarling. Snot and tears were running down her face. I remembered holding her little brother Eddie, and how he had been crying too.

"No," I said. "I came here for you."

"You going to kill me?" She stepped steadily closer.

"You're going to fall tonight, Krista. I came to stop it."

"Did the *crow* tell you that?" Her lip hooked with disdain. "I laughed my ass off when I heard that story."

"Please, Krista. Something bad is going to happen."

She jabbed the knife at me and I jumped back. "Something bad? You don't get to decide my fate."

"I'm just trying to help."

"*Messenger 93*," she said, sneering. "You'll do anything for attention, won't you?"

I surged to get around her, to get away, but she blocked my way with the point of the knife. "This was supposed to be a party for *me*," she said. "*He* was going to be here. I was going to come *back* tonight. It was going to be *amazing*." She jabbed the knife with each emphasized word. "But he showed up with *her*."

Boyd was calling Krista's name, but his voice sounded very far away. Or like it had been slowed down by one of those recording devices.

"And then *you* walked in," Krista said. She wasn't crying anymore. "With your *mask* and your *mission*."

I was cornered now. I'd backed all the way to the roof's perimeter wall, far from the fire escape, the twinkling patio, the potted plants, the city horizon. Far from the moon.

There was a sudden flapping. I didn't dare take my eyes off Krista's knife-holding hand, but the black-feathered wings clipped my peripheral vision. Then more flapping. More wings.

"What the fuck?" Krista squinted through the dark at the commotion behind me, and I took a quick glance over my shoulder.

A dozen crows had arrived. They fluttered over a power line

that came right up to the warehouse. One by one, they landed on its tubular steel rungs.

They were showing me an escape route. If I wanted it. If I dared.

Krista stepped closer and jabbed the knife to indicate the crows. "You think that's funny?"

I climbed up on the ledge. I didn't need to look beyond my feet to know it was a long and deadly drop down. *Three stories.* "No, Krista, I don't think it's funny."

Boyd stepped closer. We were a triangle. He was one point, astonished and helpless. One point was Krista wielding the knife. The last point was me, above them, balancing on a two-foot ledge. Edging to freedom.

Boyd shouted, "You're going to fall!"

But I kept my eyes on Krista as I inched along. Her eyeline ticked from me to the crows, the crows to me. Her brow furrowed. Like she couldn't understand anything that was happening.

The wind buffeted my back. I rocked for balance and Boyd yelled out. But I was okay.

I reached into my pocket. Felt for all the things I'd stolen to find Krista. Her phone, the drawing of the bird, the photo. I pulled them all out. "These are yours." I crouched down slowly and set the scrap of bird on the ledge. I laid her phone on top of it. "You stole my wallet at City Hall, so maybe we're even."

"Fuck you," she said.

"*9393*," I said, tapping her phone. "That was weird."

"How do you know that?" She stared daggers at me. "Did my mom tell you his birthday?"

9/3. September third.

"Your father's birthday," I said. Krista crushed her lips together. "I'm really sorry he's gone," I said. And I meant it.

"You're crazy."

"Remember this?" I showed her the photo. Her kissing my cheek. "Remember when we were friends?"

"I was never your friend."

"Yeah, I know." I let the photo go. The gusting wind swirled in and took it away.

Either one of us could have made the next move, but Dell came running around the elevator bulkhead. She came to an abrupt stop a few feet behind Krista and Boyd and locked eyes on me. "Messenger 93!" she screamed. White silk rippled around her like turbulent water. "I knew it was you!" A bunch of partiers and three Donation-Box Crow People arrived behind Dell. "Messenger 93!" one of them yelled. "It's her! She's here!"

Krista's face went white. She had her feathered back to Dell, to the others. Only I could see the calculations that flipped across her face. *What would they say? How would this look? One of us on the ledge, the other holding a knife.*

Fall from grace. Wasn't that another expression?

Krista *threw* the knife.

She threw it with such force that it clanged against the steel rungs of the power line that I was trying to get to. The crows flapped and screeched. Not human voices inspiring me, but birds speaking to each other in their own language. The knife hit rung after rung, *clang clang clang*ing all the way down. One of the crows lifted into the sky. It spiraled above us.

Krista started to sob. Hunched-over, shoulder-wrenching sobs. "Help!" she cried. "She had a knife!" She jabbed her finger at me. "She was going to kill me!"

Everyone froze, stuck in some sort of gawking amazement.

Boyd had his arms open like he'd lost something important. Remy arrived and joined him. Then Anusha, L.J, and Hattie came around the corner. They were checking me out. Checking with Krista. Krista was sobbing.

The crow circled overhead. I watched it, stuck in the same ring.

Dell went to Krista and put a hand on her wrenching back. She looked up at me. "What is happening?" she cried at me. "What did you do?!"

Everyone turned to me wearing the same hostile expression: *What did you do?!*

I was spiked to my spot. No words to explain myself.

Krista was supposed to fall. I was supposed to be here to stop it. Instead she was safe on the ground, surrounded by people who loved her, and I was balanced on a precarious ledge.

"Someone get the cops!" Dell yelled. "We need help." Barbie-Boy was in the crowd, and he bolted to do Dell's bidding. "Make sure you get all this," she said, stroking Krista's heaving back, to one of her friends who had her phone out and was filming.

The wheeling crow caught a downdraft. Its wings tipped and it spun towards us.

The same wind buffeted against me. I lurched on the narrow ledge. Everyone gasped.

Take the fall for someone. There was always another more difficult meaning.

Somewhere far off, a song started to play, a lo-fi synth riff that sounded vaguely familiar.

3

YOU KNOW WHEN SOMETHING bad happened to you once, and you felt the incision, and it hurt so much until it faded, and then later you remember it for some reason, and the pain repeats in your mind, reflecting and multiplying, over and over — maybe it will never end? Your pain expands times a million. Times infinity.

I closed my eyes.

The end credits of my life scrolled by.

Why had I ever left my house?

I didn't save Krista.

Krista would always hate me.

I didn't find Jocelyn.

Jocelyn was still gone.

I'd betrayed Gray.

Gray would never come back.

Everyone at school would know me now.

They would see that I made everything worse.

That I stole what wasn't mine.

That I chased what wasn't there.

It wasn't enough. It was never going to be enough.

A familiar voice came in through the void. "Don't jump." It was Boyd. "I've got you."

"Don't do it don't do it don't do it." Anusha, L.J., and Hattie.

People running. Calling out. Yelling for order.

"What are you doing?" Krista's voice in the noise. "You said it was going to be *me!*"

She will fall.

I felt the crow land at my feet. Felt it lift its wings against my legs.

The end was so close, I could hear the *shush shush* of its veins.

She will fall.

Even Joan of Arc had to die.

Maybe that's what the crow had meant all along.

I lifted my arms and let go. A falling star.

ONLY YOU CAN SAVE her.

The moment I dropped over the edge was the moment I understood.

She is me.

Right from the beginning, it had always been me.

She will fall in seven days.

You must find her.

Only you can save her.

The crow had never once said her name. I had chosen her.

I didn't want to die. Especially not like this. Random people gaping from the roof of a random warehouse at my spattered body.

My arms wheeled frantically. My legs were weights pulling me down.

The tubular power line was only inches away.

Her skill can be slow motion.

I swung my arms out. One hand caught a steel crossbar. My body jerked to a stop. A g-force so strong, it rattled my every-thing. Something in my arm ripped. There was a terrible howl. A monster coming. Then I realized it was me screaming.

I dangled and lurched in agony, trying to get a hold on the

tower. Pain scorched my shoulder. Threatened to burn off my grasping hand. A dozen crows screamed and fluttered with me. They were sharing my pain. Coaxing me on.

My free hand caught the crossbar. My feet, left first, then right, landed on the rung below. I pulled myself over the steel girder and collapsed. When I took my next breath, it felt like my first one.

The song got louder. I definitely recognized it from somewhere. A repeating refrain. Stuck on the same chords. Not a song, but a siren.

I knew then that it didn't matter that I didn't matter to people like Krista.

I wanted to be here.

You will go where you would not go. You will see what you would not see.

I looked at the sky.

The sky was blue.

The full and perfect moon was watching me.

See her, a voice whispered in my ear. *See her, see us all.*

AFTER

1

THE AMBULANCE BROUGHT ME to a hospital, siren racing, flat white light. They rolled me down hospital hallways, past traumatized people and their people. They transferred me to a bed behind a pink curtain in a large room shared with other patients. Medical staff bustled in and out. They checked me, touched me, murmured to each other. Connected me to monitors and an I.V. My roaring misery was the only sound I heard. I lost track of time. Was it night? Had morning come?

They injected me with drugs, then manipulated my shoulder back into place. Pain scorched and flared through my left arm, into my neck. Excruciating agony. My arm was cradled against my body as they tied a sling around it to keep it in place. Soon the intense twitching in my muscles relaxed, and then the moaning stopped.

The nurses left and the doctor stayed. She eyed me, her clipboard clasped against her chest. I wondered if she used her work as armor too. She asked me some questions in a low voice, all of which made me want to laugh. By then, I was delirious. But I understood she was checking to see if I was suicidal.

"It was an accident," I told her. "I didn't jump," I said. "I *fell*."

She nodded and murmured, "All right, thank you." She jotted notes.

"I swear," I said. "I was just trying to help."

She asked if I'd be willing to see a therapist for some follow-up assessments, and I agreed in a too-sunny way. I wanted her to leave — I was epically tired. But, really, how bad would it be? Maybe a mind-expert would have some answers, some enlightening perspective. The doctor smiled, patted my hand, hugged her clipboard to her chest again, and slipped away through the pink curtains.

I was ready to fall into the deepest sleep, but then my parents came in. And that was catastrophic. In an instant, every tear I'd ever smothered or hid or regretted surged to the surface.

My dad took my hand and squeezed it. My mom hovered over my beaten body. They stared at me with such wide eyes it was as if they were trying to pull me inside.

How had I forgotten them? My mother and her sweet-serious face. My father and his dorky dad grin. The comfort and security they gave me. Their tentative questions meant to prod me out of the dark. I had completely erased them. *Gone for seven days.*

I dumped my head in my mother's chest as the last week rushed back. All the jolting forces that I didn't want to remember: *alone at night, humiliated at school, getting punched on a back street, not knowing what to do, belt being loosened, dirty jeans coming down, thumb in my mouth, shivering with cold, aching with fatigue, running from terrors, dangling from a roof, preparing to die.* And all the things I never wanted to forget: *Lily and Walter, Vivvie and her friends, finding Infinity Girl again and again, the stars and the moon, so many black crows, a feather tattoo, his face close to mine, his eyes, his name, Gray.*

My parents didn't say a word, just held me as everything overfilled me and spilled.

One anguished wail escaped my mom, only once, but she caught herself.

"I'm sorry," I said to them when I was able to speak.

"It's funny," my mom said, dabbing a tear that was caught on the brim of her nose, "every time it seemed like we'd lost track of you, a little light would shine from somewhere. You'd used the credit card to buy dinner the first night. The next day, you bought some clothes and supplies at that drugstore. The day after that, Clio found your phone, so then we knew to track Krista's phone. We didn't know exactly where you were up north, but we could see that you were moving around. You were always just out of reach." She stroked my face. "But you were always there."

Little lights, I repeated in my mind. I had seen them too.

"They brought that Krista girl in," my dad said. "She's pretty messed up." He squeezed my hand. "Did you actually find her?"

I tried not to laugh. "No, Dad. She did that all by herself."

"Huh," he said like it was a whole essay on runaway girls.

It got quiet again, and then my mom said, "Your friends are here."

"What friends?" I said.

"Boyd, the girls," my mom said like of course it was them. "They're not pushing to come in, but they say they want to see you when you're ready."

But I wasn't ready. I remembered Anusha saying to me in the field outside our school, *Everything breaks*. And she was right. You have to be careful with the pieces.

"And your new friend too," my mom went on, gently holding my hand. "The one who told us that you'd come back to the city, that you were at that party." She took in a breath and held her hand to her throat. "I don't know if I was supposed to tell you that."

I guess it could've been seen as a betrayal. Him sharing the private messages I'd sent him. *Back in the city. Have one more thing to do. One last Crusade.*

Saving me from myself.

"Do you mean Gray?" I said. I could hardly say his name. "Is he here?" It didn't seem possible.

"He was helping us look for you. We had no idea you were on the roof — That you were —" Mom let out another involuntary wail. She put a hand over her mouth to stop it.

"No, Mom. I didn't — I would never —" It was my turn to stroke her arm. "I fell. It was an accident. I'm okay."

She took in a breath of air and held it and nodded at me.

"I'd like to see him," I said.

2

THE PINK COTTON CURTAINS they'd pulled around my bed popped and flailed. Hands rooting for the split. And then Gray stepped through. He stood on that one spot, just inside, not too close, clutching his black hoodie in front of his body, staring at the ground. I took him in, every curve of his face, every shift of its shape and color.

"Gray —" My throat jammed against another push of tears.

"You ran away." He wouldn't look at me. "You screwed up — and I got mad — and you ran away."

"I know. I should've taken your anger." I could barely get the words out. "I'm so sorry."

He closed his mouth in an uncertain line.

I said, "Did they find Jocelyn?"

"I don't want to tell you about her."

"I want to help, Gray. Please let me help."

"So, *help*, yes. You should help. Just not me. Not us."

My face was trembling so much, I had to use my hand to hold it in place. "I understand."

He looked at me for the first time. "You and that girl you were chasing?" The light in his eyes was fierce. "You're lucky to have everything you have."

"I know."

"You get to make choices."

"Yes."

"Jocelyn — girls like her — they have to fight."

"I know that now." I wiped a pool of wet from my chin.

"Everything she's done, everything she's still going to do, that's *her* life, *her* doing. You don't get to feel good about it."

"Wait —" I corralled my tears. Saved them for later. "Does that mean they found her?"

His breath was shaky. He spoke quickly. "The trace on her phone — Vivvie and the girls — They wouldn't leave the station until —" His voice broke and he took a long time to collect himself. I waited, not daring to hope. "They found her. Near Deerhead."

I wanted to laugh the way we'd laughed before he knew who I was.

But Gray kept his expression in check. "Her family is with her. She's safe."

"She went undercover, didn't she? Trying to find her dad's murderer." I couldn't stop filling in the blanks. "She found him. The guy in the blue Chevy?"

Gray was nodding. A quick tremor. A million times yes. But he caught himself and said with conviction, "It's not my place to talk about it. Jocelyn's story is her own to tell."

My heart spun. "You're right."

"Let Jocelyn tell it. Please —" He was pleading with both of us. "Listen to her."

There are so many things we don't understand until it's too late.

Gray loosened his grip on the hoodie. "We're on our way up there right now — Lily, Walter, my parents." For the first time, I could feel his hope. It was on the other side — where I wasn't allowed.

"You shouldn't have to be here for me," I said, my voice weak.

"It was on the way." He almost-smiled. "I'm glad you're okay."

"I'm okay."

It was quiet between us for a few moments. I expected him to walk out, but he shifted his weight, checked his boots. Then he locked eyes on me again and said, "The Messenger 93 stuff? Was that just to mess with my head?"

"No!"

"You actually believe it?"

I didn't want to rush an answer. But also, the answer was flickering around me like a trapped bird. "Something happened this week that I can't explain. The messages showed me things I never would've known. Things I'm still trying to understand. Were they real crows with real messages? Or was it all in my head — making up crows so I would help myself? I don't know ,... But it felt so … It feels so … *true*."

Gray's voice, his expression, mellowed. "I get it. Sometimes things happen that I can't explain." His face brightened slowly. "Or something will work out when it shouldn't. I get that too.

Synchronicity. Signs. All that —" He was measuring something invisible. "I don't have answers. I thought I did — Or that I would — But — I don't know either ..." He stopped to scrutinize me. Then he said, "We have to be there for each other."

"Yes." I tried a smile. A small one.

We considered each other in silence. The best thing to be caught in his gaze, even like this, so close to the end.

"I'm sorry I hurt you, Gray."

"I guess I know." This would be the last time he'd look at me like that — already his gaze was orbiting away. "You tried to do something. And I respect that."

He stepped closer, to the side of the bed. I held my breath as he reached out his hand and curved it over mine.

He kept it there forever.

Like when one second feels like eons and eras.

We shared one last soft thread of air. Then he said, "Have a good one," and he turned and left. The pink curtains drifted after him, caught his elbow, let go, then fluttered to stillness in his wake.

3

THEY DECIDED I NEEDED rest and observation, so I spent the next week at home. I got my mom to buy me a stack of those eight-inch paper squares you need for origami, a packet of sparkles, and a few packages of white sequins like the one from Vivvie's vest. I practiced with the paper a bunch of times until I managed to fold a pretty good supporting cast into existence. Obviously Vivvie's origami person was going to star as Infinity Girl.

Filming the stop-action animation took a long time, especially with my left arm still in a sling, but it was exactly the distraction I needed.

Establishing shot: *After falling into a heap at City Hall Square, Infinity Girl rises from despair. She is surrounded by the ruins of her superhero mirrors.* Props: White sequins cut into strips. Only one — Vivvie's — remains whole.

Passersby see Infinity Girl for the first time. They are shocked and repulsed by her. Cast: Twenty origami people, various colored papers, filmed to look like a bunch more.

Infinity Girl slowly gathers all the broken pieces of her superhero costume.

Narrator (Trevor): *"She accepts the hatred, pity, and anger of the people. But she is tired of being their mirror."* (Yes, Trevor's voice is exactly as dorky as you think it is.)

Infinity Girl makes her way home. Location: Camera-pan past my favorite album-covers. Arrive at bedroom window with shelves of air-plants in glass jars.

Infinity Girl works tirelessly to restore her mirrors. Props: the diamond-glinting pebble is her easel. Camera zooms in on Infinity Girl's reflection in a jagged shard.

Narrator: *"Her mirrors will have a different power now. She doesn't know yet what it will be. But she made herself who she is, and she will do it again. Breaking and remaking herself, over and over, for however long it takes."*

Infinity Girl clutches the reassembled mirrors. They absorb and channel all her light. Soon she is well enough to venture out into the world again. Location: Camera-pan of Infinity Girl walking. She wears Vivvie's perfect sequin on her head.

Infinity Girl passes Double Kross, who doesn't see her. Double Kross wields her saber. Seething with anger and frustration, she snaps her saber in half. She cuts herself on the shattered edge. Cast: Origami female with a double-cross painted on her chest, plastic stir-stick glued to her hand, watered-down red paint as blood.

Infinity Girl practices her slow-motion skills. When time slows down, she sees that there are others like her. Others who've also pieced together bright reflective parts. Cast: All the origami people, also wearing sequins, also casting light. Props: Sparkles filmed upside-down against the black feather. Applied as slow-motion effect over each person.

As Infinity Girl walks on, she reflects her light to the others. They reflect their light to her. Location: Infinity Girl walks into the distance of the fake-painting of a highway.

Narrator: *"She knows they are never going to see her the way she wants to be seen. She has to see and know herself. She knows she will never see the others the way they want to be seen. They will see and know themselves. She wants to be there because now she knows what it feels like to love a stranger."*

Soundtrack: Tandem Acorns and Last Sunny Day.

Narrator: *"She will never save the world."*

Because in all the history of time, who has ever saved the world? I mean, actually.

ACKNOWLEDGEMENTS

This book was written while on the traditional territory of the Huron-Wendat, Petun First Nations, Seneca, and Mississaugas of the Credit. This territory is covered by the Dish with One Spoon Wampum Belt Covenant, an agreement between the Haudenosaunee Confederacy and the Anishnaabe (Ojibwe) and allied nations to peaceably share and care for the lands and the resources around the Great Lakes.

I am a white, able-bodied, middle-class, cisgender woman, which gives me many positions of unearned privilege, in particular those created by settler colonialism. I am trying to understand and resist our systems of inequality, and to assist those working for change.

In *Messenger 93*, M appropriates something that is not hers, and uses it to advance her position. As the author, I wrote several Indigenous characters into this story, which involved appropriating their cultural identity and possibly benefiting from their inclusion in my work. I recognize that I was and continue to be at risk of making the same mistakes as M. Conversation and critique about this work are welcome and will be received with an open heart and mind.

I acknowledge my Indigenous educators with immense gratitude. A process of compensated consultation has taken place over several years, during which I gained invaluable gifts through their expertise, direction, counsel, and feedback on all aspects of the manuscript. Each consultant reminded me they do not speak for everyone. Any mistakes or missteps I've made on these pages are my own.

I asked permission to acknowledge my Indigenous guides here. They come from various First Nations, including nehiyaw (Cree), Anishinaabe, Mohawk, and Oji-Cree. Thank you with all my heart. Theresa Cutknife: you are a most extraordinary human, and I am so grateful we met. Your positive, gracious spirit is in everything you do. Your gifts are many, your voice authentic and powerful. Thank you for being my mentor and friend. Waubgeshig Rice: thank you for answering my call four years ago, for your kindness and patience and thoughtful consideration. Thanks for bringing your wisdom to all of us through your compassionate journalism and your incandescent fiction. Myles Thurston: thank you for being the first to sit down with me when Messenger 93 was just kindling. Thanks for your perspective and your honesty. The energy you bring to others is bright with your thoughtful kindness. Johl Ringuette: thank you for turning around that day and inviting me to come listen. Thanks for creating such a nurturing space for all of us with NishDish Marketeria, for nourishing us with delicious feasts and steaming cups of sweetgrass tea. Audrey Maracle: Thank you for your sensitivity and your considered reflections. Thanks for sharing with me, and for your willingness to go there. Every time I'm in my garden, I think of you. Thanks to Janis McKenna for introducing us, and to Brian for opening the door to that first conversation, and for sharing his perspective. Thanks to Maria Montejo at Dodem Kanonhsa, for the access to so many educative sessions, and for the time and intellectual generosity of your invited elders and speakers.

There are many people doing the heavy labor of educating us through their books, talks, and social media. I am particularly indebted to the public work of writers, musicians, and film-makers, Carleigh Baker, Gwen Benaway, Leanne Betasamosake, Cherie Dimaline, Alicia Elliott, Martin Heavy Head, Harold Johnson, Tracey Lindberg, Dawn Maracle, Lee Maracle, Alanis Obomsawin, Waubgeshig Rice, Chelsea Vowel, Joshua Whitehead, and many others. It is imperative that we learn about Indigenous issues from Indigenous voices. If you would like to join me in supporting their exhaustive efforts, please buy their books, talks, music, see their plays, watch their films, and/or donate to their platforms.

An important theme in this book is the tragedy of North America's Missing and Murdered Indigenous Women, Girls, and 2 Spirit. This is our problem as a society, and it is important that settlers understand our place in this tragedy. I encourage readers to learn more through Indigenous-authored articles and reports, including the *National Inquiry into Missing and Murdered Indigenous Women and Girls*, and investigative books like *Seven Fallen Feathers* by Tanya Talaga and *Stolen Sisters* by Emmanuelle Walter. I pledge to donate a portion of my earnings from *Messenger 93* to Anduhyaun Inc. and to Nimkii Aazhibikong.

Messages of thanks to the many others who've been integral to this journey: Olga: thank you for being my first messenger, for taking me on a journey of messages, and for teaching me how to listen for them. I'll never forget the lucid dream I had while you worked to heal me, when I saw your iridescent wings. Murry Peeters: Thank you for your questions, your insights, your keen writer's eye. Thank you for going deep deep down with me. Stephanie Nixon: Thank you for your extraordinary work in deconstructing allyship, and for your unflagging commitment to helping me refine the words. Diane Terrana: Thank you for always honing in on the problems, but also the good stuff. Thanks especially for not losing faith in this one, which gave me the courage to keep going. You are a brilliant writer, and I'm so fortunate to have you as my TRF editor. Thom Vernon and Ken Murray: Thank you for inviting me into The Group. What a joy and a privilege to hash it all out with you. You have brought me countless writers' gifts, both through your astute and meticulous notes, and through your breathtaking, mind-blowing prose. Sam Hiyate: Your heart is huge, and I'm so grateful to have you as my agent. Thanks also to all your hard-working crew at The Rights Factory. Charlotte Sheasby-Coleman: Thank you for reading every draft, for catching mistakes and balancing perspectives. I don't know if I would have been able to keep on this writer's journey if not for your continued support, encouragement, and insights. Barry Jowett: Thank you for always understanding, with no preamble, no text of explanation, what I am trying to do. Thanks for zeroing in on exactly the right key to the right vehicle, which will send the story on its rightful journey. The Cormorant/DCB team: thank you for getting on board with such enthusiasm and encouragement, for all your hard work making sure our books get out there, and for consistently pushing harder for more for your writers.

Thank you to Hannah Baron and her peers in Heather Evans' creative writing class, to Debra McGrath, Kinley Mochrie, Nicole

Radecki, Catrina Radecki, Josée Caron, Vickie Lavoie, Lori Landau, Kate Ashby and the WOWs and Broads, Sarah Perry, Carolyn Scott and Bennet, Jo Vannicola, Sean Roberts, and to so many more of you, for your countless gifts to me.

Thank you to my extended family, and to my parents and sisters—for always always being there. Thank you to Michele Ayoub: my muse, messenger, the bellwether I carry with me everywhere. Curious seeker, creative explorer, bountiful heart. Thank you to Stefanie Ayoub: my muse, messenger, the bellwether I carry with me everywhere. Delicate architect of beauty, nurturer of love. Thank you to Philippe Ayoub: my rock and my superhero. Without you, none of this is possible.

Before transitioning to writing, Barbara Radecki was an established actor with many film and television roles and hundreds of commercials to her credit. In recent years, several of her screenplays have been optioned or sold. As a screenwriter, her most recent film, *Modern Persuasion*, will be out in 2020. Born in Vancouver and now based in Toronto, Radecki was nominated for the Kobo Emerging Writers' Prize for her first YA novel, *The Darkhouse*.

We acknowledge the sacred land on which Cormorant Books operates. It has been a site of human activity for 15,000 years. This land is the territory of the Huron-Wendat and Petun First Nations, the Seneca, and most recently, the Mississaugas of the Credit River. The territory was the subject of the Dish With One Spoon Wampum Belt Covenant, an agreement between the Iroquois Confederacy and Confederacy of the Ojibway and allied nations to peaceably share and steward the resources around the Great Lakes. Today, the meeting place of Toronto is still home to many Indigenous people from across Turtle Island. We are grateful to have the opportunity to work in the community, on this territory.

We are also mindful of broken covenants and the need to strive to make right with all our relations.